BROTHERS
OF THE OUTLAW TRAIL

Four Women Surrender Their Hearts

ISBN 978-1-59789-352-7

Published by Barbour Publishing, Inc., P.O. Box 719, Uhrichsville, Ohio 44683, www.barbourbooks.com

Our mission is to publish and distribute inspirational products offering exceptional value and biblical encouragement to the masses.

Printed in the United States of America.

Reuben's Atonement

by Lynette Sowell

Dedication

This book is dedicated to CJ, my outlaw.
I love the trail we've traveled together.

Denmark, Texas, 1867

Quit your bawling, Benjamin." Reuben Wilson didn't mean to sound harsh, not with his baby brother. But a six-year-old couldn't understand why they couldn't go home. Reuben didn't care to think about what he'd left behind in Wyoming. Otherwise he'd probably want to lean back and give a good howl like Benjamin.

Benjamin's round cheeks flamed red, his eyes swollen from a day and night of crying. "I want Ma!" A few passersby on the street glanced toward them but kept on their way. Reuben hoped they'd mind their own business. Colt should be back any moment with their supplies. That is, if he didn't lose his head and draw too much attention to them.

"You can't have Ma, not with the law after us." Caleb Wilson bent closer to Benjamin. "One day, I promise, I'll come back for you. Me, Reuben, and Colt."

"You p–p–promise?" Benjamin's sobs turned to hiccups.

"Yeah, sure do." Caleb chucked him on the shoulder.

"Y'all gonna stand there jawing with the boy, or can I show him where he's goin' to sleep?" Sadie stood in the doorway of the Gilded Lily. Her booted foot tapped like a woodpecker on the boardwalk. She shoved the short-capped sleeve of her flaming red dress over her bare shoulder. "I got customers waitin' to meet the girls."

"Yeah, go on, Benjamin." Reuben kept scanning the crowded street. He considered himself a man at twenty, and he took his responsibility for his brothers seriously. "Sadie's goin' to take good care of you. She'll even give ya some spending money once in a while for helping out." His gaze darted from faces to horses to weapons of passersby. They needed to leave, and fast.

"She will, will she?" Sadie's brow furrowed. "I don't recall agreein' to pay the boy just 'cause y'all are running from the law."

Reuben flashed his attention to Sadie. "Just give the boy a quarter once in a while. He's a good boy. My ma taught him. He can read a mite, even sweep floors and do dishes. Can you help 'er out, Benjamin?"

"Okay." Benjamin hiccupped.

"We can't go back to Ma now. But one day I'll come back for you." The promise made Reuben feel as if he'd swallowed an apple core.

Pounding hooves made Reuben look up. He touched the revolver on his hip. It was only Colt, riding up on a new mount. He had two more in tow. "Got our rides, boys. Let's go."

Reuben's eyes burned as he took one last look at Benjamin. If only Caleb and Benjamin hadn't tailed them from Wyoming. By the time he and Colt had discovered the boys following, they couldn't well turn back. Not with the sheriffs of three towns hunting for them. He said nothing and grabbed the reins of the nearest mount. The other horses had been ridden too hard, and they couldn't risk stopping for long.

Before Benjamin's tears began anew, Reuben led Colt and Caleb to the edge of town.

Reuben reined in his horse and faced both of them. "We go different directions. Y'all lay low, keep your noses clean, and get a new life if you can. A year from now we meet here, get Benjamin, and go back to Ma." Colt and Caleb nodded, then spurred their mounts and disappeared in clouds of dust.

Desperation now drove them apart, but Reuben hoped they'd all find their way back together somehow.

Chapter 1

Raider's Crossing, Wyoming Territory—February 1880

Thirteen years and a heart full of memories lay between Charlotte Jeffers and Reuben Wilson. That, and his mother's coffin being walked down the chapel aisle and out the front doors. Charlotte shivered at the blast of wind that whistled through and touched them all.

The man's heart had to be as icy as the late winter air to leave his mother for so long and return but a few days before her spirit left this earth. Charlotte knew Reuben had broken Elizabeth Wilson's heart. She shoved her own childhood pain aside and prayed silently that somehow the Lord could work good out of the whole mess.

Reuben removed his hat. His calloused hands traced around the band. Lines etched his face, partly from grief and partly from a life spent away from Raider's Crossing that Charlotte could only guess at. Propriety reined her in from stepping across the aisle and telling Reuben exactly what she thought of him.

He'd grown tall, as she'd guessed he would. Broad as a fence, with arms that looked strong enough to hold up a wagon by the axle. Walnut brown hair as untamed and unruly as its owner, and green penetrating eyes that held plenty of secrets. Reuben's well-kept mustache lent a maturity to his face. If he weren't one of the Wilson boys, she reckoned he'd be yet another eligible man in town. Which didn't interest her one bit.

"They say he's a changed man."

Charlotte started at the whisper in her ear. "We'll see about that, won't we, Mrs. Booth?" She should know better than to entertain conversation with the postmistress who happened to know all sorts of interesting tidbits about folks in town.

"I heard he killed a dozen men in Colorado and New Mexico. And he's got a red-skinned wife hidden somewhere." The older woman's voice carried in the crowded chapel.

"If he's made his peace with God, his past won't matter anymore." As for the wife? Well, that was Reuben's own business. Her words sounded trite and pompous. She dropped the conversation, hoping Mrs. Booth would fall silent. This would teach her to accept a ride from James instead of accompanying her parents to the funeral.

"A fine young lady like you would do well to stay away from the likes of him. Good thing those brothers o' his aren't around, either. Scalawags, the lot of 'em." Mrs. Booth clucked and hissed, shaking her head. "Except for poor Benjamin. . ."

Charlotte wanted to distance herself from the gossip, but she was wedged shoulder-to-shoulder with the other residents who'd come to pay their respects. James sat on her other side, and she guessed he probably wondered if anyone had noticed his new buggy. She wondered where he'd gotten the money for it.

She forced her feet to keep still and clamped her hand on James's offered arm. He started rubbing slow circles on the back of her hand. Charlotte slipped her hand free from the unwanted demonstration of. . .affection? James's expression didn't exactly show affection. In fact, she couldn't quite put a name to the look on his face. It made her want to find her parents.

Other young ladies in town saw James as a fine match for an unattached female. He came from good, hardworking people and had made quite a name for himself in Laramie, or so he claimed, writing for the newspaper. Now he was back in town and writing for the *Raider's Crossing News.*

A good name was something to be proud of, unlike some names that sprang to mind. Like the one attached to the man across the aisle from her.

Charlotte glanced at Reuben and saw his expression boring into her. Her face tingled. She straightened her posture and refused to pull her gaze from his.

I know what you're all about, Ruby Wilson. No childhood loyalties will keep me from surrendering the land we bought from your mother. Leave Raider's Crossing, and we'll all be better off.

—ʬ—

A man could do only so much to make amends. Reuben sighed, the sound an echo of the prairie wind. He would never be able to make up for his ma's undeserved grief.

The tiny community had gathered for a brief service, but their faces were a blur to him among a sea of dark suits and dresses, showing respect to his ma. He would not look at them, only at the cross that hung at the front of the tiny church.

What do I do, Lord?

"Find your brothers, Reuben, and buy our old farm back." Ma's last request came to him again. "Make your pa's dream come true."

"I promise, Ma," he'd said. At that moment he would have agreed to anything, to see the glow of pride in her eyes.

Long ago, when life was simpler, he and Colt, Caleb, and little Benjamin had lived a joyous boyhood as they traveled west and helped their pa build a home. Pa had promised they would raise cattle and keep as many horses as they could.

Where had those days gone? When did joy sneak away like a bandit in the night?

Whispers drifted through the crowd after the closing prayer, and Reuben forced himself to look directly at the source of the voices. Mrs. Booth, the loosest jaw in town, and Charlie Jeffers. Reuben found himself locked in a battle of glares with the younger woman while memories dragged him away. . . .

"Charlie! Girls ain't supposed to ride like boys!" Fifteen-year-old Reuben bellowed at a honey-haired girl with spindly arms. She rode astride a straggly pony as she gave Reuben and his brothers hot pursuit across the rolling hills. He reined in his horse and watched the pair approach.

"Can, too!" Her bonnet flopped around her neck. "I can do anything you or Colt or even Caleb can!" She set her jaw and gave him a look hot enough to fry an egg.

"Go home and help yer ma." Girls! Always getting underfoot. Arguing, then sniffling and bawling when they didn't get their way.

"Stop treating me like Benjamin." Her lower lip started to quiver. "B'sides, I'm your blood sister."

Reuben spat on the ground and glared at Colt. He'd been the one to let Charlie in on their little ritual. "Blood brothers—and sister—till the stars die," they'd promised.

Now Reuben felt the heat of the same expression. He and his two younger brothers had always been fascinated with the customs of the natives in the land, but it never occurred to them the silliness of proclaiming themselves blood brothers. The only one who'd really been bonded to them through the ritual was Charlie.

Did she remember? He let himself stare until a blush swept over her face. Her once-thin features had bloomed, and her awkwardness had transformed into curvy womanhood. A brief thought fluttered through his mind. Did she still wear trousers on occasion? The caught-up hair that still reminded him of honey in sunlight and the prim neckline of her dress told him she'd put childish notions behind her.

Reuben had come to town with money in his pocket, with hopes of one day buying back his family's land, but he wanted to test the waters before he plunged in with talking about a sale. The folks in Raider's Crossing held grudges, he discovered. They also took care of their own.

Just like the dandy who'd been eyeing Charlie like she was a prized possession. And eyeing Reuben like he was a fox trying to get into the henhouse. Reuben gritted his teeth. Courting

Charlie Jeffers would be like expecting to rope the moon. Finding his brothers and getting the family land back would be nearly as difficult.

He barely remembered stumbling to the cold outside, shaking the preacher's hand, and thanking him for his words about Ma. Reuben wouldn't have been able to speak, and he didn't deserve to. He couldn't have spoken of the few happy childhood memories he owned. Just as well. He'd probably have cried in front of the town.

An older yet familiar man, who of a certainty had to be Mr. Jeffers, shook hands with Charlie's suitor. The suitor smiled at Mr. Jeffers then offered Charlie his arm. The couple left for a smart-looking buggy. Reuben seized the moment to approach Charlie's father.

"Mr. Jeffers, thank you kindly for coming." He touched the brim of his hat and nodded at Mrs. Jeffers. "Ma'am, thank you, too."

Sam Jeffers regarded Reuben's hand for a moment, then reached out to give a hearty shake. "Welcome back, son."

"Thank you." Reuben swallowed hard. "I–I've been meaning to ask you somethin' since I've been back."

"Yes?" Sam huffed through his gray mustache.

"I was wonderin' if you're needing a hand about your place. I've been working some ranches in Colorado, and I ain't afraid of hard work here." Reuben dwarfed the man by at least six inches, but somehow in his presence Reuben felt as if he were ten years old.

"I reckon I'll need some help with the horses, plus the barn needs patching 'fore a late storm sets in." Sam looked him straight in the eye. "You come on out at suppertime, and we'll talk some more."

Reuben nodded. "Yes, sir. That'll be fine, sir. I've got a room in town."

"Is that so? If you work for me, plan on staying in our bunkhouse. It's not much, but it's warm. Our other hired hands go home to their families, so you'll be on your own." Sam squeezed Reuben's arm. "Etta puts supper on the table at five, so bring your appetite."

"Thank you, sir, ma'am." Reuben watched them leave the churchyard, and he felt strangely alone.

He'd gotten used to his own company these past years after losing track of Colt and Caleb. Reuben moved back to the wooden coffin and squatted next to it on the hard ground. He had ordered a stone with honestly earned cash in anticipation of a burial come spring. But the man had accepted the money with a suspicious look in his eye.

"Lord, it's a beginning. At least Mr. Jeffers—Sam—will look me in the eye. Thank You for the chance to make things right again."

Reuben bowed for a few minutes more in wordless prayer, letting regret sweep through him until silent sobs threatened to wrack his body. He did not care that a couple of men stood nearby, waiting to carry his mother's coffin to be held with the others until the ground thawed.

"Mr. Wilson?"

He forced his face into a semblance of composure and glanced up. "Reverend. I was just takin' a moment—"

"You've walked a long road to get here."

Reuben nodded. He had arrived by stage and meant to buy a horse, but he figured the reverend was talking in a different sort of way. "Yeah, I have. I–I'm not the same person I was when me and the boys lit out years ago."

"People around here, they don't change much, I've noticed."

"I have, thanks to God and an old preacher named Reverend Mann. He told me I needed to start making amends for what I'd done." Reuben turned his focus to the wooden box before him. "It meant jail time, but Reverend Mann was right. A man sleeps easy with a clear conscience."

"Well, maybe in time people here will see the change in your life." Reverend Toms patted Reuben's shoulder. "Won't happen overnight, but you give them a chance, and they'll come around. God's grace covers all of us willing to accept it. I'll be praying you find your family."

"Thank you, sir." He watched as Reverend Toms left the yard to return to the parsonage. The preacher had been in Raider's Crossing since Reuben was a boy. He imagined the older man entering the tiny home he shared with his wife. Their children were probably grown and gone.

Would Reuben ever have the security of home and know the warmth of a family? Right now he felt as desolate as the grave. Warmth didn't linger among the dead.

He supposed he'd better get moving, back to the rooming house, and prepare himself to face the Jeffers clan. Maybe he could glean a bit of comfort from them. Although he didn't deserve any kindness, he hoped even Charlie would welcome him.

Chapter 2

He's coming here?" Charlotte's voice cut off with a squeak. She set the kettle back on the stove and whirled to face Momma.

"Your pa's talking about hiring him to help out. You know we need an extra hand around here, especially with your brother gone." Momma matter-of-factly kneaded the bread dough a final time.

"I figured Pa had already hired someone." *Reuben Wilson, coming here?* Her thoughts swirled around; then a gnawing feeling settled in her stomach.

"Thirteen years can change a body."

"Yes, you're right." Charlotte handed the bread pans to Momma. "But how do we know for certain?"

Momma reached out a flour-covered hand and touched Charlotte's arm, stopping her from moving back to the stove. "Child, I'm not telling you to give him your heart. No one's asking for that."

"I know," Charlotte whispered. She managed a smile and hoped the subject would change.

He'd made her out a fool once, but not again. At thirteen she'd trusted him with her fragile heart, only to have it tossed at her feet in a million pieces two years later when he and his brothers disappeared. Then when he reappeared, she realized she'd only squashed the pieces together, and her whole heart threatened to crumble again. This "put her in a mood," as Momma would say.

James had left after a short conversation in the front parlor earlier in the afternoon, a fact for which she was grateful. No, maybe she wanted him here by her side at supper, at least to drive home to Reuben the fact that her life did not include him. *Stop it. You'll not use another man to prove a point to someone else.*

Charlotte started heating the grease to cook the beef her family reserved for special occasions. If Reuben was like the prodigal son in the Bible, she needn't act like the jealous older brother and begrudge him some Christian hospitality.

She'd been praying about acting more like a Christian outside of church. Therefore she would do her best to see Reuben as the reformed wanderer, in need of restoration and kindness. But she would make sure the walls around her heart held firm. When she put supper on the table, a knock sounded at the front door.

Momma said, "Charlotte, open the door for our guest."

"Of course." Charlotte placed the plate of meat on the table, smoothed her apron, and headed for the front room.

As she expected, Reuben waited, turning his hat over in his hands. His bulk filled the doorway.

"Please come in." Charlotte reached for his hat. A tangle of fingers made her catch her breath.

"Your ma and pa have a nice home. I think they were building it when. . ." Reuben's voice trailed off as he took in his surroundings with a somber expression.

"Yes." Charlotte glanced at the comforts she'd grown to love. Her momma's warm knitted throws, perfect to wrap up in on a chilly night, the hand-carved rocking chair from back East, an iron woodstove that kept the front part of the house warm. "Pa finished the house not long after you and. . .you and your brothers left." The words came out in spite of her reluctance.

Reuben winced as though she'd slapped him. "What about your brother? Is he still around? He should be about eighteen by now, right?"

Charlotte shook her head. "No. Momma and Pa sent him to school. Which is why Pa needs the help now. We lost a hand recently also."

She turned her back to lead Reuben to the warm kitchen, but his strong hand on her shoulder stopped her.

"Charlie."

Charlotte closed her eyes and murmured, "It's been a long time since anyone called me that." She allowed Reuben to turn her back around. What had happened to her head? Her feet refused to take her into the kitchen.

She opened her eyes and tilted her head back to meet Reuben's gaze. Her rebellious pulse now hammered in her ears. The last time they'd been this close was the night before Reuben and his brothers disappeared. She now saw a man's face instead of a mostly grown boy, torn between loving her and running from the sins of his youth. Well, she thought he'd loved her. The fingers of her free hand tightened into a fist.

"Oh, Reuben—" Her fingers tingled, wanting to touch his jaw, which tensed with emotion. The sorrow in his eyes struck her in the gut, making her feel like the time she'd taken one of the boys' dares to leap from the hayloft onto a haystack. She'd fallen down, down, down and landed on a shallow part of the stack. The air had left her lungs with a whoosh as she slammed onto the hay-covered ground. Just like now.

"I'm sorry, Charlie. We'd gotten in over our heads. I didn't want to lead the law straight to Ma. Turns out I broke her heart anyway. We all did." Reuben raked his hand through his hair. "I didn't want to break yours, either."

The old feelings of betrayal surged through her. "I loved you once. But that was a long time ago. We're both adults now, and I'm sure quite different people." The admission of her old feelings made her face flame hotter.

"I know I'm different now. Which is what I hope you and the rest of the town will see one day." Reuben expelled a hollow sigh. "And I thank you for coming today. Your family has done me a great kindness. I'm glad my ma wasn't all alone."

"No, she wasn't." Her emotions teetered between compassion for the man before her and anger at the years they'd lost. "She prayed for you, even up until the end."

"She prayed me home."

Charlotte fell into the river of anger. "A little too late, don't you think? Why are you here, anyway?" Two stray tears crept down her cheeks.

"This place is my home. I need to make amends for what I've done." He wiped away one of her tears with his rough yet gentle fingers.

Her stomach quivered at his presumptive gesture and stepped backward in the direction of the kitchen. "Come. Supper's on the table. Pa should be washing up after seeing to the animals, and then we'll eat."

So much for building up walls around her heart. As he had done in childhood, Reuben snuck around the back and caught her unawares. No matter what he said, some things hadn't changed, but she wouldn't tell him that. Her heart accused her of being a fool not to realize that James was a lesser man than Reuben.

—∞—

All through the meal, Charlie avoided looking Reuben in the eye. Although Sam talked about the work he needed help with around the farm, Reuben felt as though he held an unspoken conversation with the woman across the table.

During the few moments in the front room before dinner, the feelings coursing through Reuben nearly overcame him. He wanted to shove through the years piled between them and take Charlie in his arms and kiss her, as he should have years ago, and promise never to leave.

What would have happened if he and his brothers had returned the money from the robbery in Colorado and come clean? Reuben imagined Benjamin, who was safe at home, and Colt, Caleb, and himself running the Wilson ranch after jail.

"So what do you think, Reuben?"

"Sounds fine to me."

"You ain't heard a word of what I've told you the last five minutes, have ya?" Sam chuckled. His molasses brown eyes glinted in the lamplight. "Ah, but you've had a lot on your plate. I can't pay you much—"

"That's all right, sir." Reuben downed the last sip of his coffee. "I'm here to figure out some things, maybe earn some respect back for my family. One thing I have learned is there's no shame in hard work."

Sam nodded. "Right you are. I was hoping Sam Junior would have wanted the farm one day, but he's got work of another kind. He's going to be a lawyer."

He appeared to change his direction of thought. "Another thing, around here we work every day except Sunday. We go to the Lord's house and worship. And you'll come with us, too."

"That's fine by me." Reuben didn't dare venture a glance at Charlie. "Another thing I've learned is a man isn't much of a man without living for God. I'm nowhere near the man I want to be, but with His help I'm trying."

That said, he picked up his coffee cup and raised it to his lips, then stopped. He'd forgotten it was empty.

"Charlotte, get our friend Reuben here another cup of coffee, would ya?" Sam gestured toward Reuben's cup, still held in midair.

A knock sounded at the front door. Sam glanced at his wife, then at Charlotte, who had moved to the stove.

"I'll answer that," she offered. Charlotte rounded the table, her skirts swishing.

She returned a few seconds later with a red flush on her cheeks. The young dandy who'd driven her home after the funeral followed close behind. Reuben didn't miss the challenge in the young man's eyes.

"I apologize for interrupting your supper, Mr. and Mrs. Jeffers. I happened to leave my hat here earlier and thought I'd retrieve it now." The man appraised Charlotte with a look that made Reuben want to wipe it from his face. Reuben found himself the focus of the mild-mannered gaze that masked anger held back like a wild bronc.

Reuben stood from his place at the table. "I don't believe I've made your acquaintance, but I want to thank you for coming and paying your respects to my ma. I'm Reuben Wilson." As if the man didn't know. Reuben extended a hand.

"James Johansson. I used to share a desk with your brother Caleb in school." James's hand clenched Reuben's in a wiry grip. "Mr. and Mrs. Jeffers, since you have company, I'll be off. But if Charlotte wishes and with your permission, may I return tomorrow evening to listen to her read?"

Sam nodded as Reuben took his seat.

"All right, tomorrow at seven. Have a pleasant evening." James put on his hat then left.

Reuben stared at his empty coffee cup and wondered if Charlotte could see that James was as slippery as a fish. From the corner of his eye, he saw her move to the stove for the coffeepot, her face now glowing crimson.

"Here's that coffee, Reuben." Charlotte was at his elbow. Her hand shook as she poured.

"Thank you. It's good coffee."

"Ma made it." She returned to the stove and kept her back to him.

Reuben ignored the barb. "Another thing, Sam. I'm going to start looking for my brothers. Part of my promise to Ma, you know. Has anybody heard from them?"

Sam shook his head. "Not since Caleb came through about five years ago. He looked wore out. Think he was pretty ashamed. Saw yer ma and left."

Etta added, "I remember talking with her about Caleb over tea. I think it hurt her again that he left, but she believed that somehow the words she shared would bring him back to following the Lord's ways."

"I'm grateful to you both for watching out for her. You gave her a fair price for the land, and she lived comfortably in town." Reuben sipped his coffee, feeling the all-too-familiar shame rising inside again. "You've been good neighbors. She said you helped her after Pa died." His throat tightened.

Etta patted his hand. "We take care of our own here, Reuben Wilson. Welcome home."

Reuben caught Charlotte's gaze. Her eyes glittered with unshed tears.

Chapter 3

"Reuben this, Reuben that!" The wind tugged at Charlotte's hat, so she grabbed the brim with a free hand. She'd tucked her other hand around James's arm. "For two weeks now that's all I've heard."

He reined in the horse pulling the buggy. "And that's all I've heard from you." Though they were on the road leading from town to her parents' farm, James drew her closer and moved in for a kiss.

His face swallowed up her vision, and Charlotte pushed James away. "Don't! Someone might see us!"

"I don't mind if you don't. I'd rather the world know I'm courting you."

Charlotte sat up straight and as far away from James as she could. "Courting? I know you've been escorting me home, but my pa never spoke to me about courting."

"What do you think I've intended, if not to court you?" James took her gloved hand in one of his. "Then you needn't feel so shy about kissing me."

Charlotte didn't know about the shy part, but kissing James

had been the furthest thing from her mind at the moment. What had been on her mind was Reuben. Every day of the week at every meal she'd seen him. In the sleepy hours before dawn she silently poured his coffee, and he smiled his thanks. Sometimes at the noon meal he'd return dusty and tired from his labors. In the evenings after supper he would listen to the family Bible readings. And at night, when she was supposed to be sleeping, she would find herself awake and wondering about the man asleep in the bunkhouse.

"Well, you're not saying anything. That doesn't bode well for me." James chirruped to his horse, and they continued down the frosty lane.

"I'm sorry." Charlotte shook her head. "I've been distracted."

"I can tell."

"Thank you for driving me home and for rescuing me from Mrs. Booth at the general store." Charlotte shook her head. "That woman tries to get news from people like a bee gathering pollen."

"I'm always glad to help a lady in a predicament. If I'd been a few minutes later, I'd have needed to rescue you from Reuben."

"No need. Reuben would never hurt me. . . ." Charlotte recalled seeing Reuben on the street. She wondered what business he had in town, especially on a workday when he should be helping her pa.

Reuben's face had lost some of its somber cast when he saw her, and she thought he might offer to escort her home, especially when she saw her pa's wagon hitched in the street.

"So what news was our Mrs. Booth attempting to wrest

from you?" James's voice held a mild tone.

"Oh, if Reuben Wilson has stolen any of our valuables—things like that." Charlotte shook her head. "Of course he hasn't. He's worked hard. In fact, I don't think Pa's paying him enough for what he's doing."

"Sounds like you're going soft on him."

"It's not like that," Charlotte stammered. "I think he needs a fair chance, just like everyone. People can change. Especially since he's a Christian."

"Uh-huh. And a leopard can change his spots."

"Really, James, you sound like Mrs. Booth."

"Charlotte, Reuben and his brothers went bad. They tore all over the place, thieving and such. You remember that robbery at the mercantile, the one they pulled right before they disappeared with Benjamin?" James slowed the buggy. "Some people are bad news through and through. There's no changing that. I'm a newspaper man. I deal in facts."

"Facts change. People can, too." Charlotte was wishing more and more she'd stayed in town and let Reuben drive her home instead.

Reuben signed his name at the bottom of the telegraph form. "That should do it. You'll be sure to let me know if you hear back, right?"

"Check in with me next time you're in town, Mr. Wilson." The telegraph operator proofread Reuben's form and accepted his fee. "It may take awhile—depending on the records and how busy the lawman is—before you hear anything."

"I suppose I'll keep waiting then." Reuben put his hat back on. "Have a good day."

He left the telegraph office and entered the brisk outdoors. Raider's Crossing's hubbub of busy citizens crisscrossed the street. Reuben headed down the boardwalk to the rooming house where his mother once lived.

Reuben touched the bankroll nestled in an inner pocket of his coat. It would have taken him too long to write a letter that made sense, so he figured he'd telegraph sheriffs for information about his brothers' whereabouts. One of the first things he'd done was write to Sadie, but his letters had returned unopened.

Please, Lord, help me find my family. I need to stay here to get the land back, and I don't know where to look for the others.

Charlie and her persistent suitor had probably already left in his snug little buggy. He had seen her earlier across the street. She almost appeared as if she wanted to speak to him.

In fact, he'd borrowed Sam's farm wagon with an ulterior motive in mind. Not just to take his mother's and family's effects with him, but maybe even take Charlie home. She'd stubbornly walked the two miles to town, claiming she wanted to get the mail and some fresh air. Probably ruined her pretty boots in the frozen, muddy wagon tracks.

A reluctant smile tugged at his lips as he entered the boardinghouse. The smell of fresh apple pie made his stomach growl.

Mrs. Beasley, the boardinghouse owner, met him by the staircase. "Mr. Wilson, good day. You've come for your mother's things?"

"Yes, I have." His throat tightened. "I won't be long."

"No worries. Take as long as you like. Here's the key." She handed him the cold piece of metal.

Reuben went to what had been his mother's room, where she'd lived the past five years or so. As soon as he opened the door, he smelled the rosewater she used to wear.

The patchwork quilt on the bed was neatly tucked under a pillow. A brush and hand mirror lay near the bowl and pitcher on the washstand, as if waiting for his mother to return. He moved to the small wardrobe and opened a door to find several dresses, worn yet well cared for.

Maybe Charlie or her mother would like them. He removed the dresses from the wardrobe and placed them on the bed. The bureau contained a few ladies' undergarments. It was odd removing those; perhaps he would throw them away.

Reuben's throat swelled, and he dashed away the tears. He needed to finish this job fast before he set to bawling. The trunk at the foot of the bed came open easily, its lock broken. Reuben stuffed the dresses, the brush, and the mirror inside. He glanced around the plain yet tidy room. Nothing else was left for him to do except gather the contents of his family legacy into the trunk and head for the Jeffers farm. Having a family around him might help him squirrel through this box to see what to keep and what to give away. Reuben corrected himself. Having Charlie next to him would help. He could force himself to wait for the right time.

—ꟾꟾꟾ—

Charlotte's eyes burned. Even by the window in the front room the afternoon light didn't help illuminate her mending very much.

But the chore was a welcome diversion that had sent James on his way. He'd unsettled her with his advance in the buggy. Before they parted, he promised he'd never make such an assumption again. Still, she didn't like the way he spoke of Reuben.

The front door opened. Charlotte didn't bother to look up when a familiar clomp of boots entered the room. They crossed the room and stopped near her.

"Could you help me, please?" Reuben stood before Charlotte, carrying a wooden trunk. "That is, if it's not much trouble."

"Help you?" He seemed to have no difficulty carrying the trunk.

"These are. . .were. . .my ma's things." His gaze dropped from her face to what he held. "Some things I want to keep, but I. . .I found a few things you might like."

Charlotte swallowed hard. She couldn't imagine having to complete such a task, didn't even want to think of it. To do so alone, with years of regret piled high. . .

"Of course I'll help." Her gentle tone surprised her. "Set the trunk beside the stove, and I'll put the kettle on for tea. It's cold outside."

"Thank you." Reuben deposited the trunk on the rag rug and sat on the chair across from Charlotte's.

She went to the much warmer kitchen and stoked the fire in the cookstove to a snappy blaze, then filled the kettle with water from the sink pump. Reuben's mere presence and humble request made her head reel, much more than James did.

Reuben needed a friend. Any romantic entanglements would only complicate matters further. Besides, Charlotte couldn't be sure that he wouldn't run again. She returned to the sitting room where Reuben knelt before the open trunk.

She found a spot on the rug next to him and lifted a simple gown and matching shirtwaist from the trunk. "What do you want to do with the dresses?"

Their gazes locked. In the harsh afternoon light, the scar on Reuben's face seemed deeper than usual. Instead of the sadness she'd seen since their reunion, she glimpsed a spark of hope in Reuben's eyes.

"You can have them. I mean, you and your ma might find them useful." Reuben turned his attention to the trunk's contents.

Charlotte folded the clothing and set it to the side. In the next layer of trunk items she found a rather large packet of brown paper tied with twine. "What's this?"

"Open it."

She untied the packet and unfolded the paper. A gown of soft silk, more than thirty years out of style, tumbled onto her lap. "Oh, it must be your ma's wedding gown."

"You can keep it if you want to. I know it's not the style ladies wear now, but maybe you can make something else from it. I don't know, but the fabric looks fine." Reuben rubbed his forehead and opened another paper packet, this one containing several daguerreotypes.

"Your ma and pa. And"—Charlotte smiled—"you and your brothers. So long ago. . ." Her eyes smarted as she wondered what had happened to the other Wilson boys.

"We were still in knickers." Reuben smiled, and Charlotte wished she could see that expression on his face more often. "I think I was all of fourteen. Benjamin was a baby."

His voice cut short, and Charlotte heard the sorrow in his tone. "Where are they, Reuben?"

"I don't know. I've written to—to the place where we left Benjamin. Never heard anything." Reuben put the daguerreotypes back into the packet and retied the string. "We were stupid, thinking we'd never get caught or that no one had wised up to what we were doing. And Benjamin? Benjamin thought we were having fun adventures without him."

Reuben settled to a seated position on the rug, and Charlotte forced herself to be quiet long enough for him to continue.

"He followed us, the little coot." Reuben shook his head. "We didn't know until it was too late. And we didn't want to risk leading a trail home to Ma."

"So you split up."

"Yeah. It wasn't supposed to be for long. Then months turned into years somehow." Reuben held up a pocket watch and let it spin on its chain. "Time moved fast."

Charlotte's heart surged with compassion. She couldn't imagine being alone in the world and knowing that somewhere out there she had kin. She placed her hand on Reuben's arm. "I want to help you. I'll write letters, do whatever we can to find them."

He covered her hand with one of his. "Thank you, Charlie. That means a lot to me."

"We're old friends. I suppose that hasn't changed."

Reuben picked up her right hand and turned it so the palm faced upward. He moved the cuff of her dress up a few inches, exposing her forearm. The simple action made her face burn. "Do you remember?"

"I never forgot." Charlotte wanted to weep out the sorrow of the lost years between them. *Lord, we can't go back.*

She stared at the faint scar from long ago when she and the Wilson brothers pledged to be blood kin to the bitter end. Back then she had no idea what that would mean. And now she had no idea if her heart was up to the challenge.

Chapter 4

The wind sliced through Reuben's thin and threadbare coat as he walked along the boardwalk in Raider's Crossing early Saturday evening. His stomach ached after enjoying an early supper in town. He'd bought a new horse, too. While in town he'd met a few more people, and the name Wilson meant little to them—other than wasn't that the older woman who had passed on sometime back? Then when they found out it was his ma, their tone changed. No questions asked, either. He supposed not everyone knew of his prodigal state.

Reuben shivered and turned down the side street to the livery. He paused once out of the wind. A warmer coat would be nice. Reverend Mann, though, had said he ought not to spend money on frivolous things like a new coat, not after how he'd squandered money in the past. To atone for this sin, Reuben waited awhile longer. He wondered when God would think it was long enough. Maybe he'd ask Reverend Toms. Reuben had no Bible, but he sure paid attention to the preaching, and Reverend Toms seemed to know the Book well.

A voice drifted down the side street and into Reuben's ears.

"Yessir, that pretty little Charlotte Jeffers comes with a fine package if I marry her."

Reuben curled his hands into fists at the sight of the dapper young man talking and laughing with other spit 'n' polished lads.

"You know her pa's going to throw in that old Wilson parcel."

His friend chuckled. "I tried to come courtin' once, but she's as cold as Raider's Pond in December."

Charlie's suitor clapped his friend on the back, and the men paused at the end of the alley with their backs to him.

"Well, my friend, the ice is beginning to thaw. I'm sure of it. If I have my way, she'll be begging her daddy to let her marry me. You know she's three years older than me?"

"She don't look long in the tooth."

The suitor—James, was it?—strutted like a rooster. "Nor the rest of her, either. People will pay good money for that land, and they're going to be paying it to me once it's mine."

Reuben turned and walked to the livery before he punched a wall or, worse, planted a fist into James's face. The man had practically sold Charlotte's dowry before he'd even married her. James had no knowledge of how to treat a lady, either.

Reuben had a right to buy that land, intended dowry or no. Soon he could make Sam Jeffers an offer. And wouldn't that throw a kink in James's spokes? He grinned at the thought.

Something didn't set right with Reuben about James. The man's expression reminded him of the sort of fellow who marked cards and hid his pistol under the table.

The warmth of the livery made up for Reuben's coat, and

the scent of straw and animal swirled around him. Reuben went to the stall where his new mount, a roan mare named Checkers, waited. She had wise eyes and looked strong. One day she'd make a fine cutting horse. He'd need to get some cattle first, though.

"Come for your horse, have you?" Mac, the liveryman, stood holding a pitchfork at the end of the aisle.

"That I have, and I thank you for the saddle." After settling the matter of payment, Reuben swung up onto the horse's back and rode out feeling a mite taller—and not because of the mount.

He had arrived in Raider's Crossing by stage with nothing but the clothes on his back and a small sack of sundries. His pa's words came to him. *You take a trip one step at a time and build a life one day at a time.* He remembered not understanding their humble beginnings when they arrived in Wyoming Territory. He wanted the riches Pa had promised, and right away.

Reuben wondered if his dissatisfaction had led him astray. The old memories accompanied him back to the Jeffers farm as he rode Checkers along the trail out of town.

—∞—

"Tell me about life on the trail," Charlotte ventured while she and Reuben sat in the parlor that evening. Ma and Pa remained in the kitchen, their soft after-supper conversation taking place as it had every night for many years. Reuben had missed supper, and Charlotte in turn had missed him. When he arrived after she put away the last clean dish, her stomach gave a lurch at his presence.

Now Charlotte knitted, or tried to knit, while Reuben sat across from her and kept her yarn from tangling. At least that was what he said he was doing.

"I don't like talking about those days." Reuben remained focused on the yarn. His eyelids drooped. Pa said Reuben put in a full day's work. Why, then, would he be here in the evening when he could be settling down in the bunkhouse for a well-deserved rest? Charlotte didn't want to think he meant to spend time with her.

"I'm sorry. I often wondered where you'd gone." She cast another loop of yarn over the needle and paused. "I'd ride out on Belle, hoping to see you coming over the ridge to our place." Her throat burned. She reworked her stitch. The blanket she was knitting for a new mother at church would never take shape at this rate.

"Well, we ended up in Texas and left Benjamin there with a. . .friend." Reuben set the mass of yarn on his lap. "Then I headed up to Colorado, got caught selling stolen horses." His face flushed.

"How—how long were you in jail?"

"Eighteen months." He cleared his throat. "The first time." The expression on Reuben's face made her think the yarn had turned into a pile of snakes on his lap.

"But you were sorry, weren't you?"

"The first time I was sorry I got caught." Reuben clutched the yarn as if it were a lariat.

"Why did you do it?" Charlotte's eyes burned. The Wilsons, she remembered, were not wealthy people, but neither were they destitute.

"The money and the challenge." Reuben sighed. "Money just ain't all it's cracked up to be. It goes too fast and makes people do crazy things only to lose it again. And challenges? Well, I could have found some better ones than stealing horses."

Charlotte didn't know what to say to the serious man who sat across from her. His shoulders slumped as if they bore a great weight.

"Reuben, I'm sorry you walked such a long road." She bit her lip. "But I'm glad you're home again."

"I'd like to say I'm glad, too." He held her gaze.

"Are you going to ask me what I've done these past years?" Charlotte tried to lighten the conversation.

"I can see you've grown up."

"Of course. What a feat that would be, to remain exactly as I was when you left." She smiled at him. There was so much she wanted to tell him—why she had never married, why in the last year she'd still looked for him when out riding Belle.

"I'm glad you're not the same. But I figured you'd be settled down with a family by now and have a posse of kids."

"Well, you can see I'm not. And I don't." Charlotte hadn't intended the words to sound so cold and brittle, but the ripe old age of thirty was two short years away.

"That young man coming around—do you think he's honorable?"

What a question. Charlotte could only say that James was polite, had some polish from schooling, and didn't seem to mind that she was a few years older than he was. Other possible suitors had no doubt been rebuffed by her deliberate disinterest.

"He has never led me to believe he isn't." At that her face

flamed, but she dared not tell him about James's attempt to kiss her.

"I see." Reuben's stare bored into her.

"I'm not getting younger." She hadn't expected to be defending herself, although clearly Reuben enjoyed the focus being off him.

"I still care about you, and I don't want you hurt." The tender expression on his face surprised her.

"That means a lot to me. I still. . ." Charlotte swallowed hard. This conversation was not at all turning out as she'd hoped. A brief getting-to-know-you-once-again, not unspoken revelations of the heart.

Reuben leaned forward. "I have something I feel I ought to tell you—only I'm not sure you'll like it."

Her heart felt as if it had leapt into her throat. "You're not leaving again?" Here she was, come full circle as she knew she would. At first she wanted him to go, but now. . .

Reuben shook his head. "It's about James."

Charlotte scooted her chair a bit closer. "What?"

A flush swept over Reuben's face. "I don't want to be accused of tale-bearing, but. . .just. . .be careful about him, okay?"

He was close enough now that she could see flecks of gold in his green eyes. She wanted to make him smile, to see them twinkle as they once did. Reuben's beard was making an appearance, and Charlotte wanted to touch the stubbly growth on his jaw.

"All right."

Reuben stood and reached for his hat. "Promise me. Be careful, Charlie. Wise as a serpent, harmless as a dove."

Her head swam, and she sat back. James. Reuben had said

something about James and being careful. But right about now what she wanted was for Reuben to kiss her, and James was the furthest thing from her mind.

Charlotte nodded mutely and watched as Reuben went into the kitchen. She tossed her knitting onto the floor.

Reuben stoked the embers in the bunkhouse stove and tried to coax some warmth into the old room. Mr. and Mrs. Jeffers had offered him their son's bedroom in the main house, but Reuben didn't think it was proper. He wasn't accustomed to living under a family's roof, not for a long time. In jail you did what you were told when you were told. The idea of being in the outside world, doing what you wanted when you wanted—well, it was hard getting used to.

"Lord, I still need Your help. I'm not sure how to behave among upright people," Reuben muttered as he folded his change of clothes. He placed them in the small trunk he had bought on a trip to town.

Had he done the right thing in telling Charlotte to be careful about James? Reuben dared not repeat the words James had used, soiled with their double meanings. He did know he would protect Charlotte, even if it meant losing her.

Reuben stared out the lone window across the stockyard and at the Jeffers home glowing with warm rectangles of light.

Losing her. He chuckled to himself. He had given up all rights to claim her heart when he rode away all those years ago. No matter what Reverend Mann thought, some things a fellow still couldn't make up for.

Chapter 5

Reuben clutched the receipt for his bank deposit, his heart pounding all the while. Now his money was safe in an account. He glanced about the lobby, but the other customers seemed to be minding their own business, even Mrs. Booth in the corner. Carved wood and iron bars proclaimed security. The bars also reminded him of days gone by, years lost and wasted. Not anymore if he could help it.

No, if God could, and would, help him. Reverend Mann would caution him in that singsong voice of his to take heed not to succumb to greed. God would help him pay if he truly showed repentance for his ways. Reuben hoped he had shown just that. Repentance.

He reread the piece of paper in his hand as he started for the front doors. If he kept all his new earnings for himself, the amount would have been larger. Paying back those whom he'd stolen from helped ease his conscience along the way.

Reuben collided with a short, squat man in a bowler hat. The man's head was tucked low against the blast of cold air that followed him into the bank. A sack fell from his hands. Paper money and coins scattered, the paper floating on air before settling on the floor.

"Oh, pardon me," Reuben said. "I wasn't paying attention." He bent to help gather some of the money.

"No harm done." The man squatted and scraped some coins onto his palm. "I was in a hurry, not paying attention myself."

"I think that's all of it." Reuben straightened.

The man stood, as well, and extended his right hand. "Howard Woodward, *Raider's Crossing News*."

"Oh, you run the newspaper. I'm"—Reuben shook the man's smooth hand—"I'm Reuben Wilson. Pleased to make your acquaintance."

"Likewise. And next time I'll watch my step."

"And I will, too." They exchanged nods, and Reuben wondered if the man's words held a double meaning. He brushed off the idea like a pesky fly and pushed through the bank doors to come face-to-face with James, also on his way into the establishment. James gave him nothing but a glance.

Reuben tugged the collar of his coat more tightly around his neck and pocketed his receipt. The ice-tinged air bit into him, and Reuben shivered where Checkers stood tied outside the bank. He needed to hurry before the freezing rain began to fall, but he had to make one more stop first.

—ꝏ—

"Too bad we haven't seen any of the other Wilson boys," Pa remarked while he stabled the animals for the night after returning from town.

"It's sad, Pa." Charlotte paused while brushing Belle's warm flank. "I wish we could do something to help Reuben." The wind had already picked up outside with the promise of another ice storm. Charlotte wanted spring to come and breathe new life across the land.

"God can make something out of nothing. He knows exactly where those boys are. Even now their ma's prayers are at heaven's throne. Perhaps she's visiting there awhile, too." Pa leaned over the stall door. "I didn't want to worry you, but I ran into Howard Woodward today at the mercantile. He was asking about Reuben."

Charlotte's throat constricted; then she found her voice. "Why's that?"

"He's missing some money from his deposit today. Claims he and Reuben were at the bank, ran into each other. Reuben helped him pick up the money."

"You don't think Mr. Woodward's saying—"

Pa raised his hand. "Don't worry. He was only asking about Reuben since he heard I hired him. I told him I'd vouch for Reuben. We haven't had anything missing since he's been here."

"It's not fair." But Charlotte didn't blame his distrust. She didn't want to trust Reuben at first.

"I know, but that's how people are. Seems like there's a few who want to give him a fair shot. I'm going to talk to him tonight, warn him in case there's trouble in the future." Pa sighed uncharacteristically. "Well, you'd best finish up. Ma's laying supper on the table." He didn't chide her for not being inside the warm kitchen and helping, and Charlotte wanted to hug him for it. She had not taken refuge in the barn for longer than she could remember and now realized why she'd loved its peacefulness as a child.

"I will." She waved at Pa and watched him leave. The barn door groaned as he closed it behind him.

Charlotte started half thinking, half praying as she brushed Belle. This afternoon of solitude was meant to be a time of speaking with the Lord, away from distractions. But Reuben and his family had somehow followed her thoughts into the barn.

She could not imagine losing her brother and not knowing where he was. Last letter she had read, his first-year studies in Lincoln were going well. She knew her parents sacrificed to send him to school, and she was proud of him.

Her thoughts turned to James. Her parents neither encouraged nor discouraged the possibility of him calling. Charlotte moved to Belle's hindquarters and started working some snarls from the mare's tail. But what did she want?

All the prayers she'd sent heavenward so far about James had been met with a resounding silence. No yes or no, no warning sign. Or was it that she didn't want a warning? Or was it because her former love for Reuben and his subsequent rejection made her leery about opening her heart to another? The thoughts chased themselves around her head.

Belle shifted her weight and nearly stepped on Charlotte's foot. She moved away in time and patted her mare's neck.

"Sorry, Belle." She'd been brushing too vigorously, and the mare had sensitive skin.

Reuben had warned her about James. She wanted to drag

the meaning out of him, but if he was as stubborn as when they were children, he wouldn't budge. Did she trust the warning? Reuben had nothing to gain. . .or did he? She thought about Mr. Woodward's questioning.

Charlotte tossed the brush onto the straw and placed both palms on her forehead. Her swirling thoughts reached a frenzied pace.

The barn door groaned open again, and a blast of air made Charlotte step closer to Belle, who snorted and moved to the edge of the stall. Another horse answered.

"Who's there?" *Please, not James inviting himself for supper.*

"It's me, Reuben." The sound of his voice made her feel warmer. And relieved.

Charlotte picked up the castaway brush and met Reuben outside the stall. He led Checkers into the barn. The young mare's ears twitched.

"Has she been a good horse so far?" Checkers turned at the sound of Charlotte's voice, and Charlotte touched her velvet nose.

"So far she's been smart and strong." Reuben grinned, a sight Charlotte hadn't seen in years. "She's the first of many horses that will run cattle."

"So you're planning to start a ranch then?"

Reuben nodded. "I want to continue what my father started. Or tried to start."

"Lots of opportunities here."

"That there are." He looped the reins over one hand and adjusted his hat.

"Where will you get the money?"

"I've got some put back. I'll save and work. I can make furniture to sell. I learned how to build tables and chairs in prison." Reuben's face flushed. Charlotte believed him and tried to calm the flutters in her stomach.

"The Ladies' Aid Society is having a box social." The words came out before she could stop them. As if he would be interested.

"Oh. When is that?"

"Saturday night." She was already fussing over her box, hoping to decorate it well. "The money is going to the children's home in Laramie."

"I will most definitely be there and bid high." Reuben swallowed. "I think about children like Benjamin and what he might have lost by not being in a proper home. I think the children need some place warm and safe to live where they can get good teaching."

Reuben turned from her and led Checkers to an empty stall. Charlotte followed.

"I hope Benjamin's all right, wherever he is. Have you heard anything yet?" She stopped and watched Reuben close the gate to the stall.

"No, nothing." The sigh he gave echoed the wind increasing outside.

Charlotte shivered. "Pa and I were talking earlier. If you need help. . ." She touched the sleeve of his coat and realized how thin it was.

He shrugged off her hand. "Thank you, but I'll be fine."

"Let me get you another coat then. You must be freezing in this one." Her breath made puffs in the air.

"No!" Reuben stepped around her.

She followed again, feeling like a puppy at his heels. "Why? Let me do something."

He whirled to face her, and she collided with him. She could scarcely breathe. He took her by the shoulders.

"I don't deserve your help. Work on your box for the social. I'll bid on that."

Charlotte nodded. "I wish, back then. . ."

He reached up to her face, then let his hand fall. "I know, Charlotte. I know."

—∞—

Charlotte sat at the table and tried to fold the thick pasteboard to make her box. Thanks to Momma's coaching, she'd managed to cook some chicken and make biscuits that wouldn't break off someone's teeth. She already had a spare length of blue ribbon tied into a bow that would adorn the top of her box.

Momma came from answering the door. James followed her from the front room. Momma's eyebrows rose so high they were nearly lost in her hairline.

"Good afternoon, Miss Charlotte." James set his hat on the table although no one had invited him to stay.

"Hello." She tried to smile and focused her attention back on the box. Now that James had seen her box and the ribbon, of course he would know which box was hers. At lunch Charlotte had left the materials at the end of the table, hoping Reuben would notice it when he came in from work. If he had, he said nothing. Not since their moments in the barn together had they spoken, except for the usual everyday greetings.

"You're quiet today."

"Ah, yes, well, I'm getting ready for tonight."

"May I see you to the church?"

The question hung in the air while Momma lurked in the background. Charlotte looked up at James. His eyes brimmed with sincerity. She recalled Reuben's warning. Reuben would not lie to her for his own gain. At least she hoped he wouldn't.

"No, but thank you all the same. I'll be riding with my parents tonight."

James snatched his hat from the table. "I see. I'll call again sometime." He turned on his heel and left the kitchen. The front door banged behind him.

Charlotte released a long, slow breath.

"I'm so glad you said no." Momma fetched a clean cloth for Charlotte to place inside her box. "Your pa and I have been talking, and we don't think James is a man you should be spending much time with."

"Why didn't you say so? I would have told him 'no' sooner." Charlotte arranged the cloth.

Momma touched Charlotte's blue bow. "You were always the headstrong one. I wanted you to see for yourself. Be patient. Your time is coming."

Charlotte tried to smile at Momma, but her eyes filling with tears surprised her. She didn't know how much longer to wait or what exactly she was waiting for.

Chapter 6

Reuben could see the white box with the big blue bow on the table at the front of the chapel. That box had to be Charlotte's. He recalled that the bow he'd seen on the Jeffers table at dinnertime was blue. He glanced in Charlotte's direction. Patches of red glowed on her cheeks.

"What am I bid for this fine supper, last box of the night?" Albert Booth held it up for all to see.

"Ten dollars!" Someone else's voice rang out. James, of course.

Heavenly smells drifted across the room. They reminded Reuben of Ma's cooking, and the memory panged him. If he wanted to eat tonight, he'd better get a move-on.

"Who else to bid on this fine meal? Remember—the money goes to Ladies' Aid."

Now was his chance. "Fifteen dollars!"

Reuben ignored the gasps of the crowd and the sharp look from James. Surely the fellow didn't plan on going as high as Reuben, who had enough cash in his pocket to outlast Mr. James Newspaper Writer. He sure hoped Charlotte had learned to cook. Enjoying her company would be enough, though, regardless of the supper.

Albert Booth grinned over at James. "Any more bids?"

"Twenty dollars." James nodded.

Reuben's stomach growled. "Twenty-five."

Now came the whispers. "Where'd he get that money?"

"Thirty!"

More roars from the crowd. James had leapt to his feet. Charlotte went pale, and Reuben wanted to tell her she had nothing to worry about.

Albert Booth stared him down. "Anyone else?"

Reuben remembered the times he had stolen, once pilfering a donation plate such as rested on the table at the front of the room. Why the Almighty had shown him such great mercy, he didn't understand. He hoped tonight would go a ways to paying Him back.

"Forty-five!"

Whoops rose up around Reuben, and someone clapped him on the back. He saw James conversing with a friend, maybe the same one he'd been talking with about Charlotte. The man showed James empty pockets.

James faced Mr. Booth. "Fifty dollars."

The look in James's eyes told Reuben he'd come to the end. Maybe the fellow didn't have such a great poker face after all. Reuben stood a mite taller.

"Sixty dollars."

The room fairly buzzed. James threw his hat on the floor while Reuben went to claim his supper box. He didn't regret the money. But he hadn't counted on the ruckus when he withdrew cash from his inside jacket pocket. Mr. Booth shook his head while he counted the money. Mrs. Booth fanned herself and appeared as though she needed smelling salts.

Reuben didn't care. He searched for Charlotte, who had her back to him and was speaking with a few of the other women from church. One younger unattached woman giggled when he approached.

Charlotte's cheeks looked as if she'd spent an hour in front of the mirror pinching them. "Hello." Her glance darted from her friends then back to him. "I had some help with the cooking."

"That's all right." Reuben found himself grinning. "Ma'am, let's sit down and have us some supper."

He turned and nearly walked smack into James.

"Where'd you get all that money?" His brows furrowed. His dark eyes held a demanding glare.

"I earned it, fair and square." Reuben clutched the box instead of going with his gut inclination to shove the man out of his way.

Charlotte tried to step between them. "James, don't."

Reuben balanced the box on one hand and touched Charlotte's shoulder. "No harm done. He realized he was mistaken, didn't he?"

James leaned closer. "You think you've got people fooled, but you haven't fooled me. Wait and see. I'll make sure this whole town sees you for the fraud you are."

"I'm not that person anymore." Reuben's stomach growled. His expensive supper was waiting, and his temper was tighter to rein in the hungrier he got.

"Keep telling yourself that."

There came Albert Booth. "Gentlemen, is there a problem?" He stood as if ready to intervene. A few in the room had stopped dining to stare at the face-off.

Reuben waited for James to answer and gritted his teeth.

"No, sir." James kept boring into Reuben with those burning molasses eyes. "But I'd keep my wallet close by if I were you."

Only Charlotte's firm squeeze in the crook of Reuben's elbow kept him from taking a swing at the man. *Lord, I sure need Your hand to hold mine back right about now.*

James pushed past them both, and Reuben released a pent-up breath.

"Son, you did good." Albert gave him a nod, then went back to his wife.

"Let's sit down and eat, and you can tell me how wonderful everything tastes." Charlotte moved closer to his side, not releasing her grip on his arm.

"Thanks." Reuben found a quiet place at a bench in the corner. He settled onto the seat. The rest of the crowd seemed to be enjoying their meals. Would his past continually trail him like this? No wonder he had delayed coming home for so long. He removed his coat and laid it on the bench behind him.

He watched Charlotte unfold a pair of napkins. She handed one to him.

"Here. Wouldn't want you to muss that nice shirt of yours."

Charlotte had their meal spread between them quick enough. He asked the blessing and wasted no time tearing into the largest piece of chicken in front of him.

"I'm glad you won." She gave him a small smile that lit the corner of the room.

"I am, too," he said around a bite of chicken. "This is one more step toward atonement."

Her face flushed again. "What do you mean?"

"You see, after I made my peace with the Lord, I promised Him I would make up for as many wrong things as I could. To show Him I was sorry. Reverend Mann said it was needful that I do."

"Needful?"

Reuben nodded. "To make sure I was forgiven."

"I believe in making restitution when you can, but, Reuben, you can't atone for your sins." She touched his hand, an act that made his throat grow a knot. He hoped no one had seen the gesture.

"You don't understand." Reuben moved his hand away from hers. "I've done so many wrong things that the scales are heavy against me. God's scales."

"What about grace?"

"What are you talking about?"

Charlotte leaned closer, close enough that he could see the sprinkle of freckles remaining on her cheeks. "God's grace and the forgiveness He gives us tip the scales in our favor. Well, better than that. He knocks the weights off the scales, and we don't owe any more."

Reuben set down the chicken bone and grabbed a biscuit. He tried to think about her words. The scales knocked clean. Not owing anymore. The thought of weights being lifted from him sounded like a breath of fresh air, the kind a man inhaled when sitting on top of a mountain.

"You don't know what I've done, Charlotte." The flaky

biscuit did little to soothe the churning Reuben felt inside his stomach. "It's easy for you. You haven't drifted off the straight 'n' narrow more than a few paces in your life."

"But I've still been wrong. I battle with—with pride, a sharp tongue, a bitter attitude. Quite often, in fact." Charlotte was trying to look him in the eye, but at the moment he found a second biscuit more interesting and wouldn't glance her way.

"Charlotte, I was an outlaw. I lived without thought of right or wrong. I don't think asking for forgiveness is all I have to do."

"Are you saying that what Jesus did for us wasn't enough?"

"Of course not." He didn't care if she saw the biscuit lolling around in his mouth. Tonight was not going as he'd planned. Not at all. He had wanted to see if there might be an inkling of love for him inside Charlotte, but instead he'd gotten tossed onto the grill over an open fire.

"Reuben, there'll always be people like James wanting to fling your past in your face. But as you told him, that's not you anymore."

He wanted to believe her, to kiss the lips on her earnest face. Right now, though, he felt as if the hangman's noose had settled around his neck.

"Miss Charlotte, I thank you kindly for the superb meal and your company." Reuben stood and nodded to her while reaching for his hat. He found his coat, which had slipped to the floor, and put it on.

"Where are you going?" Her eyes pleaded with him to stay.

"I reckon I need some air." With that he turned on his heel

and walked away. If he could but step away from his past so easily.

Reuben paused at the door when he reached inside his outer pocket and felt a piece of paper. He slid it out and found a five-dollar note.

This was not his money. The cash he'd withdrawn from the bank for supper, he'd tucked inside his chest pocket. He did not recall anyone giving him cash, either.

Someone was out to smear him, and he had a pretty good idea who'd like to try. He stood outside in the chilly air and felt a long, slow burn inside.

"Reuben Wilson?" He turned at the sound of a voice at his elbow.

"I'm Ed Smythe. . .from the telegraph office?"

Reuben's heart leapt inside him. "Have you received word?"

Ed withdrew a folded paper from his pocket. "I was hoping you'd be in town Friday, but since you weren't, I thought I'd bring this tonight."

"Well, thank you." Reuben received the paper and watched Ed stride toward a waiting team.

He read the paper.

"Colt Wilson. Inmate at Texas State Penitentiary, Huntsville." The chief warden had replied to Reuben's inquiry.

Oh, Ma. I'm making good on my promise. Reuben needed to speak with Sam as soon as possible about leaving for Texas.

When Charlotte emerged from the chapel with her ma and pa, Reuben found Checkers and watched, hoping to speak to Sam without having to face Charlotte.

The last thing he saw before riding home was Charlotte

talking to James, standing next to his buggy that gleamed in the lantern light.

"No, James." Charlotte shrugged off his attention and shivered. Her breath made puffs in the evening air. *Where did Pa go? He said he'd be right along with the wagon.*

"I'm trying to warn you." James took a step closer. "Reuben Wilson has not changed, and I'm going to prove it. One way or another."

"Whatever Reuben is, he is my friend, and I've known him practically my whole life." Charlotte glared at him as best she could. "Leave him alone." She saw Pa driving up with the team and moved away from James.

"You're not thinking clearly. Childhood fancies have—"

"I've never thought more clearly than now." The chilly air stung her hot cheeks. "In fact, it's clear to me that I don't want you to come calling—or offer me rides anywhere—ever again."

Charlotte turned on her heel and joined her parents. This was what Reuben had meant. She felt like a young child bilked out of her small coins by a huckster's false promise. Relief soon followed, and she smiled at Pa.

"Everything all right?" he asked.

"Yes, it is. Or I hope it will be."

He helped Momma and then her onto the wagon, and they headed for home.

Reuben did not come to the house after the family returned from the box social. Charlotte didn't suppose he would, but for a while she held the remote hope that he might. She had so many things she wanted to say to him.

The poor man, all he'd wanted was a good supper, and she'd kept at him like a pecking hen.

A knock sounded at the door as if in response to her thoughts. Reuben stood there holding his hat. "Charlotte, I must speak with your pa." The urgency in his voice made her stomach turn.

"Of course." She opened the door wider for him. "What's wrong?

"Nothing, but I need to leave for a spell."

"Leave?" A dozen questions soared through her mind. She turned to the kitchen. "Pa, it's Reuben."

"Well, send him in here. Your ma has the kettle on."

Charlotte followed Reuben into the warm kitchen. He stood there, shifting his weight from one foot to the other. She tried to sit without drawing attention to herself.

"Sir, I've received word of my brother Colt. He's in Huntsville."

Pa nodded. "You must go to him."

"I'm real sorry. I don't like leaving you like this. But I promise I'll be back as soon as I can."

Leaving? Charlotte's heart sank. He said he'd return but. . .

"We'll send you with a parcel of food for your trip." Pa huffed through his mustache. "Charlotte, gather some things for Reuben."

Charlotte stood, glad for something to do. That way she could listen while the men planned. She began gathering provisions.

"I'll leave on the next stage out. Can't say as I know how long I'll be."

"You take what time you need, and we'll be home waiting for you, son." Pa gripped Reuben's shoulder.

"Thank you, sir." Reuben's voice was a bare whisper.

Home. Pa had called this place Reuben's home. Charlotte's vision blurred with tears. This time she wouldn't let him leave without a word. This time things would be different. They had to.

Reuben slid the piece of paper money from his pocket and showed Sam once Charlotte had left the room. "Sir, this isn't mine."

"Well, whose is it then?"

"I don't know. I found it in my pocket tonight."

"Do you think you miscounted?"

"No, sir, I don't. The bank clerk counted the money twice in front of me." Reuben sighed. "I counted my money twice when I paid for my box supper tonight."

"That doesn't explain the extra bill."

"It doesn't. I think someone put it in my pocket, intending to frame me for stealing it. I know it's only a five-dollar note, but I'm not going back to jail again."

"Now, son, don't think that." Sam scratched his chin. "I tell you what. Let me hold onto this until you get back. We'll get it straightened out. Go see your brother. Right now you going to Huntsville is safer than staying here."

Chapter 7

Reuben felt as if he moved in someone else's dream as Sam drove him to meet the stage. He had a sack of food, enough for two men, on this trip. He was not sure what would happen, nor was he worried about that at the moment.

Charlotte had not said good-bye to him that morning. He had hoped for a glimpse of her, but in the predawn hours, Mrs. Jeffers told him Charlotte was ill. A fine time for her to get sick.

"Well, son. Here you are." Sam drew the team to a halt. "You be sure and telegraph when you get there, just so we know. We'll be praying for you and for Colt, as well."

"I appreciate that, sir." He shook hands with Sam and climbed from the wagon. Approaching hoofbeats made him look back where they'd traveled from.

Charlotte rode up on Belle. Her hair streamed back in the wind, her cheeks flushed.

"You ought to be home in bed," Sam chided.

"No one woke me." She swung off Belle's back. Her face

looked pale. "But I had to see you before you left."

Sam reached for Belle's reins. "Go on—you two talk. I'm not going anywhere."

Reuben couldn't believe he was leaving Charlotte again. But he would be back.

He escorted her a few paces away from the wagon. "Your ma told me you were sick."

"I don't care." Charlotte's cheeks blazed. "I couldn't let you leave without telling you. . ."

"I'll be home again as soon as I can. I want to see what I can do for my brother and hope to start making up for the past."

"Do you think you can do that in a matter of days or weeks?"

"I'm not going to stay there too long, but I want to make a start anyway." He studied her face and saw the fear in her eyes. "What are you afraid of?"

"That you won't come back this time."

He took her hand, which was as much as he dared. "Charlotte Jeffers, it about rips a hole inside me to think of not seeing you every day. When I get back again, I aim for a new start with you, too."

A smile crept across her face. "Well, I aim to hold you to that."

"Pray for me?"

"You know I will."

Her hair reminded him of those days long ago when she'd chase after them on her pony. She'd followed again, with the promise of love in her eyes. Now how could a fellow not return to that?

He released her hand and, without a backward glance, headed for the waiting stage.

—∞—

Reuben stood before the prison in Huntsville, Texas. His heart pounded in his throat. He had vowed never to enter such a place again. After he was admitted and the doors clanged shut behind him, he had the inclination to turn around and run. Right now, though, he was about worn out after days of travel. The bath and shave, a hot meal and a good night's sleep helped some, but now that he'd turned a couple of corners past thirty, he felt the effects of traveling.

He found the man they told him was Colt. Reuben tried not to grimace at the odor in the cell block, the scent bringing back a flood of memories. No wonder he had inhaled deeply of the outside air once he'd been freed from prison.

"Can I help you with somethin'?" His voice sounded deeper, coarser than Reuben remembered. He sat up on the straw mattress that crackled and popped under his weight.

"It's. . .it's me, Colt." Reuben felt as if he'd swallowed an apple whole. "Reuben, your big brother."

"Well, if you don't say so." Colt remained seated. "Been a long time. Thought we were gonna meet back in Denmark and get Benjamin."

"I thought we were, too." Reuben's eyes burned, and he clutched the bar with one hand. The excuses and avoidances of the past thirteen years swirled within his head.

"You look good. You come into any money?"

"The hard way. By workin' for it."

"So. What're you here for?" Colt's dark gaze dropped to the floor. Reuben remembered the way it felt. Not to be free to speak, to move.

"I came to see you. I need to ask your forgiveness. . . ."

Colt's head snapped up, and his gaze bored into Reuben. "What're you talking about? I wasn't a spineless nitwit who followed you like a pup. If anything, you would've never done half the things you done if it wasn't for my gumption."

Now this was the Colt that Reuben remembered, already wanting to pick a fight after not five minutes. Reuben smiled and let the words blow past him.

"All the same, I'm sorry for my part in what happened to our family, and I want to make it up to you."

Colt shot across the cell until but inches remained between them. If it weren't for the bars and the watchful guard, Reuben supposed his brother's hands would be clamped around his neck.

"Make it up to me? That's real easy to say when you're on the outside looking all polished like you're ready to go to a church meeting." The air crackled between them as Colt ground out the words.

"Once I was right where you are. I know what it's like. And it's only with God's help that I'm about half the man I oughta be."

A crooked grin slid across Colt's face. "Got religion, did ya? It's not surprising. Many fellows do when they're on the inside. Say a prayer, cry like a mama's boy, and start singing hymns is all you've got to do."

Reuben's heart sank. But it wasn't as if he really expected

Colt to greet him with any measure of brotherly love.

"I have to go now." Reuben glanced at the guard. "But I'll be back."

Colt ambled over to the bunk attached to the wall and sat. "Suit yourself. I ain't going anywhere."

—∞—

Charlotte stared at the telegraph in her hands. "Arrived safe Huntsville. Pecan Street Hotel. RW." The seven days he'd been gone so far felt like seven years. She trudged along the boardwalk and saw her family's wagon. Her parents were still about, Momma at the mercantile and Pa on his errands. They never complained about having an old maid daughter, but today she felt as useless as a holey, worn-out dishrag. She might as well join Momma at the mercantile. She'd said something about purchasing some new fabrics for spring dresses.

The bell clanged over the shop's door as Charlotte entered. Momma looked up from the dry goods. She clutched a bolt of cloth to her chest and smiled.

"They have some nice-looking fabrics over here."

Charlotte nodded and joined Momma. "We got a telegraph from Reuben. He made it." She fingered the flower-sprigged navy blue. Normally the color would appeal to her, but today the prettiest pattern had no interest.

"I'm glad." Momma moved to the thread and gave Charlotte a glance. "You don't look too happy."

"I miss him, Momma."

"That's good. But is that all that's eating at you?"

She shook her head. "I'm afraid that he won't. . .he won't come back."

"He promised, didn't he?" Momma's pat on the hand wasn't reassuring. "You need to have faith in the man you love and faith that God will watch over him while he's gone."

"You. . .you can tell how I feel about him?" Charlotte touched her burning cheeks. "Is it obvious?"

"Like the sunrise on a clear day. To me and your pa, anyhow."

Mrs. Booth moved from her place behind the post office window. "Ladies, how are you today? Do you think spring is about here yet?"

No, but I think you're here to see if you can catch a tidbit about Reuben.

Aloud, Charlotte said, "We're fine, thank you. And I do believe a thaw is on the way."

"Oh, I certainly hope so." The older woman leaned closer. "I think if another ice storm came upon us I'd give up and move back East." Charlotte almost hoped she'd sensed a freezing bite in the air outside.

Charlotte felt the toe of Momma's boot press hard enough on her own to cause her to stifle a yelp. Same as always, Momma probably had her figured out.

"Mrs. Booth," Momma said, "do you remember how much the Ladies' Aid raised at the box social?"

"Over a hundred dollars, thanks to Reuben Wilson." Mrs. Booth's stare at Charlotte made her blink. "I hope that was some supper you fed him. Although, honestly, seein' him flash that money when he paid for his box got me a bit worried."

"Whatever for?" Momma placed her hand over Charlotte's as she spoke.

"Where'd he get that cash from?"

"He's been working hard," Charlotte interjected. "He was working his way home and saving money before he returned here."

Mrs. Booth nodded. "It wouldn't surprise me if he's trying to get his gang back together and rob us all blind. Didn't I see him leaving on the stage not a week ago?"

Charlotte glanced at Momma. Reuben had asked that they not tell the full nature of his errand so as not to get tongues wagging in his absence.

She let Momma speak. "Reuben is away seeing to a family matter." Then Momma's face closed up tight. A customer clanged into the store at that moment, and Charlotte wanted to breathe in relief.

Mrs. Booth humphed and stomped back toward the post window. "I think the sheriff ought to know. Forewarned is forearmed." Her boots clunked on the wooden planks as she moved to the postal window and put on a fresh smile.

Momma kept silent for a moment. Then, "I'm proud of you for not saying anything. Nearly every time I see that woman and speak with her, I find myself on my knees apologizing to God for something I said."

"Some people bring out the best in us, and, well. . ." Charlotte couldn't get her mind off Mrs. Booth's words. Reuben. Getting the gang together. He'd told her he promised his ma he'd find his brothers.

She hoped Reuben hadn't faltered in his desire to get back

the family ranch. *What if he finds his brothers and they run off again?* Charlotte pushed back the idea. Have a little faith in the man you love and in the Lord, Momma had told her.

Help me, Lord, to do just that.

Chapter 8

"You're back." Colt still sat on the mattress in his cell. The other inmate snored from his bunk along the opposite wall. Reuben had arrived after supper, hoping to have a better visit than yesterday.

Reuben couldn't decide if Colt had asked him or told him. Either way, Reuben knew he wouldn't give up on building a bridge to reach his brother.

"Yes, I'm here."

"Why?"

"I. . .I promised Ma I'd find you." Reuben's throat caught. *He doesn't know about Ma.*

"Does she still care? Doesn't she know I'm here?" Colt almost sounded like a little boy again.

"She does care. . .well, she did." Reuben swallowed. "Ma. . . Ma passed in February. I got back to Raider's Crossing a few days before she. . ."

The Adam's apple bobbed in Colt's neck. "I'm glad she wasn't alone." He looked lost.

"No. She never quit prayin' for us, either." Reuben wanted

to reach through the bars and hug Colt, but he figured he'd probably get slugged. "The Jeffers family bought Pa's land."

Colt nodded. "What about that little girl they had, the one always chasing you on her pony?"

"Charlotte? She's there." And Reuben knew he should be with her.

"I see. Guess she's plenty old enough now for you two to get hitched." A wry smile teased the corners of Colt's mouth.

"Yeah, she is. If she'll have me." Reuben's heart panged. "If she'll take a fellow with a past like mine."

Colt shrugged. "See—now that's what I meant yesterday. You pray a few prayers, dress right, sing some church songs—yet you still ain't fixed. I don't need that. I don't have the time."

"But God's forgiven me. I've turned from my wicked ways." Reuben found himself gripping the bars as he had yesterday.

In three steps Colt stood at the bars that separated them. "Then, big brother, tell me why you look like you're still carrying a sentence on your shoulders. Either this religion works enough for you to tell me about it, or it don't."

Reuben drew in a shuddering breath. "Colt, I want this to work. The way I did things didn't. I've got no other choice. I know I can't do this without God."

"Always the serious and responsible one. Ruby, there's some things a man just can't keep taking responsibility for. You need to learn when to let go." Colt ambled back to his bunk and sat down.

Colt's words slammed into Reuben like a well-planted fist. He would have welcomed the fist more than the words.

"Colt, how much longer do you have in here?"

"I get out real soon."

"You're welcome to join me in Wyoming. I'm going to get our land back, and I'd like your help building what our pa lost." Reuben felt like he was begging. "It won't be easy, but having family around will make the burden lighter."

Colt appeared thoughtful. "I. . .I can't. I've got somewhere else I need to be. You ain't the only one who made a promise."

Reuben had to leave it at that. "All right. But, Colt, if you need me, you get word to me. You're my brother, and that don't change."

With that, Colt hung his head. "You take care now, Ruby."

That night Reuben could not sleep, alone in a strange town with his long-lost brother not far away. The late-night rumble of carriages, the sound of a piano somewhere, and laughter and muffled voices from downstairs reminded him of how much he missed Wyoming. He longed for the sound of the wind whistling in the bunkhouse eaves, the pop of burning wood in his stove, and the occasional call from one of the cattle. Even the mournful coyote. Most of all he wanted to hear Charlotte's voice.

Instead, he heard Colt's words that pierced into his soul. Since he couldn't sleep, he figured he might as well pray.

Kneeling on the hardwood floor as Reverend Mann had said a man ought to pray, Reuben began.

"Lord, I've been trying to do what's right in Your eyes, but I still"—he drew in a shuddering breath—"I still feel like I'm not good enough. I know I've done all those things Colt said, but the idea that You've forgiven me just doesn't add up."

Charlotte's words at the box social chased Colt's words around Reuben's mind.

"Now, Lord, I'm not saying what Jesus did for me wasn't enough. It was plenty for one thief on the cross. And I have a feeling he and I aren't much different."

Reuben paused and heard only the sounds of the traffic outside and hotel noises below. He touched his face, and it was wet with tears.

"Remember me."

The weight on Reuben's shoulders nearly suffocated him as he remained on his knees, his head bowed. Colt was right. He'd worn the past like his old coat and dragged it along behind him like a string of chains when it got too heavy. The bitter realization made a flood of tears burst from inside, tears he'd never let himself shed since that day in Denmark.

"Please release me from this, Lord." Now he was blubbering like a five-year-old. "I'm not sorry about getting caught. I know what I've done was wrong."

A quiet breeze drifted in the window, and it held a hint of early Texas spring.

I make all things new.

The silent words wrapped around Reuben and swallowed up the weight that covered him. He felt as if he'd dropped a heavy load.

Reuben imagined he was out riding Checkers and had cast a burden on the trail. He could picture himself looking back at the heap lying in the dust. Sure, he'd owned up to it, but he wouldn't carry it any longer. Then another rider came up on a horse that glowed brighter than fresh cotton. This rider took up Reuben's load and slung it over his shoulder. His smile hit Reuben like the sun's glow.

Let's ride together.

Reuben opened his eyes to see the blanket on his bed in the hotel. It was time to go home.

Charlotte flung back the covers and rolled out of bed. The new dress with its sprigs of flowers hung on the dress form in her room. She and Momma had worked to finish the dress before Reuben returned home—today!

The simple telegraph lay on the washstand, and Charlotte had dreamed of the message the whole night:

"Returning. Arriving Wednesday on stage. RW." She hoped and prayed that Reuben's errand was successful.

She hurried through her simple chores and helped Momma make breakfast but didn't change into the new dress until it was time for them to leave for town.

Why had she doubted? For an instant, Charlotte wondered what dark thing lay in store for them.

"Sorry, Lord. I didn't mean to borrow trouble. Go before us today and guide our steps. Watch over Reuben on his journey." She stood before the looking glass that hung on the wall over the washstand and pinched her cheeks. Color sprang into them.

"You ready?" Pa called at her door. "Don't know exactly when that stage will arrive, but I'd like to be there. The team's waitin' outside."

"I'll be right there, Pa." Charlotte paused and glanced

back into her bedroom. A spinster's bedroom. The room of a woman who waited for a broken promise to be fulfilled. No, not quite broken. Just delayed. She regretted the lost years she had spent, not in idleness certainly, but in waiting. But some things, some people were worth waiting for.

Momma was fastening the bow under her chin when Charlotte entered the kitchen. "Sam, I don't see why you're going, too."

"Etta, the other boys have things in hand around here till we get back. Besides, I need to speak with Reuben." Pa showed them a folded piece of paper money. "He asked me to keep this while he was gone—says he doesn't know how it came to be inside his coat pocket and didn't want to be caught holding this money."

Charlotte eyed the money. "You think someone might be trying to make it look like he's stealing again?" No, not Reuben. But all that money at the social and him at the bank—the idea made her blood boil.

Pa nodded slowly. "If Reuben's in trouble, he needs all the friends he can get right now."

She looked at Pa. "Why didn't you tell me?"

"Didn't want you to spend your time worryin' while Reuben was gone."

Charlotte grabbed her shawl and followed them into the late winter chill. Borrowing trouble? She suddenly felt as if they'd bought a whole pile of it.

Days spent on the stage left Reuben with a short scruff of

beard and a weary heart. He hadn't expected his brother to rush to him with open arms. He hadn't expected his faith to be shaken to its crumbly foundations, either.

The buildings of Raider's Crossing loomed ahead. Home. For good or ill, Reuben would stay. He squinted from his place on top of the stage. Better on the outside freezing than inside below with a screaming baby and folks smelling of travel.

Reuben caught sight of the Jeffers' wagon, and his heart leapt when he saw Charlotte. The first thing he wanted to do, after getting a bath and shave, of course, then speaking with her pa, was take her in his arms.

Then he saw the fear on Charlotte's face.

Another sight made his heart fall. There stood the sheriff, Mr. Woodward, the newspaper man, and James Johansson.

Be my shield, Lord. I have no defense but the truth.

Reuben waited until the stage rolled to a stop. He climbed down, his heart pounding a drumbeat. Charlotte ran to him and wrapped him in a strong hug.

"I don't believe it. They're wrong," she whispered in his ear. "You should have told me about the money."

"I didn't want to worry you," he whispered back.

Fresh tears came from her eyes. "You sound like Pa."

"I consider that to be a compliment."

"Miz Jeffers," came the sheriff's no-nonsense voice, "you need to step aside."

She did so slowly, her hands curled into fists. "You've got no proof."

"Have I done something wrong, Sheriff?" Reuben looked him in the eye.

"That remains to be seen, Wilson." The sheriff nodded in the direction of Mr. Woodward and James. "You need to come down to my office and answer some questions. Mr. Woodward is asking that robbery charges be lodged against you."

Chapter 9

Reuben's eyelids drooped as he sat in the stiff-backed chair across from the sheriff. He didn't know how many times he repeated the same answers to the same questions.

"Like I said before, I only made one deposit and one withdrawal. Check the bank records."

The sheriff kicked back in his chair and leaned against the wall. "Mr. Woodward here says he started noticing money missing about the same time you arrived in Raider's Crossing. And he told me about the time y'all bumped heads at the bank, money going everywhere.

"I'm sure it's mighty tempting to a man in your position to see a month's worth of wages going across the floor."

Reuben curled his hands into fists at his sides. *A man in your position.* "Sheriff, I'm not that kind of man anymore. I've earned my money from hard work, not thieving."

James stepped forward. "And you have enough to throw down for a silly supper? What, were you trying to impress her father?"

It would take but one punch to fell this dandy.

Reuben sucked in a deep breath. "I don't recall the sheriff allowing you to ask questions. In fact, I don't know why you're here in the first place." He glared at James, who shrank back to the corner. "You've had it in for me since the day I came here. Wouldn't it be something else if you were the one causing all this trouble?"

James licked his lips. "Howard, tell him about the accounts."

Mr. Woodward began. "I've been missing money, here and there, five to ten dollars at a time, from the subscription receipts." He tossed a ledger onto the table. "Sheriff, start from the beginning of this year."

"I'm not a man of numbers, Woodward." The sheriff thumbed the pages. "What'm I looking at?"

"The missing amounts are circled, right here. Somehow between the newspaper office and the bank, the money goes missing." Mr. Woodward pointed to the last entry. "See here? Last Tuesday, five more dollars missing."

Reuben sat up straighter. "Mr. Woodward, I believe you've got a thief, and I know it's not me. I was in Huntsville visiting my brother in prison on that date. The Jeffers family has two telegraphs I sent, on my arrival and right before I left. And the prison has a record of my visits."

James's face had turned the color of paste. "Wh–what?"

Mr. Woodward turned to face James. "You told me you had seen Reuben that day in town. Unless he can work some kind of trick, I don't see as how he can be two places at once."

James bolted for the door, but Reuben stuck out his foot and sent the man flying. Not quite a punch, but at the moment it would serve the cause of justice.

Charlotte saw Reuben leaving the sheriff's office before Momma and Pa did. "He's coming out!" She picked up the hem of her skirt and ran for him. "What happened?"

He smiled at her, his green eyes alight in a way she hadn't seen in years. "It was James all along. Seems he had a hankering for a new buggy and other things. Figured a few dollars here and there would help. When I came to town, he started getting greedier."

"So that explains it. I wondered how he got that buggy." She shook her head. Reuben offered her his arm, and they walked along to her parents' wagon.

"He looked squeaky clean around me." Reuben shrugged. "Get enough rumors flying, people will look the other way at what's under their noses. Howard Woodward didn't quite suspect me, though. But he had an idea something was up when Mrs. Booth mentioned me being out of town on the same day James said he saw me on the street passing by the newspaper office."

Charlotte laughed. "Thank you, Mrs. Booth, for sharing information! I never thought I'd say that."

Reuben's chuckle made her go all warm inside. "Yes, and thank You, Lord."

"What about Colt? How is he?"

"About as well as you can expect in prison. I offered him a place here with me one day, but he's got somewhere else in mind. He showed me something, even though he didn't want to listen about God changing him." Reuben stopped and took

Charlotte's hands in his. "He showed me I was wrong, thinking I could earn my forgiveness. Like if I did enough good, it would cancel out the bad. It's hard sometimes, still, thinking about what I've done, but I'm ready to start looking forward."

Charlotte smiled. "Me, too. And one day I'd love to see Colt and thank him."

"You two going to talk each other to death?" Pa's voice carried over the wind that held the hint of early spring. "In case you didn't know, it's freezing out here."

Reuben tied a knot in his necktie. He could never get used to feeling gussied up, but when a fellow proposed marriage, he couldn't take a chance at appearing in less than his best. Sam had told him to make sure he joined them for supper. Maybe he was a tad overdressed for a Wednesday night supper, but he figured he wouldn't be comfortable even in his everyday work clothes.

He crossed the yard to the main house where the scent of supper drifted from the kitchen door. Charlotte's and her ma's laughter joined the smells that made his stomach growl louder. After a week of jerky and stale bread, a supper of beef and potatoes would go down well. *Thank You, Lord, for true freedom.*

"There you are!" Charlotte stood in the doorway and drew him inside with her hand. Her smile made him feel warm to his toes. She squeezed his hand, and he raised her hand to his lips. The blush that swept over her face reminded him of the days in summer when they'd tear around on horseback and she'd leave her sunbonnet at home.

Sam entered the kitchen and surveyed the table laden with food. "Son, I almost feel like sending you away again so we can eat like this every night."

"Now, Sam," his wife chided. But she beamed, as well, when he tugged on her apron strings.

Sam asked the blessing once they were all seated around the table. "Lord, thank You for this food. Bless it to our bodies and our lives for Your service. We thank You for delivering Reuben from the snare of the wicked today. Thank You, as well, for bringing him home again. Amen." At that Reuben tightened his grip around Charlotte's hand.

"Sir," he ventured once they filled their plates, "I must talk to you about something important, before I lose my nerve and before I eat and lose my supper at the idea of speaking to you."

Charlotte's father set his fork down next to his plate. "Well, if it's all that important, I'd like to hear it before I eat."

"Two things." Reuben tugged at his necktie. "First, I love your daughter. I always have, and I always will." He could feel her face glowing from where she sat opposite him. "I haven't been a Christian man for many years, but I'm learning. Once I can provide for her properly, I want to marry her, and I'd like your blessing." His throat hurt after the long speech.

Sam nodded. "I appreciate you asking me first. I see Charlotte's answer on her face."

Reuben reached for Charlotte's hand. "I love you, Charlie Jeffers, till the stars die. I was stupid and selfish many years ago, but I promise you I'll never leave our love behind again. We were only children, but even then I knew. . ."

"I did, too." A tear slid down Charlotte's cheek, and she grinned as she dashed it away with her free hand.

"Now." Sam punctuated his sentence by slamming his palm on the table so hard his coffee cup jumped. "How do you propose to provide for my daughter?"

Reuben cleared his throat. "That's the second thing I'd like to talk to you about. I want to buy back the land my family used to own. I don't have enough money yet to make you a good offer, but I'm working on that."

Sam picked up his fork and stabbed a bite of meat on his plate. He swirled it in some gravy and popped it in his mouth. Reuben could almost see the man's mind working as he ate.

Reuben followed Sam's lead and popped a piece of meat into his mouth although his appetite had fled. He swallowed it without even noticing that it was so tender it melted in his mouth. Then he paused and smiled at Charlotte. They had so many things to talk about.

At last Sam broke the silence. "I can't sell you that land."

Reuben felt his shoulders sag, but he refused to let Sam see the dreams crumbling inside him. "I. . .I see."

"I'm going to give it to you."

"Sir—" Reuben's throat tied itself in a knot to match his necktie.

Sam raised his hand. "No. Cut that out. I know what you're goin' to say. You don't deserve that. Maybe not. But this is what we'll do." He took another bite.

"What's that?"

"I'm going to give you the pick of the spring calves this year, seein' as how you're going to help me with the calving.

You raise those and add to the small herd I know you can buy." Sam sipped his coffee. "Then, for the next three years, all the female calves your herd bears will be mine."

The room seemed to spin around him. "You'd do that?"

"We both want the same thing. I want my little girl cared for. I want you and Charlotte to work that parcel. . .together."

"Oh, Pa. It's a dream come true." Charlotte squeezed Reuben's hand.

Sam smiled, a rare sight Reuben hadn't recalled since working for the man. "That it is."

Epilogue

Charlotte and Reuben rode out to their future home. The March breeze spoke of living things and new chances. The Wilsons' soddy would be snug until Reuben had completed repairs on the main wood-frame house, abandoned for years. Charlotte could hardly wait to make the place their own.

"Think we'll be courting for long?"

"I don't know," Reuben replied. "I think your pa knows we spent many years apart. I think a summer wedding is fine. Except I'd marry you tomorrow if I could."

"My dress isn't finished." Charlotte studied his expression. "I know you're wanting a short walk to the altar, but I'm not getting married in my Sunday dress. I've waited too long for you to take shortcuts now."

"I know." He smiled that Wilson smile she loved so well.

They halted the horses, and Charlotte swung off her horse. Reuben did the same, and Checkers and Belle strolled on long reins as they munched the new grass.

Reuben took Charlotte's hand. "I need to be getting back

soon, but I wanted to have a few minutes of quiet. Promise me one thing?"

"Of course."

"Help me keep looking for Caleb and Benjamin."

"You can count on me." She would sprout wings and scout the land for the two men if she could.

"It doesn't matter if they don't want to come home. I want to know they're safe and well, and if they need help, I want them to know I'm here." Reuben blinked, and Charlotte thought she saw a few unshed tears.

"We'll find them together." She squeezed his hand tighter.

"That's how I always want it to be." He pulled her into his arms. "You and me, together."

"Till the stars die," Charlotte whispered just before Reuben kissed her.

LYNETTE SOWELL

Lynette Sowell's early love of books sparked her love of story and sense of adventure. She works as a medical transcriptionist for a large HMO during the day. In her spare time she loves to write, read, travel, and spend time with her family. Lynette hopes she's earned the title of honorary Texan after making it her home for nearly fifteen years. Its wide skies and open spaces have fed her creativity. She lives with her husband, two kids by love and marriage (what's a stepkid?), and a herd of five cats who have them all well trained. You can visit her Web site at www.lynettesowell.com.

The Peacemaker

by DiAnn Mills

Chapter 1

Texas 1880

When Anne Langley became a widow, she vowed her children would know Jesus and never go hungry. She'd accomplished those things and more. Standing on the back porch of her white-stone home that faced east, she sipped from a mug of strong coffee and watched the sun slowly expand the horizon in shades of purple, orange, and pink. She inhaled the beauty around her—the kind of beauty that only God could paint. Morning had come to life with color and promise for the day. Heaven's beams gently illuminated the hundreds of acres Anne called the Double L.

All this gives me a reason to go on. Thank You for Your love and those mercies that are new every morning, just like Your book says.

The door squeaked open behind her, and the sound of boots tapping against the wooden porch revealed her visitor.

"Mornin', honey," Anne said without turning to greet her daughter.

"Another pretty one, isn't it?" Fourteen-year-old Sammie Jo leaned in close to her mother.

"I believe you're right." Anne wrapped her arm around the girl's shoulder. This winter Sammie Jo had shot up like a weed after spring rain, and her body had begun to look more like a young woman. Anne wasn't ready for that. In a few years, she'd be shooing away the young cowboys like flies on. . .on what comes natural.

"We're leaving right after breakfast?" Sammie Jo lifted a mug of coffee to her lips. She drank it black like her mother. The steam rolled off the top in a mystic dance before disappearing into the air.

"And not a minute later. Your sister doing all right?"

Sammie Jo nodded. "She hates not going. Says she feels better."

Anne chuckled. "Nancy should have thought about what those green dewberries would do to her stomach before she ate so many."

"Mama, those had to taste terrible, and she got so sick."

Anne shook her head. "Curiosity gets the best of Nancy. Reminds me of your daddy."

"Ever wish we were boys?"

"Never. But I do think some of the ladies at church believe I've turned you into them."

Sammie Jo laughed. "I feel more comfortable in my boots and jeans than dresses."

Anne kissed the tip of her daughter's nose. "Me, too, but we best keep that tidbit to ourselves. Let's see what Rosita has for breakfast. The sooner we help the others round up strays, the sooner you and I can do a little hunting."

"Is Clancy going with us?" Sammie Jo turned her head slightly, peering up with sky blue eyes that mirrored her daddy's. The look always caused Anne's heart to remember the man she'd loved.

"I don't think so. He's taking a few of the men to the upper ridge. Fence needs mending."

Sammie Jo frowned. "He's getting too old for all this hard work. Needs to settle down and spend out his days in a rocking chair. And his aim's getting bad. I beat him with my rifle in target practice last Saturday."

"Do you want to be the one telling him that?"

"No, ma'am. Clancy would chase me with a branding iron."

Anne hugged her daughter's shoulder again. They had a good life. For five years they'd worked hard and made the Double L Ranch the largest in this part of the state. And she intended to keep building it into an empire. Vast herds of longhorns and a line of fine quarter horses made her proud. A few eligible men had eyed her ranch and come courting. Didn't need a single one of them except Clancy, who was like a daddy to her and a granddaddy to the girls. Hadn't been a man since Will who interested her or could tame her stubborn nature.

Will used to call her *Mustang*. She smiled. Most women would have slapped a man silly for calling them a horse, but Anne took it as a compliment. Those traits helped make her strong when Will took sick and died. Her girls would have a good life ahead of them with money for education back East, and they'd not be dependent on a man to survive.

God had smiled on the three Langley women, and she

prayed He'd continue for a long time. Two tragedies in a lifetime were enough.

—∾—

Colt Wilson could taste the freedom. It lingered on his tongue like thick honey, and when he swallowed, his whole body felt the excitement. His fingers trembled like a kid with a fish on a hook. For six years he'd worn chains and worked like a fool to pay his debt to the state of Texas in Huntsville Prison. Now, as he placed one foot in front of the other, he could see the steel door that led to sweet liberty's sunshine. No more bug-infested food and bedding down with rats, and best of all, no more jumping every time the man jammed a rifle barrel in his ribs.

"Good luck to ya," the guard said. "You're a smart man, Wilson. Don't get yourself in here again."

Colt nodded and offered a grim smile. Prison life did that to a man: made him slap on a fake smile when he wanted to fight, laugh when he wanted to cry, and respect those who held his life in their hands. Years like what he'd endured made a man take stock in what he stood for—and what he'd do and not do when he got out.

The heavy door swung open, creaking like the gates of Hades releasing one of its own. Colt inhaled the freshness of life. Air so pure he gasped to make sure he hadn't died and gone to heaven by mistake. He'd shaken off the shackles that had physically bound him, but he couldn't shake the memory of the man who had allowed him to be turned in to the law. Those shackles tightened around his heart, and the key lay embedded in bitterness. The hate threatened to overtake his good sense, but Colt had long since promised himself never to set foot in a jail again. He had no future unless he got rid of the past.

He knew the right way to live, and he'd abide by the law. But first he had a matter to settle.

Inside of a week, he found a job with a rancher. He enjoyed the hard work, especially when he got paid for it. The solitary life with a few ranch hands for company settled well with him. The sound of bawling cows was like music, certainly better than gunfire or fighting men.

Summer heat sent sweat dripping down his back, but he'd take these sweltering temperatures above the stench of heat fused with filthy men any day. His mind drifted to the days ahead, and the more he pondered on ranching, the more he realized he could do a whole lot worse than punching cows for the rest of his life.

Two months later, Colt had a few dollars in his pocket, a good horse, and a worn saddle. With a Winchester strapped to his saddle and a saddlebag full of provisions, he headed toward a little town outside Austin called Willow Creek. Before he could get on with his life, Colt needed to see a man face-to-face.

Heading back home to Wyoming needled at him. Seeing his brothers again might be good, but he didn't know where to begin. They were a sorry lot. All of 'em bent on breaking the law. That most likely had been part of what killed Ma. Maybe his brothers would turn around their way of thinking before their pasts caught up with them. At least Reuben had learned from his mistakes, even if he did get religion. Colt remembered his eldest brother visiting him in prison. Colt had no desire to listen to Reuben's God-business, but it did grieve him to learn of Ma's passing.

Colt rode into Willow Creek and headed straight for the general store. Storekeepers always knew the goings-on and could give him directions. He lifted his hat and banged the trail dust from it on his jeans before stepping inside.

"Howdy." He grinned big at the balding man behind the counter.

The man greeted him, and they talked a bit about the dry weather and the sore need of rain.

"Say, I'm looking for an old friend of mine. Haven't seen him in years, but I know he was from these parts," Colt said.

"What's his name?"

"Will Langley."

The storekeeper rubbed his whiskered chin. "I hate to give you the bad news, but Will's been dead nigh on to five years."

Colt pasted a sorrowful look on his face. "Sorry to hear that. What happened?"

"Accident at his ranch. An ax went through his leg. Got gangrene and died."

"What about family? Anyone I can pay my respects to?"

"His widow owns a ranch not far from town. I can tell you how to get there."

"I'd be obliged," Colt said. "It's the least I can do."

Colt took note of the road to the Langley ranch and headed back to his horse. Disappointment snaked through him. Will's widow probably didn't have anything but a rundown piece of no-good property. He'd ridden all this way, though. Might as well take in a few more miles. Hard to make a man pay when he was dead. Bad luck had dealt Will Langley a rotten hand, but he felt sorry for the widow. A woman always seemed to suffer for loving the wrong man.

Revenge is bad for the soul. He could hear his daddy lecturing him, although he'd been dead for years. Unfortunately, whatever folks told him, Colt had a habit of doing the opposite and usually with a heavy dose of temper. Even Reuben had been afraid of him. Colt's ugly disposition was what got him behind bars in the first place.

No matter what he ended up doing, he had to stay to himself, keep his temper in check, and be careful not to rile anybody. Colt clenched his jaw. Will Langley being dead was probably good. Colt would most likely have lost his temper and ended up back in Huntsville prison for life or in a hangman's noose.

Colt followed the storekeeper's directions and rode straight onto a ranch so wide and green he wondered if he'd made a wrong turn. Herds of cattle grazed over rolling pastures, and when he strained to look again, he saw some of the finest horseflesh this side of the Mississippi. *Will Langley's widow owns this ranch? This may be my lucky day.*

Colt rode right up to a ranch house that was about the fanciest he'd ever seen. This part of the country was known for its abundance of stone, and the Widow Langley's ranch used lots of it. He dismounted about the time a young girl stepped onto the front porch with a rifle in hand. She wore a tattered hat pulled down over her eyes. Couldn't tell what she looked like.

"What's your business, mister?" the skinny, half-sized woman said.

"I'm here to see a Mrs. Will Langley."

"What for?"

"Business. What's your name, little girl?"

"I'm no little girl, and you haven't any right riding on my land and asking me who I am." She raised her rifle and aimed straight at him.

"Be careful. Do you know how to use that thing?"

"No matter, since I'm about to blow a hole right between your eyes if you don't ride on out of here."

"Sammie Jo, put down that rifle before I take a switch to you." A woman's voice rose above the quiet. "That's no way to treat a man just riding in off the trail."

Colt expelled a ragged breath. For a moment, he thought he'd meet his Maker by way of a girl. He swung his attention around to a woman dressed like a man. A very pretty woman, tall and with hair the color of deerskin. She must work for the widow.

He yanked off his hat. "Thank you, ma'am. I'm looking for Mrs. Will Langley. Her husband is an old friend of mine."

The woman lifted her chin and eyed him curiously.

"I'm Mrs. Will Langley. What can I do for you?"

Chapter 2

The color drained from Colt's face, and sweat dampened his back. He'd had a better reception at Huntsville Prison on his first day. This was Will's widow and his daughter? In Colt's opinion, Will was the one who needed sympathy. Whatever happened to defenseless women? If Will died of gangrene in his leg, these two probably offered to cut it off.

The girl called Sammie Jo lowered her rifle and propped it against the side of the porch. A younger girl dressed in jeans and boots slipped through the door and stiffened to about four feet tall. She placed her hands on her hips and scowled.

"I smell him clear over here," the smallest girl said. "Doesn't he know what a Saturday night bath is?"

"Hush, Nancy. You mind your manners," Mrs. Langley said.

What is this? Have I died and gotten what I deserve?

"State your business, sir. I have a ranch to run." Mrs. Langley crossed her arms over a green plaid shirt. She nodded toward the girls. "Meet me in the horse barn. We'll talk about your punishment for treating this man shamefully. Right now, you two apologize."

When the girls hesitated, she repeated her request—a little louder.

"I'm sorry," the two girls echoed and hurried toward the barns.

Colt dragged his tongue over dry, cracked lips. He'd never done well talking to women. "Your husband, ma'am, was a friend of mine."

"He's been gone for five years."

"Yes, ma'am. I've been drifting."

"In prison, no doubt. What's your name?"

He started. "Colt Wilson."

"A friend of Will's, you say?"

"Yes, ma'am." Alarm—the strength of a tornado—twisted through him. He best be riding out of there before she questioned his business with her departed husband. If Will had told his wife what he and Colt had done, she most likely would have killed him on the spot.

"Are you wanted?"

"No."

"What were you in prison for?"

Didn't your husband tell you? He shifted from one foot to the other. "Bank robbery."

"Kill anyone?"

"No, ma'am."

"Ever kill anyone?"

"Only to defend myself."

"Likely story." She glared at him. "Need a job? From the horse you're riding, you must not have stashed away the money."

The question caught him by surprise. "Why would you give me a job since—?"

"Since you just got out of prison? Because you knew Will and because I just lost two hands."

Did he want to work for this woman? For that matter, did he want to spend five more minutes with her? Unpredictably, he heard himself saying, "I'd be grateful."

She pointed to the bunkhouse. "Take your stuff over there and ask for Clancy. He'll show you where you'll sleep and what he needs you to do." She whirled around to follow the girls. "Don't waste any time. I'm short-handed and have too much work for you to dillydally."

"I'll do a fine job for you, Mrs. Langley."

She stopped in her tracks and turned around. A little cloud of dust spun up from her heels like a miniature dust devil. "Don't make me regret hiring you, or I'll be the one squeezing the trigger."

A lady boss? Why had he taken this job? He came looking for Will's widow, thinking she might be in a bad way and know a little about her husband's past dealings. Instead, he'd been waylaid. Sure, she had a pretty face and owned a large ranch, but this was downright degrading. Colt swung a look after her. Mrs. Langley might dress like a man and give orders like a man, but she didn't walk like a man.

—∞—

Anne studied her two daughters inside the shadows of the

horse barn. Some days she wondered if she'd done the right thing by making them strong and feisty. After seeing their behavior toward Colt Wilson, she realized she'd stepped over the boundaries between strength and inhospitality.

Sammie Jo crossed her arms over her chest and tapped her foot. Nancy had her familiar stance of planting her chubby hands on her hips.

"I'm ashamed of both of you," she said. "What have I taught you about manners?"

"I didn't like the way he looked," Sammie Jo said.

"And I didn't like the way he smelled," Nancy said.

"Hmm. Is that what the Bible teaches?"

"No, ma'am," they chorused.

"Look around you." Anne pointed toward the horse stalls. "Do you like what you see and smell?"

"Not really." Sammie Jo wrinkled her nose. "Needs a good cleaning."

"And you two are going to do that very thing." Anne almost laughed at the horrified looks on their faces.

"Mama, that's too hard a punishment." Nancy's eyes widened, mirroring the same shade of blue as her sister's.

"I'd rather take a whippin'," added Sammie Jo.

Anne shook her head. "That's too easy. You can think about good manners and what the good Lord requires of us while you're cleaning stalls." She nodded at her precious daughters and headed toward the sunlight filling the doorway. "You can watch the horse-breakin' before you start your work."

Giggles broke from behind her, but she dared not turn around or she'd relinquish the stall cleaning. Anne had shoveled them a man-sized job, but she hoped it taught her sassy girls a lesson.

Colt Wilson. She searched the cobwebs of her mind for the name. Nothing tore through the many memories of Will and their countless hours together. Near the end he'd told her many things, but a wayward man by the name of Colt Wilson wasn't one of them. Maybe he followed the law back then. Given time, she'd find out the truth. If she'd learned anything over the past five years, it was how life dealt every man and woman a bushel basket of mountains and valleys. How people handled those happenings made them who they were today. She'd hardened through it. . .maybe too hard.

Anne shuddered. Where were her brains in subjecting Sammie Jo and Nancy to an outlaw—or rather a past outlaw? And what about the good hands who worked for her? Some men never shook off the habits that had thrown them behind bars. Still, a nudging at her heart had told her to offer him a job. And she sure hoped it was the Lord and not stupidity.

"Mrs. Langley, are you riding?" Thatcher Lee asked.

She surfaced from her reverie and waved at the young man standing with the other three hands. She laughed at the seriousness on his face—barely eighteen years old and her self-proclaimed protector. Or maybe he had his eye on Sammie Jo in a few years. That thought curdled her stomach.

"Ah, yes, I am. In fact, I want that bronc you're afraid of."

"The sorrel stallion?" Thatcher Lee asked.

"You bet. I see you have him ready. About time I showed you men how to ride."

Clancy strode up to the corral with Colt beside him.

"Anne, that horse is mean. You could hurt yourself real bad. Why not let me sell him?"

"Are you kidding? How many times in the past few years have you seen me back down from a good fight?" She laughed again.

"When he tosses you on the ground I'm not helping you up." Standing with his back against the sun, Clancy's shoulder-length silver hair glistened, his Apache heritage evident from every inch of him.

She opened the gate and headed toward the stallion, which snorted and pranced. Clancy might be right. Thatcher Lee held the reins and tried to settle the horse. Oh, this one would cause her to taste dirt more than once.

"Be careful, Mama," Nancy called. Sammie Jo knew better than to object.

Fearfulness ruined Anne's concentration.

Lord, I have a foolish streak, and I know it. Seems like I always have to prove something. She grabbed the reins, stepped into the stirrup and swung onto the saddle. As if stung by a swarm of bees, the horse reared. Anne dug her knees into his sides and held on. Her heart raced, pumping excitement through her veins. That quickly, his head touched the ground, and his rear legs aimed for the sky. If she hadn't watched the stallion's habits, she'd be lying in a heap of bruised flesh looking up at the sun—and listening to Clancy scold with an "I told you so." It could happen yet.

About the time that thought emptied her head, she lost balance and hit the hard ground. Thatcher Lee headed her way, but she waved him off and spit out a mouthful of dirt.

The young man grabbed the stallion's reins, and she mounted the horse again.

With a twist of powerful muscles, the horse jerked and twisted in midair. She heard nothing, saw nothing, and concentrated on the massive animal beneath her in an attempt to sense its every move. After several minutes, the stallion began to slow. Good thing, for she was ready to give the job to the nearest ranch hand.

Some days she didn't have a lick of sense.

Finally, the stallion ceased its rearing and snorting and allowed her to walk him around the corral. The others shouted her on. She tossed them a smile. *This is the last time I'm doing this.*

When she finally dismounted and handed the reins to Thatcher Lee, she thought her legs had turned to matchsticks.

"You all right?" Thatcher Lee whispered.

"Yeah," she said. "If I mention doing this again, remind me I have two daughters to raise."

From beneath his hat he nodded and grinned.

Anne glanced at Clancy, who narrowed his eyes. No doubt he had his lecture all worked out. She deserved it. Her gaze swept to Colt. Curiosity rested in his dark eyes. Usually admiration greeted her from the ranch hands.

Pride goeth before destruction. That's why she wasn't breaking any more horses.

Anne glanced at her girls standing on either side of Clancy. Nancy's face had turned ashen. She'd apologize to her baby girl. Shame had made its point. She walked over to her girls.

"Good job, Mama." Sammie Jo lifted her chin.

Anne nodded and cupped Nancy's quivering chin in her

hand. "I won't be breaking any more horses, darlin'."

The little girl swallowed hard and swiped at a single tear rolling over her cheek. "Thank you."

She caught Colt Wilson's gaze again. This time he offered a thin-lipped smile.

"Young'uns have a way of setting us right," he said.

Fire burned her cheeks. "I'd appreciate it if you'd keep your remarks to yourself."

"Just making an observation, ma'am."

"I can take care of my girls just fine."

"I reckon so."

His words were like kindling on a crackling fire, but she dare not lose her temper in front of the girls or Clancy. What made matters worse was that he'd spoken rightly. To prove herself equal to a man, she'd risked her life, but she didn't need him pointing out the truth. And that's what made her even angrier.

Chapter 3

Three days later, on Saturday night, with a belly full of smoked ham and beans, Colt brushed down his mare in the ebb of daylight. He'd already decided to take an evening ride and think through the mess he'd gotten himself into. Decisions needed to be made soon, because his idea of a good job didn't mean taking orders from a woman. He'd looked up Will for a reason, and those reasons still needled at him.

The sound of sloshing water snatched his attention. He watched a couple of the ranch hands hustle about heating water over a fire and adding it to a watering trough in the middle of the barn.

"What's going on in there?" he asked Thatcher Lee.

"Bath night," the muscular young man said.

"Why?"

" 'Cause we smell. Mrs. Langley demands it."

"Why?"

Thatcher Lee scowled. "For church. We all go to church on Sunday morning with Mrs. Langley and the girls."

Colt laughed. "Not me. I haven't set foot in a church since

my ma carried me on her hip."

"Well, on the Double L, you either get to church or hit the road."

Irritation bubbled up inside Colt, but he swallowed it. This wasn't the first time he'd heard strange notions coming from Anne Langley. The more he thought about the Double L, the more he realized she had to know about what he and Will had done. Where else had she gotten the money to build up this ranch? He'd learned from Clancy that Will had purchased it about a year before he had the accident.

That meant a portion of this fine acreage was Colt's. All he had to do was convince her of his partial ownership. Except every time he considered Anne Langley as a business partner, his insides shook.

"What if I don't have any clean clothes?" Colt asked.

"We have extras."

"I'd rather take a bath in the creek."

Thatcher Lee tossed him a cake of soap. "Me and Clancy feel the same way. I'm on my way now. You might as well join us."

"Since I don't have a choice, I reckon so."

A bath and church. This woman would drive him crazy. He nearly laughed aloud. The sight of the Langley women stepping into church with their jeans and boots instead of dresses and bonnets must amuse the locals. No matter. He'd catch up on his sleep during the sermon.

Sunday morning he dressed in clean clothes and stomped the dirt and manure off his boots. He mounted up with the rest of the hands, thinking his brothers would never let him live this one down. Clancy had a Bible. No wonder the old

Indian didn't curse or tell a good story now and then. As far as drinking, he doubted if Clancy did that either, since the boss lady didn't allow it on the ranch.

Up at the house, Colt did a double take. The Langley women sashayed onto the front porch dressed like fine ladies. Why, they looked quite fetching—especially Mrs. Langley. All three had ribbons in their hair and wore shoes instead of boots. But what he noticed the most was how Mrs. Langley curved out nicely in a corn-colored dress, and her walk still took his breath away.

Stop it, Colt. You'll get shot for such thoughts. He lifted his hat and brushed back his hair, hoping no one could hear what raced through his mind. Every time he considered Will and the boss lady married, he simply couldn't picture it. Will's take-charge nature and the strong-willed woman Colt secretly called "Boss Lady" would have been like fire and dynamite. And he wouldn't have wanted to be around for the explosion.

Oh, he should be fair. The boss lady did have her gentle moments; he'd witnessed her tender side with the girls and Rosita—and even Clancy.

The small church stood out in the middle of nowhere with plenty of room for wagons and horses to crowd around the wood-framed building. He expected folks to be solemn, but they were laughing and calling out to each other as if they were on a picnic. Peculiar. Real peculiar.

He swung over his horse and watched Clancy help the boss lady and her daughters down from the wagon as if they'd break in two. Mrs. Langley sure played the part well.

Colt waited as long as possible before he mounted the

wooden steps to the church. Spending his morning with Bible thumpers didn't appeal to him. Not at all. He took his place on a bench with the other hands while Clancy sat with the Langley women. The arrangement made it easy for Colt to sleep and her not to know.

The preacher stepped up to the front. "Open your hymn books to 'Shall We Gather at the River?' "

Colt grinned. The man must have been at the creek last night when he, Clancy, and Thatcher Lee took their baths. In the next instant he closed his eyes, and that was all he remembered.

—∞—

Anne could barely hear Preacher Rollins for the snoring behind her. A quick glance told her it was Colt Wilson. Later she'd tell him what she thought of desecrating the Lord's day by sleeping in church. Heathen. She must have been touched in the head to hire him on the spot last week.

But that day she had no choice after firing Hank and Thomas for pulling their guns on Clancy and Thatcher Lee. The two had been caught red-handed cutting a few head of cattle from the herd. Since then, the other hands tried to keep up with the work, but it was nearly impossible. A week later and ten more longhorns were missing. She'd filed a report with the sheriff, but the man had laziness written across the seat of his pants and a nagging wife that wanted him at home.

Hank and Thomas held their own with a gun, and the thought frightened her a bit—not for herself, but for the girls and the other men. Anne blinked. Surely Colt wasn't working with them on this. He'd known Will, but Hank and Thomas had never met her dearly departed husband. Colt's riding in must have been a coincidence. Anne didn't believe in coincidences any more than she did in fairytales. God must have purposed Colt Wilson to arrive at the exact time. He looked like neither an angel nor a saint—and he didn't snore like anything heavenly, either. Why God might have brought him into her life was beyond her thinking.

This morning when Anne caught sight of Colt all cleaned up, he looked right handsome. And he did have those big gray eyes with flecks of gold. . .and eyelashes a girl ought to have. Too bad he was an outlaw, and most likely he wasn't worth the lead to send him to kingdom come.

She inwardly scolded her wandering thoughts and focused on the preacher. God knew how she felt about all this, and He'd handle it. But, oh, how she wanted to take off after those two cattle thieves herself.

—m—

Colt sprang from his bunk. Rifle fire cracked a second time. In the dark, he grabbed his pants and rifle then tore through the bunkhouse with Thatcher Lee right behind him. In the light of a full moon and a sky filled with stars, Clancy leaned against the side of the bunkhouse, fully dressed. Before him stood Sammie Jo.

"What are you shooting at this time of the night?" Clancy asked. "You could have been killed by one of us."

"I got him." Sammie Jo's voice rose in the stillness. She held up the tail of a coyote. "He won't be stealing any more of our chickens."

"Well, I reckon you did." Clancy laughed.

"Rosita was carrying on something awful yesterday with another hen gone."

The excitement in Sammie Jo caused Colt to burst out laughing. The Langley women never ceased to amaze him.

"You hightail it back to bed, and I'll get rid of that coyote," Clancy said.

"I want him skinned."

"Sure thing. You and I'll do it tomorrow."

"Can we make a hat?"

"I suppose. Now get going before your mama finds you missing."

Sammie Jo gave the old man a hug and raced toward the main house, but Thatcher Lee caught up with her. Colt watched them disappear into the darkness. That gal acted just like her mama.

"I'll never understand women," he said in the stillness.

"You mean Sammie Jo or Anne?" Clancy asked.

Colt shrugged. "Neither one of them is like any woman I ever knew. I never had sisters, and my ma acted. . .well, normal."

"She hasn't always been this way," Clancy said. He studied Colt. "I hear you knew Will."

"We had some business together."

"You best keep that business to yourself. Anne doesn't need to hear any of it."

"I figured so."

Colt gazed out into the night, as though staring after Thatcher Lee and Sammie Jo. His thoughts narrowed in on what Clancy must know about Will, and what the boss lady didn't know.

"How fast are you with a gun?" Clancy asked.

"Fair. I prefer a rifle."

"Stick around here until a few matters are settled. Anne's going to need all the help she can get."

"Trouble? What kind?" Colt asked. An image of Huntsville settled on him like a bad case of the backdoor runs.

"The kind that can get a body killed. I buried Will, and I don't plan to bury her or them girls." Clancy released a heavy sigh. "She may look and act tough, but that's a cover for something else. And"—he turned and stared at Colt face-to-face—"we didn't have this conversation."

"Why me?"

"I see more in you than I reckon you do. This might be your one chance to straighten out your life."

Colt bristled. "What do you mean?"

"I'm no fool. You ride in here looking for a dead man, which means you've done time. No family. No money. No purpose in life. No relationship with the Lord. But I do see a shred of decency."

Colt swallowed hard and was grateful for the darkness hiding him from humiliation—and anger.

"No need to answer," Clancy said. "Will you stick around until the trouble's gone?"

"I need to know what kind of trouble."

"Let's take a walk." Clancy headed out into the blackness toward the corral, and Colt followed. More out of curiosity than interest.

"Thatcher Lee and I caught two of Anne's men rustling cows. They would have killed us if Anne hadn't ridden up and surprised them. She run 'em off, but they threatened to burn her place to the ground with her and the girls in it."

Those words did set off Colt's temper. The two men needed a hangman's noose.

"What about the local law?"

"Aw, the sheriff says those two are long gone, but I don't believe it for a minute. Besides, ten of our cows are gone."

Colt let the silence filter his thoughts. He didn't much care about getting shot or interfering in someone else's trouble, but threatening womenfolk wasn't right. Another thought entered his head. By helping the boss lady with this problem, she might feel grateful enough to give him what was rightfully his. That thought pricked his conscience. He didn't have any business taking advantage of a woman, even a woman like Anne Langley.

I've gotten mean and hard. But if I don't look out for myself, who will?

"What do you say?" Clancy asked.

"Yeah, I'll stick around to help," Colt said.

He made his way back to his bunk and tried to go to sleep. His mind sped ahead about his predicament. He kept learning new things that interrupted his original plans. Anger surfaced again toward any man who would threaten a widow and two little girls. At least they weren't defenseless. Those two hands who'd rustled cattle might have had other things on their mind. Maybe they got wind of Will's activities before he died. Maybe stealing a few cows was to cover up for something else.

A short while later, Thatcher Lee eased onto his bunk beside Colt's.

"Took you long enough," Colt whispered.

"We were talking."

Colt nearly came out of his bunk. "That gal is fourteen years old. Too young for you to be thinkin' on courtin' matters."

"You ain't her pa."

"No, but I knew him well enough to figure out what he'd have done to a young whippersnapper after his little girl."

Thatcher Lee mumbled something under his breath.

"Give her about three or four years, and let her grow up proper. Filling her mind with woman things instead of letting her find out about life on her own is downright wrong." With those words, Colt turned over away from Thatcher Lee's bunk.

From Clancy's bunk, he heard a muffled laugh.

Chapter 4

Colt leaned against the corral fence and pumped the well over the watering trough. The day had been a scorcher, and his mouth tasted as dry as the dirt beneath his feet. He'd been working at the Double L for more than three weeks, and not one more cow had been stolen. His fears about the two men using thievery as a cover for something else were unfounded. He had no doubt they'd long since left the territory.

Water began to flow from the spigot, and he cupped his hands for a cool drink. Once he doused his face, he stood and glanced up at the house. Why did he stay? Was it the money, or was it about being a decent man?

With no answers, his gaze focused on Nancy high up in a live oak tree. How did she get herself up there? And how did she plan to get down? He walked over there until he stood beneath the branches of the tree.

"Miss Nancy, how did you get up there?" he asked.

He saw the little girl rub her nose. A faint sob escaped her lips.

"Are you stuck?"

"I think so."

Colt shook his head. "Did you climb up there?"

"Yes, sir. I tried and tried. Then I got the ladder and finally made it. It fell, and I couldn't figure out how to get down."

He wanted to chuckle but thought better of it. "Can you make your way to the lowest branch?" On the far side of the tree, the ladder rested on the ground.

She nodded and slowly descended until her bare toes touched on the branch.

"Jump and I'll catch you," he said.

"Promise?" Her lips trembled—a trait he'd seen when the boss lady had ridden the bronc.

"Promise."

"And you won't tell my mama or Sammie Jo or Clancy?"

"I promise."

She took a deep breath and jumped right into his arms. Made him feel real protective.

"Are you hurt?"

"No, sir. Would you put me down before someone sees?"

He grinned. "Sure, and I'll keep our little secret."

He set her on the soft ground, and she scampered off. Shaking his head, he picked up the ladder and headed to the barn. His swaybacked mare awaited him to join the others.

"Thank you."

Colt swung around to find the boss lady speaking to him from the back porch.

"You're welcome." He waved and continued on.

"Got a minute, Colt?"

Great. Wonder what he'd done wrong. The tongue-lashing

over sleeping in church had kept him awake the past two Sundays. Bored, but awake.

"Is there a problem?" he asked.

"Not at all. Do you have time to take a ride with me?"

His heart felt like tumbleweed in a windstorm. "I imagine so."

He put away the ladder while she retrieved her horse, and he helped her saddle it.

"Will used to saddle my horse," she said. "He always took the time to make sure it was tight." She tilted her head, looking real pretty. "Then I decided I needed to do everything myself."

He handed her the reins. She'd never talked to him before like he was a human being. But he'd wanted her to.

"I can see Will taking good care of you," Colt said.

"That's what I want to talk about."

This must be it. She wanted to settle up on the money owed to him.

As they rode out across the pasture, Colt searched for conversation. His dealings with women in the past hadn't been proper, and the women hadn't been real ladies.

"I understand you told Thatcher Lee to stay away from Sammie Jo until she grew up."

"Yes, ma'am. Sorry if I spoke without asking you first."

"Not at all. I appreciate it. She wasn't listening to me or Clancy. Of course, she's a lot like me."

Colt smiled.

"Tell me about Will and the times you spent together."

How much dare he say? The man lay buried on his ranch. His wife did better than any woman he'd ever met, and his daughters weren't afraid of anything—except Nancy and tall trees. Still, defaming the dead seemed wrong, even if it meant Will went to his grave with the knowledge of Colt's money.

"What do you want to know?"

She hesitated as though carefully choosing her words. "I know my husband didn't live according to the law. He confessed a lot to me while dying."

Like the whereabouts of what belongs to me?

"And if you came here looking for money, you might as well turn around and head out of here, 'cause I don't know anything about it."

Colt's spirits sank to his toes.

"What I want to know about is the man," she said.

"Mrs. Langley—"

"The name is Anne."

"All right, Anne. This is real difficult for me. Will and me did things I'd rather not discuss with a lady."

"I'm your boss—and Will's widow."

Sweat streamed down the side of Colt's face, and it had nothing to do with the heat. "He had a way of leading out in a situation that showed real guts. I mean, he didn't ask a man to do anything he wouldn't do."

She nodded. "Go on."

"He never lied or killed anyone that I knew about."

"How much money did you two steal?"

He was afraid she'd ask that. "Twelve thousand."

"I never saw any of it. My folks left me money to buy the ranch."

They rode on in silence while Colt contemplated his miserable existence. No future.

"Did he speak to you about his family?" she finally asked.

"No. Didn't know he had one until I looked you up." He pondered over his conversations with Will, then turned his attention her way. "But he wasn't unfaithful to you."

A faint smile greeted him. "I'm glad to hear that. He always said he loved me and the girls. Thanks."

"You're welcome."

"I have another matter to discuss with you."

Dread inched over him. The last topic nearly drained him.

"Do you think any other men might be looking for him because of money—or revenge?"

"I honestly have no idea."

"If you think of anyone, would you let me know? I have my girls and my ranch to protect."

"Why did you give me a job?"

"God told me to hire you."

"God?"

"Yes, the one we worship on Sunday mornings while you pretend to listen."

He laughed. "That must be the one."

"Someday when you least expect it, God is going to grab your attention."

"Yes, ma'am. He'd have to shake me good."

"Oh, He can, Colt. And it wouldn't hurt you to be talking to Him now and then."

Anne kissed Nancy's cheek, then watched her slip into dreamland. Her daughter had confessed to the tree adventure, not realizing her mama had seen the whole thing.

Nancy had sighed and folded her hands over her chest. "Mr. Colt helped me down out of that tree and held me like I was a baby kitten," the little girl said.

"He must have thought you might break."

In the lamp's light, Nancy's face grew strangely solemn. "I thought I might. Mama, I just kept looking up in that tree and wondering what it would feel like to sit in its branches like a bird. I couldn't stop myself. Then the ladder fell, and I was scared."

"Sweetheart, curiosity is good, but you have to back it up with a little common sense."

"I'll try, but it's hard."

Anne blew out the lamp. "Ask Jesus to help you."

"I did—for the next time."

"I'm proud of you. Now close your eyes. I'm going to sit right here until you go to sleep."

Anne never tired of watching her precious daughters sleep, and she did so tonight until darkness concealed Nancy's features and Colt's face took over.

Buried beneath the hardened man was a soft heart. She'd seen it with Nancy today and heard about it from Clancy. All of Anne's frettin' hadn't deterred Sammie Jo from chasing after Thatcher Lee, but Colt had handled Thatcher Lee quite nicely. Today he'd chosen his words carefully so as not to mar Will's image. Anne liked that.

Her husband might not have obeyed the law, but he'd loved her and the girls. And she'd loved him, too. The times he'd been gone on business must have been the times he robbed banks and other folks who had money. She hated that part of his life. It made her feel dirty. The girls should never find out about their daddy—no reason for them to learn the truth.

Until recently Anne hadn't looked at another man. Strange that Colt Wilson had captured her attention, but she liked his rugged looks and quiet mannerisms. Her heart must lean toward lawless men. He was rough and tough, and his language hadn't been graced by the inside of a grammar book, but he had some good in him. She prayed the Lord would touch him for heaven before he got himself into trouble and was killed.

Anne made her way to the open window where a slight breeze swayed the curtains. Her gaze trailed to the bunkhouse. Loyal men lived there—men who respected her and worked hard. Had it all been worth the struggle of just day-to-day living? As she turned to leave Nancy to peaceful slumber, she caught the silhouette of a man staring up at the stars. She studied him and wondered if it was Colt contemplating the future, maybe thinking about her.

Odd that she should care.

Clancy, Thatcher Lee, and Colt rode around a grassy ridge and along a thick forest north of Double L land. Clancy had something on his mind, and twice he'd dismounted to look at the ground. Obviously his part-Indian eyes detected a trail.

"Where are we going?" Colt lowered his voice to speak to Thatcher Lee. He knew better than to worry a concentrating man.

"My guess is that he has an idea about those missing cows."

"Glad I'm packing my rifle," Colt said.

"I never killed a man."

"Here's hoping you don't have to. But I tell you this, if it's them or you, you'll squeeze the trigger."

Colt scanned the area around them. Between the woods and the rounded hills, unseen men could be watching their every move. He pulled his rifle onto his lap. Thatcher Lee did the same.

Clancy halted his horse and raised his hand, signaling for them to stop. For long moments, he observed the terrain and waited. Finally he motioned Colt and Thatcher Lee to see what he'd found. At the foot of the hill below them were Double L cows.

"Where're Hank and Thomas?" Thatcher Lee asked.

"Not where I can see 'em." Clancy slipped off his horse and led the animal into the woods.

The two men followed. Colt admired the old man's skill and confidence.

"Thatcher Lee, you stay here while Colt and I do a little scouting."

The young man frowned.

"You heard me. Colt and me have done this kind of thing before. I don't want to be taking you back full of bullet holes." He didn't give Thatcher Lee a chance to argue but took off toward a path that led around the hill. Vultures circled overhead.

Neither man spoke. Their bodies blended into the sights and sounds of nature. Peacefulness always masked the stalking of trouble. They moved hunched over through the woods and crawled through the low-lying areas until they were within several feet of one of the grazing cows.

"I didn't see a sign of anyone," Clancy whispered. "But that doesn't mean they aren't ready to ambush us."

Colt pointed to a clump of trees adjacent to where they lay in tall grass. Clancy nodded. A cow bawled. Squirrels chattered. Birds sang. A sultry wind blew around them. The old sensation of excitement flowing through his veins swept over Colt as he made his way alone. All thoughts left his mind except the task before him. Once he made it alone to the other side, he drank in the surroundings.

His eyes narrowed. To his far right he saw a man sprawled face down on the ground. The grass was stained red. A few feet beyond him was another man on his belly. Brush hid the second man's upper body. Two vultures picked around the area.

Colt studied the two men for signs of life. He motioned to Clancy and crawled closer. Once he joined him, they'd figure out what had happened here.

"Hank and Thomas," Clancy said a short while later.

Both men had bullets in their heads, their hands tied.

"This is worse than what I thought," Clancy continued.

"You and I both know about Will," Colt said. "It's been over five years since he died, but I can't help but think this is related."

A bullet whizzed past his ear. A second caused a gasp from Clancy as it ripped open flesh in his shoulder. A third lodged in Colt's thigh.

"If you ever thought about praying, now's the time," Clancy said.

The fire burning in Colt's leg fueled his temper. He yanked his rifle to his shoulder and fired repeatedly into the brush where the shots had come from.

"You go ahead and talk to God," Colt said. "Ask Him to send Thatcher Lee our way and cover us while we hightail it back into those woods."

Clancy aimed and fired. "That's a start."

Chapter 5

"God was looking out for you two," Anne said once she'd yanked the bullet from Colt's thigh and wrapped clean bandages around his leg.

"I know He was." Clancy winced as she dabbed whiskey on his open flesh. "That hurts as bad as the bullet tearing across my shoulder."

"Don't complain," Colt said. "You weren't the one she dug into with a knife."

Sammie Jo peered over her mama's shoulder. "That looks real bad, Clancy. Makes me wonder if you and Colt might up and die on us. Daddy's leg didn't look any better than you two."

"Sammie Jo." Anne whirled around to face her daughter. "I thought I asked you to pray for these two men, not bring death knocking at our door."

"Yes, ma'am."

Colt's leg throbbed, but he managed a nervous chuckle. "Sammie Jo, are you afraid of anything?"

"No, sir."

He studied her young face, so stubborn and innocent.

"Life's hard, Sammie Jo. One day you'll find what you're afraid of. When you do, face it."

She frowned at him. Oh, that gal had a lot to learn.

"Sammie Jo, you run along and draw water for Rosita," Anne said. "I need to talk to these men."

Once the girl had left the bunkhouse, Anne turned her attention to doctoring Clancy.

"We didn't see anyone," Clancy said. "If it hadn't been for Thatcher Lee, we'd have been as dead as Hank and Thomas."

Anne studied Thatcher Lee. "Did you see them?"

"No, ma'am. They were like ghosts. I kept firing into the brush where the shots came from while Clancy and Colt crawled away."

"I'm not sure what to think about this," she said. "Those men need burying but not at the risk of getting our men shot."

Colt squeezed his eyes shut and tried desperately to forget the pain in his leg. Drinking the rest of that bottle of whiskey was mighty tempting, but Anne didn't permit drinking—for any reason.

Colt cleared his throat. "We need to keep our eyes open until this is settled. I wonder about Hank's and Thomas's enemies and why they didn't take the cattle." He wasn't about to mention Will's name with Thatcher Lee standing there.

"Maybe this will get the sheriff off his lazy backside and doing his job," Clancy said. "We'll see him tomorrow morning at church."

"Neither of you is going to church." Anne wrapped a clean bandage around his arm. She nodded at Colt. "You can snore right through the sermon."

"And I don't have to take a bath?" Colt grinned through the pain in his thigh. He found himself captured by her deep blue eyes.

Anne shook her head. "No, you can smell like a dirty barn for another week."

"Good," Clancy said. "I have the whole morning to preach to Colt. High time that man knew about Jesus."

"No rest for a wounded man?" Colt asked.

Anne laughed. "You two can pester each other for the next week. Because neither of you can smell trouble, I've got to help the other hands."

Clancy chuckled. "I love your kind heart."

Colt fixed his gaze on her. Was she lingering a little on him? Or was it his imagination? Maybe he'd grown weak in the head with the bullet wound. But for now he'd enjoy Anne's special treatment.

The seriousness of the situation hit him hard. Anne and those girls were in danger. He knew it as well as he knew his own name.

Anne left the two alone to go help Rosita with dinner. Colt glanced at Clancy. Without asking, Colt understood the old man felt the same way. And here they were shot up like two mangled coyotes.

"Are you still praying?" he asked Clancy.

The old man nodded. "Wouldn't hurt for you to do the same thing."

"I'm not ready for religion, but I'm glad you're on speaking terms with God. I'm worried about Anne and the girls."

Clancy nodded. "She likes you, Colt. I can see it in her

eyes. She hasn't looked at a man like that since Will."

"Naw. She's just glad I wasn't killed today, and she doesn't have to go looking for another ranch hand."

But Colt wondered. He didn't deserve as fine a woman as Anne. Neither did he deserve two spunky girls like Sammie Jo and Nancy. But the thought made him feel good—real good.

—~—

Anne tried to concentrate on helping Rosita with dinner. Instead, her thoughts raced with the shooting—Hank and Thomas dead for no visible reason. . .Clancy and Colt shot. . .and why?

She'd never had any trouble like this. Hard work was one thing. Raising two daughters and running the ranch left her tired and oftentimes grumpy. But murder downright scared her.

Had Will left enemies who just now decided to whip out calling cards? Her husband had confessed to so much law breaking. At the time, she hid her fright and focused on keeping him comfortable. A dying man usually had a wagonload of regrets and things he wanted to say. He hadn't given her names or mentioned that her life and the girls' lives were in danger. Five years had passed since then. Surely this was something completely different from Will's acquaintances seeking revenge. She hoped so. She prayed so.

A twinge, like a knife twisting in an open wound, startled her. The trouble began just before Colt arrived. Was he a part of this? She shook her head to dispel the frightening thought. He'd been in prison before coming to the Double L, which caused her to suspect him, but today he'd been hurt worse than Clancy. She refused to believe he'd taken part in what happened. Perhaps God had sent her an outlaw to run off outlaws. Peculiar thought. For certain, she wasn't in the business of second-guessing the hand of the Almighty.

"Mama, do you like Mr. Colt?" Sammie Jo asked.

Anne turned the soft biscuit dough in her hands. "He's a good worker, and he helped save Clancy's and Thatcher Lee's lives today."

"I mean, do you like him?"

"Sammie Jo, I'm not sure what you mean." But Anne understood exactly what her daughter meant, and she had no intentions of answering.

"Do you like him the same as Daddy?"

Anne's heart pounded like an Indian drum. "Why ever would you ask me such a thing?"

"Because I see the way you look at him and the way he looks at you."

"I think your dreamin' on Thatcher Lee has gone to your head." Anne hoped her words sounded gruff.

Sammie Jo giggled. "You answered my question. How would Daddy feel about you takin' up with an outlaw? Especially one who's a heathen? The way I look at it, you two could marry up and then have other outlaws at the ranch looking for work and free food."

"Child, I'm going to take a switch to your backside if you don't stop pestering me. Do you understand? No more such foolishness."

"Yes, ma'am."

Out of the corner of her eye, Anne saw a grin spread over

her daughter's face. Mercy, did the whole world see her interest in Colt Wilson?

—∞—

"We're having church," Clancy said.

Colt wanted to sleep. His leg hurt. Clancy's arm had to hurt, too. Irritability inched through his veins like a slow-rising flood.

"Can't do that," Colt said. "Anne told us to sleep. We need to heal and get back to work."

"God said to honor His day."

"Still can't. We didn't take our Saturday night bath."

"Fine. I'm reading from the Bible, and you can lay there and listen."

Clancy fumbled under his bunk while Colt rolled over to head back to sleep.

"Doesn't your arm hurt?"

Clancy chuckled. "Yeah, but when I think about what our Lord did on the cross for me, it makes no difference."

Colt moaned. *Here it comes.* Preaching with a one-man congregation. Next Clancy would be asking him to confess and head to the creek to wash away his sins.

"This morning the good Lord's leading me to read from Genesis, the story of Jacob and Esau."

"And who are they?"

"Brothers who never got along."

Colt blew out an exasperated sigh. "I have three, and we fought all the time we were growing up."

Clancy cleared his throat. "Lord, we ask Your blessing on

the reading of Your Word. Make sure Colt listens. I'm beginning in Genesis chapter 25, verse 19."

Colt half listened, half dozed through the story about twins named Jacob and Esau. One was his daddy's favorite, and the other was his mama's. Colt had been a part of such a family. He hadn't been anyone's favorite. All of a sudden, Clancy had his attention.

"You mean Esau sold his inheritance for a bowl of soup?"

"Yep. He must have been powerful hungry."

"More like a fool." Colt opened his eyes. He'd listen a little more. "How did those two get in the Bible? One is a fool, and the other lies to his own daddy."

"The Bible is full of sinful people. I know you've heard the preacher say how none of us is perfect. Now will you hush and let me finish?"

So Colt listened. Jacob had to take off because Esau threatened to kill him for getting the inheritance. His mama sent him to live with her people. Then Jacob fell in love. Colt was beginning to understand how that felt, too. "None of those fellers is decent," he said. "Jacob worked seven years for Rachel, then got stuck with her ugly sister and had to work seven more years." He started to say more, but Clancy shot him one of those "shut up and listen" looks.

The story went on, and Colt started to drift off to sleep until Clancy got to the part about the angel breaking Jacob's leg and how he limped to meet Esau. Jacob was scared his brother was going to kill him, and Colt understood those feelings, too. He'd been a horrible bully to his brothers. It worked out for Jacob and Esau, but those men had been real bad.

"What do you think?" Clancy asked.

"I'm thinking on it. Jacob wasn't much better than an outlaw until he wrestled with the angel. He turned himself into bein' a decent man after that."

"What about you?"

Here comes the confessing-your-sins part. "What about me?"

"Looks to me like you're changing into a different man from the one who rode in here. God must be wrestling with you, too."

Colt didn't say a word. Clancy closed his Bible and placed it back under his bed.

"I'm going to rest a little," Clancy said. "My arm's on fire."

"And my leg feels like someone branded it."

Me, wrestling with an angel? The only thing I wrestle with are all the things I've done in the past—and if I'd ever be good enough for Anne and the girls.

Chapter 6

Waiting for his leg to heal gave Colt plenty of time to think about what had happened the day he and Clancy were shot. Repeatedly he walked his mind back through every moment of that day. He recalled the way the wind blew and questioned if the birds he heard were actually calls made by men. Sights and smells lingered in his thoughts. When he'd crawled through brush and grass, he'd seen no signs of men.

The mystery of it all puzzled him, and he and Clancy filled their waking hours talking about who could have done the killings.

"If I believed in ghosts, I'd say they fired on us," Colt said.

"Does seem real strange, and I was quite a tracker in my day." Clancy rubbed his whiskered jaw. "I even wondered if a small band of renegade Indians could have done it. But nothing I recall showed any signs of 'em."

"I've laid here three days thinking about this and haven't come up with a thing." Colt glanced around. "I'm fixin' to use the crutch Thatcher Lee made for me and get out of this bunkhouse for some fresh air."

"Walkin' around helps. At least I can get out of here. I imagine the bunkhouse feels like pris—." He stopped himself. "I'll help you the best I can."

"We've turned into a couple of helpless old men," Colt said.

"Speak for yourself. I've got another twenty good years left in me."

Colt glanced at the old man's silver hair and weather-beaten face. "How many lines can your face hold?"

"As many as it takes to make sure Anne and the girls are safe and you find the Lord."

"He doesn't want me, Clancy. I don't like church, and my singing sounds like it came from a hollow bucket."

"Oh, He wants you powerful bad. You just don't have sense enough to realize it." Clancy stood and grasped the makeshift crutch. "I don't always like the preacher's sermons, either, and my singing sounds like a hurt wolf. It ain't about that at all. It's about realizing you need something you don't have. Something that is more powerful than what any man can get on his own."

Out of respect for Clancy, Colt kept his thoughts to himself because he wasn't in the mood for preachin'. The pain in his leg felt like liquid fire. Truth be known, he'd been thinkin' on God and the stories Clancy had read to him from the Bible. The story about Jacob and Esau had hit close to home. Clancy said they were true, and lately Colt hoped they were.

Sweat streamed down Colt's face by the time he hobbled out of the bunkhouse and made his way to a shady tree—the one Nancy had climbed. He sat beneath it and stretched out his burning leg. Frustrated with the time it was taking to heal when he wanted to ride out to where the shooting took place made him want to tear into the first man who crossed his path.

"Can you leave me alone?" he asked Clancy. "I need time to think about a few things."

"Sure. When God is working on a man, he needs time by himself."

Clancy made his way to the barn, and Colt felt a little guilty for letting the man think he had religion on his mind. Leaning against the oak tree, he closed his eyes and willed the throbbing to end.

"Mr. Colt."

Nancy's sweet voice didn't irritate him at all. That little girl had stolen his heart.

"What can I do for you?"

"That's what I wanted to ask you." She sat in the grass beside him, her bare feet caked with dried mud.

"You been wadin'?"

She nodded. "I was looking for frogs. I found a little one." She reached inside her overalls and pulled it out. "I'm going to feed him some tasty bugs."

He chuckled. "I always thought little girls played like they were grown women."

"Sometimes I do. I like both."

"What about Sammie Jo?"

"Mama makes her learn cooking stuff, but she'd rather be ridin' or explorin'."

Alarm weighed on Colt's mind. "Promise me something."

She gazed up at him with huge, trusting eyes.

"Promise me you and Sammie Jo won't go explorin' very far from the ranch."

"Why? Because of what happened to you and Clancy?"

"That's right. This leg of mine hurts powerful bad, and I wouldn't want you to hurt, too."

She nodded. "I promise. Sammie Jo's braver than me, so I'll tell her what you said."

"Would she listen to anyone besides you and me?" Colt recognized the older girl's stubbornness and figured she'd do the opposite of what he or Nancy asked.

"Maybe Thatcher Lee. She's still sneaking around and seeing him." Nancy stared into Colt's face. "He's a grown man, Mr. Colt. Mama would whip her good if she knew."

"I'll say something to Thatcher Lee." As if he hadn't before.

"Thank you." Nancy grinned. Her attention focused on the utmost tree branches. "I sure appreciate you helping me down out of this here tree. Sammie Jo laughs at me getting scared easy."

"Takes a real smart gal to stay away from danger, and you and Sammie Jo are real smart."

Nancy wrinkled up her nose. "She thinks she knows everything."

Colt frowned but kept his thoughts to himself. He feared Anne's oldest daughter might need to learn a few of life's lessons the hard way.

—∞—

Anne lifted the canteen to her lips and drank deeply. She

worked sunup to sundown to take up the slack until Clancy and Colt were healed. Bone-tired, she prayed God would give her strength to continue on. Sammie Jo enjoyed helping, but Anne believed her enthusiasm had a lot to do with Thatcher Lee. Twice Anne had caught her talking to him when they thought no one was looking. Thatcher Lee knew better, especially if he wanted to keep his job. Anne would have cut him loose a long time ago except he was a good ranch hand and she needed help. No matter that her daughter looked older. Sammie Jo had a few years of growing and maturing before Anne allowed a young man to come courting.

The object of her frustration rode toward Anne with Thatcher Lee alongside her. Sammie Jo's face flushed red—and Anne knew it had nothing to do with the heat.

"Where have you two been?" Anne asked.

"Roundin' up strays." Thatcher Lee tipped his hat. Always the mannerly one, which kept his body free of buckshot when it came to Sammie Jo. "Won't take long to move the herd into the upper pasture, Mrs. Langley."

Anne screwed the cap back onto her canteen. "That job took both of you?"

"Yes, ma'am. Sammie Jo had a lot of questions about ranching."

Anne focused her attention dead center on Thatcher Lee's eyes. "She has a mama for that. If I don't have the answers, I'll find them. Do you understand what I mean? She's fourteen years old, not eighteen."

"Yes, ma'am." Thatcher Lee's lips turned up slightly.

Anne bit her tongue to keep from using words a good

Christian woman had no right to use. But this was her daughter, and she'd work this ranch without Thatcher Lee if he didn't stay away from Sammie Jo.

After dinner when the sun had slipped just beyond the horizon, she stopped by to see how Colt and Clancy were doing. Clancy had been cleaning out stalls one-handedly, most likely to chase away boredom.

"I need to talk," she said to Colt. "Do you feel up to limping outside?"

He grabbed his crutch and made his way beside her. She caught a few looks from the other hands as though they suspected something going on between them. Right now she wasn't in the mood to ask what they were gawking at.

"Thatcher Lee and Sammie Jo are sneaking around." She blurted out the words in a mixture of anger and near-tears. Not at all as she intended.

"From what Nancy said to me today, I don't doubt what you're telling me. Looks like that little talk I gave him went nowhere. You want me to have another one?"

"I told him earlier to stay away from her. I hate to fire him. He's a good hand, but I'm not risking my daughter's future on a two-bit cowboy."

"Maybe he needs to know what you're thinking. I don't mind telling him he's looking at getting fired."

"Thanks. The only reason I'm asking you is because Thatcher Lee respects you, and he and Clancy have had their problems in the past." She feared her request made her look like a whining female.

Colt smiled, and it spread across his face. She could get

used to his smile and the way he seemed to care about her daughters.

"Were Hank and Thomas friends with Thatcher Lee?"

She crossed her arms over her chest. "Always. He was real angry when those two were caught with Double L cows. He and Clancy tried to talk them out of cattle rustling, but it didn't do any good. Sure glad I rode up when I did, or he and Clancy would have been dead."

Colt appeared to take in her every word. That made her feel a little uncomfortable but in a special way. Mercy, she'd gotten as bad as Sammie Jo with Thatcher Lee.

"Why do you ask?"

He shrugged. "He's young. Maybe what Hank and Thomas did—and later finding them dead—makes him want to talk to someone who'll listen."

"Maybe so." She sighed. "I'll talk to him—see if I can be that ear instead of my daughter." She laughed. "Raising daughters is hard, but I guess raising boys wouldn't be any easier. Any suggestions?"

He hesitated. "I think if my ma had taken the time to rein me in when I bullied my brothers, maybe I wouldn't have ended up in prison. She worked hard and didn't have time to listen when we needed to talk. But girls? I don't have nary an idea."

"No sisters?"

He shook his head. "One of my brothers took up with a woman who had a little girl. The woman did anything he asked, and it nearly got her killed. That's what worries me about Sammie Jo and Thatcher Lee. She's so young and. . . Excuse me. Sammie Jo is none of my business."

She glanced at the house. A lot of wisdom rode under Colt's hat. And she understood exactly what he meant about Sammie Jo. Anne hadn't spent time with another man except Clancy since Will died. Her head warned her not to lose her heart. Colt was a strange man. His eyes were hard, but sometimes she saw a spark of genuine decency.

"There's some milk cake left over from dinner. Would you like a piece and some fresh coffee?"

"Sounds real good, Anne. Do you mind if I check on Miss Nancy? She found herself a friend today—a frog."

Anne smiled. "She's taken with you, Colt." *And so am I.*

Chapter 7

Three weeks after the shootings, Colt climbed on his horse and attempted to do his share of the work. The longest three weeks since prison. Strange how he'd always taken walking for granted. Now he counted the days until he could make his way around the ranch without limping. Nancy said he looked "grumpy," but some of the other ranch hands had more colorful words to describe his aggravation.

He had a few suspicions about what was going on at the Double L. With nothing to do but think and read, he'd watched the men to see if any said or did anything out of the ordinary. One man stayed foremost in Colt's mind, but until he found evidence, he'd keep his mouth shut and his ears and eyes open.

During the fourth week, Colt, Clancy, Thatcher Lee, and two other hands rode together for fence mending. It wasn't one of Colt's favorite chores, but he was just glad to be in the saddle instead of flat on his back. Anne and the girls joined them in a wagon with the fixin's for a noon meal. Already the sun beat down hard. They needed rain, and the cracked, parched earth proved it. Midsummer in Texas gave a whole new meaning to *fire and brimstone*.

Anne smiled and waved from several feet away. Nancy called out to him. Even Sammie Jo waved—a first since she'd made it known how she felt about him interfering with her and Thatcher Lee. Lately Anne made sure Sammie Jo stuck to her side. Colt had talked again to Thatcher Lee and told him their boss was ready to fire him. So far the young man had steered clear of Sammie Jo.

Clancy had done nothing but grin all morning.

"What's so funny?" Colt asked.

"Oh, I'm in a good mood. Thanks for returning my Bible," he said.

"Yep, I saw you readin' it," Thatcher Lee said. "Next you'll be preachin' like Clancy."

Colt laughed. "I'm not getting religious, so you two can wipe those holy looks off your faces. I like the stories."

"I'm right tickled you're reading it," Clancy said.

"Yeah, it shows." Colt wasn't about to comment on his interest in God. But interest was all he had. Anne took a lot of stock in a man who knew God, and he wanted to know why.

Sitting in his saddle, listening to the familiar creak of the leather, and taking in the surroundings lifted his spirits; he felt a rare sense of peace. He'd grown to care for these people, something he never thought would happen. Before his release from Huntsville Prison, he hadn't cared about anyone but himself. His life had changed, and he believed it was for the better.

Glancing to the right of him, he saw Anne slow the wagon until she drove beside him. He'd resolved to stay clear of her, but this morning it was real hard. He dug his heels into his mare and caught up with Clancy.

"You doin' all right?" Clancy asked. Sweat dripped from his forehead.

"Yeah. I'm glad to be earning my keep again."

"Good to see you on a horse and your face not all screwed up in pain. Any other ideas about what happened?"

"A few."

Clancy glanced around. "So do I. Got my eyes on him."

Colt nodded. Whether they suspected the same man or not didn't matter. They both were anxious to find out who'd done the killings—not to mention who'd shot the two of them—and get 'em handed over to the law. He'd feel better when all of this trouble was settled.

Anne. She made an ordinary day fill up with sunshine. Colt sensed his heart had taken a plunge well-deep. While waiting on his leg to heal, he'd considered collecting his pay and riding out. Seeing her every day and realizing he'd never be good enough for such a fine woman depressed him. She'd loved one outlaw and ended up a widow. What more did he have to offer? Sure, he'd left the past behind, but what he'd done surfaced in his mind every time he thought they might have a good life together.

The day's work nearly wore out Colt—not so much the fence mendin' but the heat. His leg ached as he limped to the corral with Clancy. He sensed the old man had things to say. At times it seemed like the two of them had the same mind.

"Neither one of us is men who talk much about what we're thinking." Clancy leaned on the fence. "I enjoy teasin' you and pushin' you to think on the things of God. But accusing a man of murder is different."

"I agree." Colt sighed. "I'm still not sure if I should say what I suspect."

"Don't blame you, and I've known him longer than you."

"Ever have any problems with him?" Colt asked.

"You know the answer to that."

"What kind of trouble?"

Clancy shrugged. "Not enough to pin murder on him. He slacks when it comes to working unless Anne's watching. Don't like 'im. Never did. And I try to look for the good in a man."

"Did you ever see him slipping away?"

"Sure have. He stuck close to Hank and Thomas until I caught those boys stealing cattle."

"I thought both of you caught them." Colt's mind raced with accusations.

"Nope. Just me, and then he rode up."

"He isn't getting out of my sight."

"Mine either. Although I can't figure out why he would have murdered Hank and Thomas."

Colt hesitated. Recollections of what he and Will used to do settled in his mind. "Maybe they knew too much about Will's business, or he just got greedy."

Clancy glanced behind them. "Hey, Thatcher Lee."

The young man joined them. He placed his foot on the fence rail. "I'm real worried about Mrs. Langley and the girls."

"We are, too, son." Clancy stared out into the ever-darkening shadows. A few horses made their way toward them.

"I want whoever has caused this trouble found," Thatcher

Lee said. "I think the only reason the women went with us today was because it left no one there to defend them."

"This is their home," Colt said. "I know our boss can handle herself, but she shouldn't have to tote a rifle to protect what's hers."

"Well, count me in on what needs to be done," Thatcher Lee said. He stroked the head of one of the horses. "I wonder about our good sheriff. He's never around when you need him, and he's plum lazy." With those words he turned and strode off toward the stables.

"What do you think?" Clancy asked.

"Nothing's changed. I just want to know why."

—∞—

In her bedroom, by the light of the kerosene lamp, Anne counted the money in the cash box, the money she used for payroll. Last month it all balanced out, but this month she was two hundred dollars short. Where had it gone? No one knew where she kept it. Someone would have to search her room to find it. She kept it at the bottom of the leather trunk with the girls' baby clothes and her parents' Bible on top. Rosita? The sweet lady never set foot in Anne's room. No, Rosita had not taken the money. But who had?

She shivered. Cattle rustlers. Murders. Money gone. Hard work and sleepless nights she could handle, but this shook her. Will would have known what to do. He'd have strapped on his Colts and cleaned up this mess.

Strapped on his Colts. The Peacemaker. Colt Wilson.

Her mind must be slipping to linger on a man who was

most likely as rotten as her husband.

Anne shoved the cash box back into the trunk and eased down onto her bed. It squeaked, as it always had. She lay back on the quilt, the one her mother had given her on her wedding day—one of the few memories of Will that didn't hurt. He'd lied to her and broken the law, and maybe he'd brought down this trouble on his family. Betrayal stalked her day and night, and she didn't want to love a man who'd do the same thing again. Why couldn't she fall in love with a man who wasn't an outlaw?

Burying her face in her hands, she cried until not a single tear was left. *Oh, God, what am I to do? I have Sammie Jo and Nancy to raise. Someone is murdering my ranch hands and stealing my cattle and my cash. A near-man has my Sammie Jo's attention, and Colt Wilson is too good-looking and so very kind.*

"Mama."

Anne blinked, wiped her face, and took a deep breath. "Yes, Nancy."

"My frog's gone."

"Come on in, honey." Anne stood from the bed.

The door opened, and Nancy broke into tears the moment she saw her mama. "He's run away. I just know it."

"Are you sure?" For certain if the frog had died, Rosita would have taken care of the matter.

"Can we go find Mr. Colt? He'll know where to look for Mr. Frog."

Anne sensed the color drain from her face. "Honey, we can't bother Mr. Colt. He's worked very hard today."

Nancy sniffed. "But he's my best friend. He never laughs at me, and he talks to me like I'm all grown up."

Oh, Colt has stolen more than one Langley woman's heart. She bent to her daughter's side. "Perhaps we can find your Mr. Frog. I'll help you."

Nancy wrapped her arms around her mama's neck. "It's no good, but we can try."

Anne grasped her daughter's hand and the lamp. Together they made their way through the house, looking here and there for one lonely frog. Satisfied it wasn't inside, they stepped onto the porch.

"Mr. Frog," Nancy called, "you don't have to hide. I'm here."

"Miss Nancy, did you lose your frog?"

At the sound of Colt's voice, Anne's legs felt like quivering matchsticks.

"Yes, sir. He's run off."

Colt mounted the back porch steps. He bent down to Nancy. "I'll look, but you know what?"

She shook her head.

"I think he's missing his frog friends. I know you take good care of him, but I bet he wants to be with his family and friends. What if you lived with him? Wouldn't you miss your mama and Sammie Jo?"

"I would, sir. And I'd miss you, too." She swiped at her eyes. "I want him to be happy. I'll let him be free."

"Your daddy would be proud of you." Colt stood and shoved his hands into his jeans pockets.

Alarm took over Anne's senses—the missing money and all the trouble at the Double L. "Nancy, why don't you run along and get ready for bed?"

"Good night, little one," Colt said. "Don't forget to tell

your sister good night."

Nancy started to protest, but with a lift of her mama's chin, she disappeared inside. A few moments later, Anne stared into the shadows at Colt.

"You have a good evening, ma'am."

When he turned to leave, curiosity got the best of Anne. "Were you needing to talk to me?"

He shrugged. "No."

"Then what were you doing up here?"

"I'd rather keep that to myself if you don't mind."

Anger simmered to a fast boil. "You're snooping around my house, and you don't want to tell me why?"

"That's what I said." He stiffened.

"Maybe you know more about what has been going on than you're telling."

Colt said nothing.

"Are you keeping something from me? Or are you involved?"

His fists clenched. "If that's what you think of me, then I'm clearing out of here tonight."

Regret washed over her. She rubbed her shoulders. "I don't think you're against me," she said softly. "Colt, you know something you're not telling me, and I don't like it at all."

"I'm not in the habit of accusing a man without proof."

"What did you see here tonight?" she asked, barely above a whisper.

"Nothing."

Clancy appeared from the shadows. She held her breath.

"Anne, Colt won't tell you what's going on, but I'll tell you. In fact, I'm part of it, too."

"I want to hear all of it." She whipped her attention to Clancy.

"We've been keeping watch on the house and barns at night. One night I do it, and Colt does it the next."

Anger smoothed to near tears. She grabbed the porch post. "I'm sorry. I thought. . .I thought. . ." She swallowed the lump in her throat. "If I'm to trust anyone, it's you two."

Colt stepped forward then back. He raked his fingers through his hair. "I'm heading back to the bunkhouse. Enough for one night."

"That's what I came to tell you," Clancy said. "He's missing."

"Who?" Anne asked. "You have to tell me." Her voice rose higher. "Please tell me."

Chapter 8

Anne trembled in the shadows, a different side for Colt to see. In all of the times they'd been together, she'd been strong and fearless—bossy and full of spirit. He wanted to reach out and hold her, take care of the situation and put her mind at ease. But he couldn't.

"Anne, I don't have proof," Colt said. "I spent too many years in prison to accuse an innocent man. Clancy and I suspect one of the hands, and we're watching him. I can't say anymore."

Her shoulders lifted and fell. "I'm sorry, and I understand. Don't know what's got into me."

"I do," he said. "You have a family and a ranch. It would make a person question everyone around 'em—especially someone you trusted."

She nodded. "Thanks." She peered around him to Clancy. "After Will died, it took that feisty old man behind you to toughen me up."

Clancy chuckled. "You had it in ya. You just didn't know it."

"What can I do to help?" Her attention focused on both men. "Won't do any good to tell me 'nothing.' I can't sleep or think right, and I won't until this is settled."

Colt wished he'd spent more time with his mother so he'd know how to convince Anne of her foolishness. "I guess keep your eyes open. Nancy and Sammie Jo wander off a lot. Might be good if you'd make sure they stick around the ranch." He forced a laugh. "Although Sammie Jo can handle herself, there's no point in her walking into a snake pit."

"I agree," Clancy said. "Both girls have a streak of stubbornness when it comes to telling them they can't do something. Kinda like their mama."

"I'll make sure it sounds like it's their idea—and include Rosita with this, too. She could find things for them to do. I want the girls to be cautious but not afraid."

Colt thought about Will. He should have been more careful and held on to this woman. Any man would be proud to. . .

"Cattle's missin', too," Clancy said. "We brought back the ones Hank and Thomas stole, but now there's twenty or so gone."

"So we're looking at a real greedy man." Colt glanced toward the bunkhouse. "If you two don't mind, I'm going to take a little look around."

"Got your rifle?" Anne asked.

"Yes, ma'am. I've used it a time or two."

"I'd still like to know who you two suspect."

"If you run him off, then we don't have a chance to catch him. At least this way Clancy and I can make sure he or they are stopped." He hoped his optimism reassured her.

"I'll be along in a bit," Clancy said. "I want Anne to take a look at my shoulder."

Colt stepped down from the porch steps and headed toward the bunkhouse and barns. Leaving Anne with Clancy gave him an opportunity to back away from her soft voice and the yearning in his heart. She made his senses go loco.

Studying the shadows, he doubted if anyone would be stupid enough to do anything with him and Clancy out checking on things. Usually it was just one of them, like he was taking off to the outhouse or couldn't sleep.

The full moon helped light the corral and the surrounding buildings. He walked to the back of the barns, along the fences, and then to the bunkhouse. The beds were occupied except his and Clancy's. Had their suspect guessed what was going on and crept back to his bunk? This cowboy was one clever *hombre.*

He eased onto his bed and stared up at the ceiling, not really looking but pondering the situation. While in prison he thought he'd done enough thinking for a lifetime. Obviously not, 'cause he couldn't figure out what was going on at the Double L.

"You and Clancy all right?" Thatcher Lee whispered.

"Yeah. Clancy's shoulder is botherin' him, and I made sure he got to Miss Anne's before changing his mind."

Colt listened to the snores around him. Tonight, like so many nights before, he pretended to sink his toes into the boots of the murderin' cattle rustler who had made life miserable for Anne and tried to figure out how to stop him. He remembered the days when his own mind wrapped around the best way to deceive innocent folks. Odd—now he was on the other side. He understood how folks felt when robbed of their property or when someone they knew was killed.

Whoever had been up to no good would slip soon. His confidence would overcome his good sense, and he'd start making mistakes. Colt planned to be right there when it all broke loose.

"Too bad," Thatcher Lee said. "She'll fix him up. G'night. Big day tomorrow."

—∞—

Anne examined Clancy's shoulder by the lamplight in the kitchen. She thought it had been healing fine, but infection oozed from it.

"Why didn't you tell me about this sooner?" She blew out an exasperated sigh, remembering the infection in Will's leg.

"I was taking care of it myself. Used some aloe leaves on it, and it does look better." Clancy sat at the table while Anne poked at his sore arm.

"It needs to look a whole lot better." She held the light over his shoulder for signs of red streaks. "Lucky for you I don't see any blood poisoning."

"What can you do for me?"

"I'll clean it up and use some whiskey to burn out some of the infection. Probably wouldn't hurt for me to squeeze a little aloe on it. In the morning I'll take the wagon into town for medicine. I need supplies anyway. Nearly out of sugar and coffee."

"Can't do that. We need the wagon to haul feed for the cattle."

She opened the pie safe and pulled out a bottle of whiskey. A clean towel lay on the kitchen table. "Then I'll ride in by myself. Faster that way."

"With all the trouble we're having around here?"

She tapped her foot against the wooden floor then dabbed the wound with the whiskey, watching him wince. "Do you want to go with me?"

"Oh, I'd be a lot of good with a hurt shoulder."

Concern mixed with fear shadowed Anne's calm composure. Clancy was running a fever and needed more than she could do. A woman in town knew a lot about herbs. An extra day made a lot of difference. "I'll ask Thatcher Lee to ride along."

"I'd rather you take Colt—in case of trouble."

All the way to town with a man who leaves me tongue-tied? "What about one of the other hands?"

"What's wrong with Colt? He's good with a gun, and I won't have to worry about you. Is it because you've got feelings for him?"

Anne sensed her face aflame. If Clancy had guessed her secret, had anyone else?

"Don't worry. I haven't told a soul. But I do think it's a good idea to have him go along with you."

She realized he'd backed her into a corner. No way out but to ask Colt to escort her. "All right. I'll ask him first thing in the morning."

"No need. I'll do it when I head back to the bunkhouse."

Barking orders seemed the easiest way for Anne to cope with trouble. "Don't go out with the men tomorrow. Stay here and keep Rosita and the girls company."

"I did toughen you up, didn't I? Before Will died, you'd have packed up the girls and left for the city."

"Times change." Her voice softened. "I love you like a

father, don't you know that?"

Clancy nodded. "I'm a bit partial to you, too." He peered at his shoulder. "The aloe is helping a lot. In another day it'll be fine. I only asked for you to take a look at it 'cause I can't see what it looks like. You don't need to go to all this trouble."

She forced a smile through her weariness. Clancy's shoulder just added to more of her worries—like a stall no one wanted to clean. At least she could do something about Clancy in the morning.

Spending the day with Colt tomorrow would cause her a sleepless night tonight. A handsome man had no room in her head or her heart.

Colt had given up on any sleep tonight. If he hadn't enough on his mind, now he had to ride into town with Anne. She made him nervous with all the men around. What would happen during the several hours alone? He'd most likely fall off his horse.

He glanced at Clancy and doubted if he slept, either. His shoulder probably throbbed each time his heart beat. And it had to hurt powerful bad for him to ask Anne for help.

Lord, would You heal Clancy's shoulder? He's an old man who works hard. I'd rather him go see You years from now.

Colt nearly jolted out of bed. Was he praying? When did this happen? His heart pounded like thunder rumbling on the prairie. Taking a deep breath, he eased back onto the bunk. He must believe in God, or he wouldn't have prayed. When he thought through the last few days, he realized his trust in God had grown while trust in himself had slipped away.

This must be what Clancy had been talking about. God would reach out and snatch him when he least expected it. In the middle of frettin' over Anne and the ranch, Colt had shaken off his independence and depended on God—not his rifle, his mind, or anyone around him.

Do I feel any different? He touched his chest as if God might have made him a new heart. According to what he'd read in the Bible and from listening to Clancy talk, if he believed and died this very minute, he'd live with God.

Heaven was a whole sight better than the other place, and he'd been real close to that. Reuben would be real pleased about this, but his other brothers would laugh good and hard about this one. Colt didn't care what any man thought. Strange how his mind had moved from thinking on himself to thinking about God.

He'd been hooked like a fish on a line and didn't mind a bit. He thought men found God when trouble had them next to death—like in the middle of a shootout or with a body full of holes lying next to 'em. This was an ordinary night. Nothing special, except Clancy's shoulder needed doctoring.

Telling his friend crossed his mind; Clancy would want to know. And Anne. . .wonder how she'd take the news? Or was he supposed to keep quiet?

Guess he should pray a little more and do it right. From what he'd read, Jesus took the blame for his ornery soul, and he needed to thank Him and ask Him to take over his rotten life.

Chapter 9

Colt took a glimpse at Anne's saddle to see if she'd brought two canteens of water. The day promised to be another scorcher. Once assured she'd be fine, he swung up onto the saddle.

"This will be a hot one," he said. "Sure you don't want me to take care of business in town? You could stay here and tend to Clancy."

Anne shook her head. "I'd feel better if I could talk to the woman who knows herbs. Could be we're doing all we can for Clancy, but I'm hoping for a remedy to bring down his temperature and stop the infection." She turned in the saddle to view Rosita. "It'll be late when we get home. The horses will need to rest a bit in this heat before pushing them the fifteen miles back."

"We'll have a good day." Rosita wrapped her arm around Nancy's shoulder and kissed the top of her head. "Expect a berry pie when you return."

Anne adjusted her hat beneath her chin and nodded at Colt.

He waved at the girls and Rosita, but Nancy threw him a

kiss and giggled. That little gal sure had his heart—just like her mama. Sammie Jo, on the other hand, looked like she'd just as soon blow a hole through him.

They'd ridden for about thirty minutes at an easy gallop when they slowed the horses in the heat. Colt considered some kind of conversation, but his tongue wouldn't form the words. This was hard. Real hard. He wanted to tell her about makin' a decision for the Lord, but the words stayed in his head.

"Do you see storm clouds gathering, or is it my imagination?" Anne finally asked, relieving Colt of the worry of talking.

He peered to the north and studied them. "Sure looks like it, and we sorely need the rain."

"I don't mind getting wet."

"Me either. But I hate riding out in the open during a thunderstorm."

She laughed—that musical ring that sounded like a sweet song. "Why, Colt Wilson, have I found something you're afraid of?"

"If you're referring to thunder and lightning, then you're right. I don't relish the thought of getting fried up like a slab of bacon."

She laughed again. "So what are you going to do when we're caught in the middle of it?"

"Pray." The moment the word slipped from his mouth, Colt thought better of it.

She started, and a wide smile spread over her face. "When did this happen?"

He sensed his face heat up. "Last night, thinkin' on Clancy."

"Does he know?"

"Naw. Not sure if a man's supposed to tell folks about these things. Like I was bragging or trying to look religious."

"Colt, I'm so happy for you."

She sounded like she was going to cry, which made Colt more nervous than before.

"Huh, thanks."

"Do you want to talk about it? Did it happen after we talked?"

What had he gotten himself into? "It happened later, and I do feel right uncomfortable. I have to get used to this a bit."

"Oh, I'm sorry. I am proud of you, and Clancy will be so happy." She took a glance at him. "All right. We'll talk about something else."

Good. He'd rather get caught with bolts of lightning jabbing on all sides of him than talk about finding God in a smelly bunkhouse.

"Are you going to tell me who you and Clancy suspect? It's making me crazy not knowing which one of my men is a thief and a murderer."

He wished she'd run out of words. "No. Can't do it."

"Even if it makes me so mad I can't see straight?"

"Yep."

Long moments followed, but he refused to give in.

"How about your thoughts on bringing in some fine quarter-horse stock?" she asked.

For the next several minutes, Colt told her everything he knew about horses, anything to keep her off the subject of God and the trouble at the Double L.

"Nancy sure likes you," Anne said.

He chuckled. "She asked me to marry her when she grows up."

"Oh, my. What did you tell her?"

"That we'd wait and see how she felt then."

"She said to me, 'Mama, Mr. Colt is right handsome; don't you think so?' "

He sensed her peering at him.

"Colt, you're blushing."

"No, I'm not." But he felt plum silly, even if it was little Nancy making the claim. Truth be known, he wondered if Anne thought he was pleasing to look at. Not that it mattered.

"Colt." She spoke quietly as if something might be wrong.

"Yeah."

"Have you been avoiding me lately? I mean, I said some ugly things to you last night, but for days now you've acted like I offended you."

He scratched his jaw. "Well, some of the others were saying a few things that weren't, uh, proper."

"Like what? You and me together?"

Had she not heard the jeering? "Yes, ma'am."

"I appreciate your gentlemanly ways, but I wish you'd have said something to me about it instead of acting like I'd made you mad."

"You're my boss."

"I'm still a woman."

Colt whipped his attention her way. Tears were streaming down her face. What had he done wrong? "I didn't mean to make you cry."

"I can't figure out why I'm crying anyway."

What was he supposed to say now? "Do you need my handkerchief? It's a clean one."

She shook her head and pulled out one from her shirt pocket. "Sorry. This is new to me."

What's new to her? Him finding God? What the others were sayin'? "I don't understand. What the ranch hands were saying made you cry?"

She glanced at him and blinked. In the next instant, she spurred her horse and raced away.

For sure Anne had him confused. He hesitated and hurried to catch up. The remaining miles into town were spent in silence, and that made him real glad.

—∞—

The longer Anne and Colt spent in town, the darker it grew until thunder cracked and lightning flashed in the distance, but Anne sensed it was coming closer. Within minutes a torrent of rain pelted the dusty streets.

"Sure glad I already have the herbs for Clancy." Anne pulled her slicker over her head as they stood under the overhang of the general store. "I'm ready for it to rain like this for three days, but I want to get back to the ranch, tend to Clancy, and make sure my girls are fine."

Thunder crashed down around them, and lightning streaked across an angry sky. They were dry, but water poured off the roof in buckets.

"We're staying right here until the storm lets up," Colt said. "It's moving toward the ranch, and we can be right behind it."

"I hope the girls' outing didn't get ruined."

"I thought you were keeping them close to home."

His voice held a twinge of alarm. She appreciated this man; he reminded her of Clancy in many ways. Since Colt had found the Lord, he'd taken on more of those traits. Her heart was betraying her, and if she didn't mask her feelings better, he'd know for sure.

"Don't worry. Rosita took the girls berry-picking, and I sent Thatcher Lee along to keep them safe. Rosita won't hesitate to tell Sammie Jo to keep her distance from him."

Colt punched his fist into his palm.

"What's wrong? They're probably within shouting distance of the Double L."

"Who'd hear? Clancy? The rest of 'em took feed to the cattle."

"Why are you so upset?" Suddenly realization hit her hard. Anne's stomach churned. "It's Thatcher Lee," she whispered.

"We only suspect him."

"But you have to be wrong. He's always been a hard worker, and he and Clancy tried to stop Hank and Thomas from running off with my cattle. And. . .and what about when you and Clancy were shot? He rode in and saved you." By now, she fought the sobs choking her throat.

Another clap of thunder shook the roof above them as if a bad omen had taken root in her fears.

"I don't have proof." He lingered on every word as if trying to convince himself.

"Tell me why you think it's Thatcher Lee."

"Here's what Clancy and I think. Thatcher Lee, Hank, and Thomas were good friends. They often rode off together, but no one ever questioned where. Clancy said the three were hired on at the same time."

She nodded and clenched her fists.

"Clancy was the one who discovered what Hank and Thomas were doing. Thatcher Lee simply rode up and stopped it. When we were shot, he stayed behind. He told me he'd never shot anyone before, and so we thought it best for him to stay clear of danger. When we were fired on, one man was doing the shooting. When Thatcher Lee joined us, the shooting stopped. And the bullet taken out of my leg was from a revolver like the one he carries." Colt paused. "Do you really think he's interested in Sammie Jo, or do you think he has something else on his mind?" He shook his head. "I'm sorry, Anne. I should have put that a little more delicately."

Anne gasped. "My babies. Thatcher Lee has my babies."

An ear-piercing burst of thunder drove her into Colt's arms. He held her tight, and she stayed there.

"I'll ride back and make sure everything is all right," he said.

"I'm going, too."

"I could be wrong about Thatcher Lee. That's why I didn't want to accuse him."

Anne swallowed hard. "But everything you told me is true. I wish I knew why or what he wanted. I'll blow a hole clean through his skull if he's hurt one of my girls." *I wonder how the good Lord feels about that.*

"Do you know where he came from?"

"He never said; neither did Hank or Thomas. They needed jobs, and I needed hands."

"Doesn't matter. He wants something you've got, and he's not afraid—"

"To kill for it." Anne despised her own words. *Nancy, Sammie Jo. Her beloved Rosita.*

Colt pushed her at arm's length. "I'm heading to the ranch."

She nodded. "Let's go." Hesitation stopped her. "Colt, you don't have to do this. You could be hurt if you're right about Thatcher Lee."

"I care too much for those girls—and you—to stand by and do nothing."

Anne sank her teeth into her lower lip. Later she'd ponder over his words, but not now.

Amid nature's fury, the two rode toward the ranch with the understanding that man's fury was often harder to reckon with.

—∾—

Soaked clear through to their clothes with water dripping from their slickers, Anne and Colt raced toward the ranch. In what seemed like the worst storm he'd seen in a long time, Colt finally saw the outline of the house and barns. How he prayed those girls were safe inside with Rosita. His spurs dug into the mare's sides.

He jumped from his horse and hurried up the back porch steps before Anne could dismount. He threw open the door and called for Rosita, then Sammie Jo and Nancy. Nothing but the sound of the rain on the roof met his ears.

"Are they here?" Anne asked from the doorway.

Colt turned slowly. "No. Where do they normally pick berries?"

"Near the edge of the woods on the eastern side."

"I'll start there. They could be taking shelter from the storm." He refused to comment on the rain washing away their tracks or what Thatcher Lee might do to the womenfolk. "We need to check on Clancy. He might know something."

Clancy rested on his bunk. All he could do was apologize for not keeping a better watch on the house. "Get on out of here. You're wasting time." He patted his shoulder. "I'm doing fine. Now go."

In the next moment, they were on their horses again and riding toward the eastern section of the ranch. If Thatcher Lee did have them—and he meant harm—Colt knew he'd forget the faith he'd garnered the night before.

No, I won't. For once I'm listening to God.

But Colt feared the worst. He'd been among desperate men too long, and he didn't trust Thatcher Lee at all.

Chapter 10

Anne pointed to where the girls often did their berry-picking. She attempted to calm the raging fears threatening to overtake her. Her mind recalled all the times Thatcher Lee had been overly polite and the way the other hands avoided him. Why hadn't she seen through him? *Oh, God, please keep them safe.*

A rush of memories from those days when she lost Will and the tragedy after his death washed over her like the rain blinding her vision.

"I can't lose my girls," she said as the horses made their way along the outer edges of the woods. The tracks she wanted to find weren't there.

Colt swung his attention her way. "I may be wrong about Thatcher Lee, and if I am, you'll probably fire me."

Emotion poured from her heart and eyes. "I could never fire you, Colt. I love you." There. She'd said it.

His eyes widened.

She must confess her heart. "I'm not sure what will happen here today. Only God knows. But I sent Will to his grave without forgiving him and telling him I loved him. I won't make that mistake again." She took a deep breath. "It cost me more than losing my husband. It cost me his son."

"Anne, I'm so sorry."

"It was my own fault. I couldn't pull myself from the guilt and grief when Will died. I was expecting, and the baby came early. If it hadn't been for Clancy, I'd have been buried alongside the baby and Will." She studied his kind face, the face she loved.

"Clancy has helped us both."

She realized Colt didn't know what to say, and she had no idea how he felt about her. "That dear man made me get out of bed, forced me to eat, and read to me from the Bible about God's strength. He lectured me about taking care of my girls, and that was only the beginning."

Colt offered a nervous grin. "What else?"

She met his smile with one of her own. "Taught me how to shoot and give orders, and all about ranching. Riding broncs was my idea."

"He did a good job." Colt glanced away, then back again. "I'm not good enough for you, Anne. Look at what I've done."

"Look at what you've become—a new creation in Christ."

He paused. "Maybe so." His gaze returned to the ground, and he dismounted. "They were here. Must have left when the rain started. We can follow these tracks."

"How many?" she asked. If more men were involved, she and Colt were outnumbered.

"Rosita, the girls, and one man. I pray I'm wrong about Thatcher Lee. I really do."

Colt followed the trail through the mud. The small band was on horseback and headed to the place where the shooting had happened. What Thatcher Lee had done to Hank and Thomas settled on him hard. He glanced around—lots of rocks and trees to hide behind—easy for Anne and him to be ambushed. He turned his mare and circled behind where he thought Thatcher Lee had gone.

"Isn't this where you and Clancy were shot?" Anne asked.

"Yeah, and I don't understand why he brought them here. This would be the first place I'd look." He hesitated. "He wants us to follow him. He's planned this for a while." Colt refused to say what else he feared. He prayed Thatcher Lee had gotten too sure of himself and had made a few mistakes that would help Colt free Rosita and the girls. "We have to walk from here. Are you sure you want to do this?"

The look she threw him left no question about her determination. Colt loved this woman. Maybe when this was over, they'd have a chance.

The rain beat down harder, causing him and Anne to slip more than once in the mud. But if they were having a miserable time in the weather, so was Thatcher Lee. The man had a short fuse; this might not be good.

At a spot he believed gave him cover behind Thatcher Lee, Colt motioned for Anne to stop. He bent low and covered the next several feet alone. Over a slab of overhanging rock sat Thatcher Lee, Rosita, and the girls. From Colt's stance, he could see that the captives' hands were bound. Colt assessed the terrain and crawled back to Anne.

"I need you to follow me, no talking, and move as quietly as you can. When I motion to you, stay put. Cover me while I circle in around Thatcher Lee."

"So he does have my girls?"

"I'm afraid so." His mind raced with the best way to seize Thatcher Lee without endangering the others. But one thing needed to be resolved with Anne. "Remember what you said about Will dying and not telling him how you felt?"

She nodded and swiped at the tears.

"I'm telling you now that I—I love you." He spun around and crouched through the brush with Anne behind him.

At the designated spot, Colt pointed to where Thatcher Lee held his captives. Without another sound, he crawled to where he prayed God would give him an advantage over the man in the distance.

The closer he crept, the louder he could hear Thatcher Lee.

"My mama and Mr. Colt and Clancy will get you," Nancy said.

"Shut up. Your mama and Colt are gone into town, and Clancy can't do a thing with his shoulder. By the time they get back to the ranch, they'll find the note in the kitchen."

Note? He hadn't seen one. Knowing Thatcher Lee's intentions would have helped.

"Why do you want us?" Rosita asked. Through the brush, Colt could see a huge bruise on the side of her face.

"Well, Rosita, Anne's husband has hidden a sizable amount of money on this ranch, and I want my share. I figure she'll give all of it to me in exchange for you ladies."

"You're a liar," Sammie Jo said. "And to think I stole money from Mama because you said you cared about me—wanted to run away with me. You're worse than a rattlesnake."

He laughed. "Your daddy was a no-good thief. He's got money stashed all over this place."

When Sammie Jo protested, Thatcher Lee told her exactly what he planned for her—and it wasn't pretty.

Dirty animal. I'll tear him to pieces for what he's saying to that sweet, innocent girl.

Colt inched closer. He trusted God for guidance and to keep everyone safe. No matter what he had to do, Colt would not let Thatcher Lee hurt those girls or Rosita any more than he already had. Huntsville Prison sounded like a good place for him.

A stick snapped. Even in the rain the sound rang out like an alarm. Thatcher Lee whipped his attention toward Colt and took aim. Sammie Jo jumped from where she sat and pushed him off balance. Colt bolted into Thatcher Lee and pinned him to the ground. In the next breath, Colt wrestled the revolver away from him. He wasn't sure how Sammie Jo managed to get her hands untied, but the moment Colt had the revolver fixed on Thatcher Lee, she flew into his arms.

"I was so afraid," Sammie Jo said. "He lied to me and said horrible things about my daddy."

"It's all right." Colt patted her back with his eye on Thatcher Lee. "I've got Thatcher Lee, and your mama is right behind me."

"I'm sorry for all the things I said and did to you." Sammie Jo cried the way he'd seen Nancy do that day in the tree.

"No matter." He heard Anne thrash through the brush and head for her girls.

Colt shook his head at Thatcher Lee. "You are one stupid man. Now you're going to find out the hard way what it means to break the law."

"I see what you're doing," he said. "You're playing up to Anne for the money."

"There's no money," Colt said. "I don't know where you got your information, but Will Langley didn't leave a cent behind when he died."

Anne touched Colt's back. Her hand felt soft and warm, and he intended to get used to having this woman around.

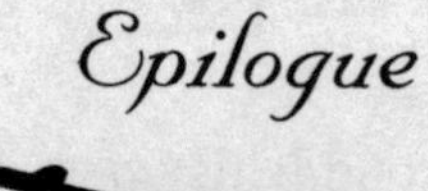

Two years later

"Papa Colt, I don't want to go back East to finishing school." Tears brimmed Sammie Jo's sky blue eyes. She was so pretty that he wanted her to pack a derringer.

"Yes, you do," Colt said. "You're going to learn how to be a fine woman. Oh, I know you can ride and shoot like a ranch hand, but your mama and I want you to learn all the things that will make you a lady."

"But who will take care of little Stephen and Nancy and Clancy?"

"It'll be hard, but we'll manage."

"But I'm scared."

Colt stifled a chuckle. Since the incident with Thatcher Lee, Sammie Jo had found more than one thing that scared her. "Nancy's growing up just fine. Your little brother has me and your mama, and Clancy would never want anyone else to take care of him."

Sammie Jo reached up and hugged him tightly. "Take care

of everyone while I'm gone."

He laughed. "We'll just pray the good Lord gives me wisdom."

Colt felt an arm around his waist and knew it was his beloved Anne. How he could be blessed with the love of this fine woman still amazed him.

"Let her go, honey. She needs to catch the train," Anne said.

Colt took a deep breath and escorted Sammie Jo to the train steps. "I love you, little lady. We'll see you soon." He waved and watched the train until it disappeared out of sight.

"You have tears in your eyes," Anne said.

"Yes, Papa Colt, big ones," Nancy said with a giggle.

"Oh, I just love my family," he said and winked at Anne.

"And we love you," Anne said and planted a kiss on his cheek.

Strange how he amounted to nothing until the good Lord slapped a wanted poster on his hide and taught him how to love. Life was good. Very good.

DIANN MILLS

Award-winning author DiAnn Mills launched her career in 1998 with the publication of her first book. Currently she has nineteen novels, fifteen novellas, a nonfiction book, and several articles and short stories in print.

DiAnn believes her readers should "expect an adventure." Her desire is to show characters solving real problems of today from a Christian perspective through a compelling story. About this one she says, "Living in Texas, I've come to love the stories about brave men and women of the Old West who struggled against lawless men and the odds of nature to build this country to what it is today."

Six of her anthologies have appeared on the CBA best-seller list. Three of her books have won the distinction of Best Historical of the Year by Heartsong Presents, and she remains a favorite author of Heartsong Presents readers. Two of her books have been awarded Short Historical of the Year (2003 and 2004) by American Christian Romance Writers. She is the recipient of the Inspirational Reader's Choice Award for 2005 in the long contemporary and novella categories.

DiAnn is a founding board member for American Christian Fiction Writers, a member of Inspirational Writers Alive, Chi Libris, Christian Authors' Network, and Advanced Writers' and Speakers' Association. She speaks to various groups and teaches writing workshops. She is also a mentor for Jerry Jenkins's Christian Writers' Guild.

She lives in sunny Houston, Texas, the home of heat, humidity, and Harleys. In fact, she'd own one, but her legs are too short. DiAnn and her husband have four adult sons and are active members of Metropolitan Baptist Church.

For more about DiAnn, visit her Web site: www.diannmills.com.

Outlaw Sheriff

by Kathleen Miller Y'Barbo

Dedication

To my nephews Daniel, Brian, and Ben Y'Barbo,
DJ Holman, William and James Heintschel, Jeremy Bodden,
Craig and Blake Adams, and Brant and Drew Goss.
May God bless you in mighty ways!

The Gentiles shall see thy righteousness, and all kings thy glory:
and thou shalt be called by a new name,
which the mouth of the LORD *shall name.*
ISAIAH 62:2

Chapter 1

Dime Box, Arizona—March 1881

Caleb Wilson tilted his hat down over his eyes then thought better of it. No, he'd ride into town head held high. If the Lord saw fit to give him a clean heart and a new start on life at the age of twenty-seven, the least he could do was act like it.

Even if it might get him thrown in jail—again.

He tasted trail dust and smelled the result of two straight weeks of going without a decent scrubbing. The heat of summer wasn't yet upon them back in Texas, but out here in the Arizona Territory there seemed little change between the seasons.

In the past his westward wanderings wouldn't have taken him any farther than Tombstone, where he would find a spot at the Crystal Palace Saloon and drink his dinner before encountering trouble, usually in the form of a woman. Not wishing to come across any of the Clantons, his former partners in crime, Caleb pushed farther west until he found the tiny town of Dime Box. He'd never heard of the place, and he hoped they'd never heard of him.

A trio of respectable folk looked up from a wagon filled with supplies as he passed the mercantile. Caleb hesitated before tipping his hat at the men.

The nearest to him, a skinny fellow not far out of knee britches, called out a "howdy" while a man of a few more years lifted his hand in a wave. The look on the older gentleman's face, however, reminded him he was a stranger here.

If he were still a drinking man, he'd be reaching for his flask about now. Instead, Caleb tightened his grip on the reins and reminded himself that a healthy dose of the Good Book was better for him than a round of gut-burning refreshment.

His mount trotted easily down the rutted road, oblivious to lesser horseflesh whose tails fought the flies and dust without success. The livery loomed ahead, and Caleb aimed the horse in that direction. The animal had done him proud on the trail to this place, and tonight she'd be rewarded with a better place to rest and a pail of oats. It was the least he could do considering she'd saved his life more than once in the past month.

His bad leg ached as if it still had a bullet in it, and he grimaced as he sat up a little higher in the saddle. Soon as he got where he was going—wherever that was—he'd have to give some serious thought to ending his trail-riding days.

Caleb sighed. If only it were that simple.

From a fellow inmate in Texas he'd heard tell that Reuben was looking for him, no doubt to put the gang back together. Well, he'd have none of that.

Even if Mama had gone on to Jesus, he still had the thought

of her disapproval weighing hard on his mind. If only he hadn't gone back to see her one last time. Hadn't made the promise that led to his meeting the Savior and taking Him to heart. Oh, he was grateful the Lord met him at his mama's bedside back in Raider's Crossing, Wyoming.

Nothing could compare to the moment when his mama led him to the Lord.

He'd promised her then that he would make something of himself. That he wouldn't come back to Raider's Crossing until he'd become a new man, someone she could be proud of.

So far the only part of that promise he'd fulfilled was the first half. Some days he'd wondered how things were faring with his brothers. More often than not, he wondered about little Benny. He'd be a man now, having grown up with no men to show him the way unless the Lord had intervened.

Yeah, and you put him in that spot, Caleb. You and your brothers.

That knowledge pricked his conscience. Dropping him off at Miss Sadie's place had seemed the right thing to do at the time. Looking back with the eyes of a new believer, Caleb knew differently. But then that went for most every decision he made before he started involving the Lord in his business.

If only he could go back in time and make the changes he longed to make. If only he could start everything over.

The scent of greasy meat beat out the other odors that trailed him, and Caleb's stomach complained. Scratching the spot where his beard itched him most, he gave a full minute's thought to parking his mount in front of the source of the grub and satisfying his belly before he cleaned his hide.

He gave the source of the smell a second look. Set between

a dry goods store and a doctor's office, the building looked as if it were about to fall down under the weight of the dust and grime it wore. Blistered paint was peeling from warped boards, and the front door listed to the left. Second-floor windows were half-covered with shutters that were missing most of their slats, and a tattered curtain covered in faded roses hung from the one in the middle. Just below, a hand-lettered sign proclaimed the place as MA'S KITCHEN.

If the woman standing in the doorway was Ma, he'd have to pass. More than a few years past her prime, she wore faded calico and a frown and carried a black iron skillet like a prized weapon. From inside came the faint sound of breaking glass followed in quick succession by a man's raised voice and a barking dog. Ma, however, never flinched.

As Caleb rode by, the woman lifted the skillet in his direction. Whether in warning or greeting, he couldn't say. Just so as not to get on her bad side, he called out, "Top of the mornin', ma'am."

She responded with a shrug before disappearing inside. *So much for charming the ladies.*

At that thought Caleb had to chuckle. The first thing he'd asked the Lord after his baptism in Cane Creek was for Him to take away the skills he'd possessed at wooing women. Wouldn't you know He'd answer that prayer right away?

He reached the livery and turned the mare over to a boy of no more than nine or ten. Thoughts of Benny returned, and he shook them off as he tossed a coin in the lad's direction.

"I'll double that if she's fat and happy with a good brushing when I return," Caleb told him.

"Thanks, mister. I'll take good care of her." The boy took

the reins and tipped his cap before turning toward the stable.

"Say, there," Caleb called. "What's your name, young fellow?"

The lad stopped short to give Caleb a toothy grin. "Edmund, sir. Edmund Francis Thompson Junior."

Caleb returned the smile. "Well, Edmund Francis Thompson Junior, my horse and I thank you."

He watched them until the horse disappeared into a stall at the back of the stable. A moment later the boy emerged, then quickly returned with a brush, a blanket, and a bag of feed.

Satisfied that his horse was cared for, Caleb headed for a bar of lye soap and a shave.

Caleb walked out of the barbershop a good while later feeling like a new man. His complaining gut was the only remnant of the man who had ridden into Dime Box, and he could fix that in no time.

The barber told him about a boardinghouse a block off the main road where a man could fill his belly and rest his head on a clean mattress for a reasonable price. The proprietor, he'd been told, ran a respectable place. No drinking and no carousing. And no tobacco.

As he stepped onto the broad boards that made up the porch of the nameless rooming house, Caleb noticed an old shingle hanging next to the front door.

"No drinking, no carousing, and no tobacco." Caleb chuckled. "Least I was prepared. Not that any of that would be a problem."

"Well, I'm glad t'hear it. I run a respectable place. Don't

cotton to no one but law-abiding citizens."

Caleb's grin was genuine as he met the gaze of a red-haired woman. She looked to be around his mother's age, with laugh lines etched at either end of her broad smile.

"The name's Wilson." Giving thanks for having such a common name, Caleb reached out to shake the woman's hand, surprised that she grasped his fingers in a strong grip. "And I reckon I qualify as a law-abiding citizen. I haven't broken a law in nigh on to two years. Does that pass muster with you?"

She looked him up and down, and for a minute he felt like a prized piece of horseflesh. "Pleased t'meet you, Mr. Wilson. Round here they call me Widow Sykes. Now come on in here and set yourself down. That growling stomach of yours is bad for business."

Caleb tipped his hat and followed his hostess inside. The dining room was sparse but tidy with a long table down the middle and benches running along each side. He estimated that during mealtime the place could easily seat two dozen hungry folks. Since it was the middle of the afternoon, Caleb was the only diner.

When the widow came through the door with two platters of food, Caleb rose to help her. "Set yourself down, young man. I've been doin' this since before you were even thought of." She met his gaze, and her expression softened. "I do appreciate it, son. Your mama ought to be proud she raised such a gentleman."

Caleb swallowed hard and rubbed his freshly smooth jawbone. Well, he'd fooled her, hadn't he? "Thank you, ma'am," he managed as he tied the red-checked napkin around his neck.

Twenty minutes later Caleb had feasted on beef stew and rock-hard biscuits and was contemplating whether to wash his pie down with cold milk or buttermilk when the door swung open. The man who walked in looked as if he'd ridden longer than Caleb and hadn't quite met with the soap bar yet. Of course he planted his dusty bones within spitting distance of Caleb.

"Howdy," the fellow said, and Caleb responded with a tip of his head.

He stabbed at the pie with his fork and kept his attention focused on the plate. Last thing he needed was a confrontation with a stranger. Caleb knew he'd probably be run out of town on a rail once the good citizens of Dime Box got wind of his past. He just hadn't expected it would happen before he had a good night's sleep.

The Widow Sykes came back through with buttermilk and poured him a glassful without asking. When she disappeared into the kitchen, Caleb set down his fork.

"Me, I hate the stuff," the stranger said. "I hear tell they make it from sour milk. Now, you tell me who wants to drink sour milk when there's fresh to be had."

Just to be ornery, Caleb took a healthy swallow. He'd gotten used to the vile drink at his mama's table. Now he had it for old times' sake. Never, however, had he learned to like it.

The fellow watched Caleb set the glass back on the table, then shook his head. "Name's Thompson." He stretched across the table to shake Caleb's hand. "Ed Thompson. When I'm not on the trail, I've got the Lazy T Ranch just north of here. Oh, and I'm the mayor around these parts."

"Pleased to meet you, Mayor Thompson. You wouldn't be kin to the young man at the livery, would you?"

Ed chuckled. "Depends on what he did. Oh, and call me Ed."

"He's a fine young man." Caleb removed the napkin from his neck and took a swipe at his lips. "Good with horses, too, far as I can tell."

"Well, I'm right glad t'hear it. I never know if he's gonna behave for his mama like he does when I'm around." He glanced down at the trail dust on his shirt, then back at Caleb. "I apologize for the way I look. I'm hungry as a bear, and wouldn't you know I'd come home the day of my wife's quilting bee? I'm not about to show up to a hen party. Better I fill my belly here, then slide in the back door once the ladies are gone."

Caleb muttered an agreement, then reached for his hat.

"Hold on there, stranger. I don't believe I caught your name."

Caleb froze. His breath caught in his throat. His name? As with the Widow Sykes, he said, "The name's Wilson."

For a moment Ed said nothing. Then something akin to recognition seemed to cross his face. "Did you say Wilson?"

"I did." Caleb took a step back, eyes narrowed. If the Lord saw fit to allow trouble with the first man he met in Dime Box, then so be it. He'd just have to take it as a sign to move on and start his new life elsewhere.

Ed rose and rounded the table to grip Caleb's shoulder. "*You're* Cal Wilson?"

Cal Wilson? He did ask the Lord for a new name just as it said in the book of Isaiah. Still, setting the man straight seemed the right thing to do, even if it meant having to high-tail it out of town before sunset.

"Well, my mama named me Caleb, but you got the Wilson part right."

Ed Thompson took him by the shoulders, all the while grinning like he'd just found gold. "Well, now this *is* a surprise. I been looking for you nigh on a week."

Caleb swallowed hard. So there was another bounty on his head. By turning himself in back in Texas, he thought he'd gotten out from under all the trouble he'd put himself in.

"You don't look nothin' like I expected. You sure you're Cal Wilson?"

"Like I said, Mama named me Caleb, sir. That's generally the name I go by."

"Guess I got it wrong then, but you're definitely the one we been lookin' for."

Caleb thought a minute before responding. "What for?"

"You're an odd fella, Cal. It's all in the telegram from Dodge City. I believe I've got it somewhere back at the house. You want me to fetch it and show you?"

He exhaled a long breath and set his hat back atop his head. "Reckon we ought to mosey on to the jailhouse and get this over with then."

Ed Thompson shoved the last of his biscuit into his mouth, then washed the crumbling mess down with a healthy swallow of coffee. When he finished, he rose and swiped his palms on the front of his shirt. With a nod in Caleb's direction, he said, "Reckon so."

The man spoke with such happiness that the old Caleb would

have slugged him for sure. But then the old Caleb would have been on the fastest horse out of town. Rather, Caleb found himself slowing his stride to keep pace with the sheriff as he headed willingly to jail.

Again.

Chapter 2

New Orleans, Louisiana—May 1881

Lydia Bertrand glanced around her room one last time, then allowed May, her mother's maid and now hers, to help her down the stairs. Were she capable of tears at this moment, she might have shed them.

If only Papa were here. Surely he would stop this madness. Surely he wouldn't allow Mama to ship me off as if I were some package headed for the Western frontier.

They stepped into the courtyard. The fountain gurgled, and the leaves dripped with sparkles of raindrops from a rain shower Lydia hadn't even noticed. Beneath her feet, the centuries-old bricks shone as if freshly painted. It seemed as if God had washed the courtyard clean in anticipation of her arrival.

She stopped short and grasped May's hand. "Mama said Papa's in New York." She whispered lest Mama be nearby. "What say we turn in our tickets for passage north? I'm sure once he hears what Mama has done he will overrule her."

May gave her a sideways look. "First off, chile, New York

City's bigger'n any place you or I's ever been, and we don't know where your papa done gone there. Ain't no way to find a man lessen you know where he's done gone." She paused. "Second, your papa loves your mama more'n either of us can understand. They's put together by the Lord, and they fit like hand-in-glove. Your mama, bless her heart, was a strong-willed chile. Your papa, he lets her have her way, now don't he? You really think he gonna overrule your mama on somethin' she's so set on doin'?"

Unfortunately, Lydia couldn't disagree with anything May said.

"That's right. You know I'm tellin' the truth." She looked as if she wanted to say more. Instead, she turned her head and made a soft clucking sound.

"Go ahead and say it, May."

"All right, I will." She paused. "I wonder iffen the good Lord ain't behind this." At Lydia's incredulous look, May shook her head. "The Bible said we reap what we sow. You done sowed a whole bunch of trouble dancin' in that fountain at school, Miss Lydia."

Again she couldn't deny it. "So what do I do, May? This is serious."

May seemed to consider the statement for a moment. "Chile, how big is your God? 'Cause my God is bigger'n any human plan."

Nodding, Lydia felt the beginnings of hope stirring.

"Well then." May placed her dark wrinkled hand over Lydia's, then squeezed. "If it's the Lord's intention that your mama get her way, there's nothin' you can do about it less'n you intend to jump outta His will. You wantin' to do that, Lydia Bertrand? You wanna go against the Lord Almighty?"

Lydia's heart sank. Disobedience had always come so easily. "No," she said softly. "Not this time."

"I didn't think so." May looked past her, presumably to the coachman. "She ready to go." Returning her gaze to Lydia, May smiled. "You the spittin' image of your mama. Difference is, by the time she was your age, you were runnin' around makin' trouble and she had lost your two brothers to the yellow fever." Her face softened as if remembering all over again. A moment later she stiffened her spine and blinked hard. "It's time you left here and made your own way in the world. What you think about that?"

Lydia glanced back at the house, and something sharp twisted in her gut. Was that Mama who let the lace curtain fall in the window above the door, or had the breeze caught it?

"I think she's banishing me."

May released her hand to envelop Lydia in a hug. "She not banishin' you—she sendin' you forth. Now let's us get a-goin'. Ain't no use to tarry when the Lord's got plans for both of us."

"May I help you in, Mademoiselle Bertrand?"

Lydia sighed as the same coachman who had handed her out of the carriage this morning now helped her back in. Two trunks and a carpetbag later, they rolled out of the courtyard onto Rue Royale with May seated beside the driver.

This time Mama definitely was nowhere to be seen.

Lydia reached for her journal to record the moment, then thought better of it. Whatever the Lord had for her, it was better she not speculate in her current frame of mind. Nor should she dwell on the feelings she now found raging inside her.

Instead, she cast her gaze down to the travel voucher in her hand and tried to pray.

When her jumbled hopes and cares refused to form a coherent thought, Lydia settled for leaning on the assurance that the Holy Spirit had taken her mutterings to the throne. As she glanced up front to where May sat, Lydia saw the older woman bow her head.

The rest of the trip to the train station seemed to go by quickly, as did the first leg of Lydia's journey west. By the time she and May landed on the doorstep of the Menger Hotel in San Antonio, Texas, she'd almost gotten used to the idea of being sent forcefully into the world.

Lydia slept soundly and might have missed breakfast to linger beneath the covers except for the noise from construction on the hotel's new east wing. This time when she prayed, she found the words to ask the Lord for a way to escape her current situation. While He did not respond immediately, Lydia had no doubt He was behind the plan she began to concoct.

As she handed the cream-colored letter to the gentleman behind the front desk and bade good-bye to the Menger Hotel, Lydia felt her heart grow lighter. Mama might hold the key to Lydia's immediate future, but eventually Papa would prevail. As soon as he heard of her troubles, he would surely come to her rescue.

All she had to do was bide her time until he arrived. She held that thought all the way across the rest of Texas and into New Mexico. By the time the train came to the end of the line and they transferred to a stage for the rest of the trip, the thought had become a prayer that she took to the throne every time they lurched over a rough patch of trail.

When not in prayer, Lydia contemplated how best to spend her time. Papa had long ago listed pertinent scripture verses in the front of her Bible, and she turned to them now. Chief among them was the one she called her life verse.

From the sixty-second chapter of Isaiah, she ran her finger over Papa's bold backward-slanting script. "And the Gentiles shall see thy righteousness, and all kings thy glory: and thou shalt be called by a new name, which the mouth of the Lord shall name."

To Lydia's surprise, May began to giggle. When a stern look did not silence the older woman's mirth, Lydia closed the Bible and shook her head.

"What's so funny, May?"

"Read that verse again, Miss Lydia." When Lydia complied, May doubled over in laughter. A moment later she gathered her wits. "I'm not laughin' at you, I promise. It's just that. . ." She pointed to the Bible. "Well, the good Lord, He do have a sense of humor."

The stage jolted to a stop, and Lydia braced herself. "What are you talking about?"

"Well, now, He say right there that you gonna be called by a new name. You see it?"

The coach lurched into motion once more. "Yes, I see it, but I repeat: what's so funny?"

"It's just that in all the years you were claimin' this verse as your own, did you ever think God would be doin' exactly what He says there?"

Lydia set the Bible aside and massaged her temples. The dull ache that had begun in New Mexico threatened to bloom into a full-fledged headache now that they'd left the state behind.

She closed her eyes and sighed. "Honestly, May, I have no idea what you mean."

May touched Lydia's sleeve. "You gettin' a new name now, aren't you, chile? Maybe you need t'stop blamin' your mama and start thankin' your Lord for makin' good on His promise."

When the reality of the statement hit her, Lydia could only groan.

"You know He goin' with us, now don't you?" May grasped a handful of Lydia's traveling frock and blinked hard. "I been prayin' for protection for you since you been borned, Miss Lydia, same as my mama did with your mama. The good Lord, He listen then, and He's kept you safe in spite of yourself, now hasn't He?"

When Lydia nodded, May continued.

"So when your mama told me what she had a mind t'do, I says to myself, is this of the Lord or is this somethin' else? Well, I set to prayin' and askin' for Him to stop the foolishness of this if it wasn't where He wanted you to be." She leaned forward. "Next thing you know, she gets word from that woman at the school that you'd done a dance in the fountain. Well, that's when I knowed for sure this was somethin' that had to happen."

Lydia leaned against the seat until the broken spring caused her to shift positions. She looked out at the passing landscape, so different from her New Orleans home, as she contemplated May's words. They made no sense.

"You can't mean that my mother planned this *before* I got myself sent home from school, May. That just isn't possible."

May sat back. "Oh, it's more than possible. She been pondering on this plan for more'n a year. She say she was worried about your future. Your papa, he knowed about it, too, and he thought it was a bad idea, but only because he wanted you close by. I know he was much aggrieved by what might happen to you after he and the missus was gone."

Lydia let May's words sink in. "If that's true, then why did he let me be sent off to Georgia to Miss Potter's?"

"He thought you were being sent off to learn how to teach the young'uns. The reverend, he figured that'd be a good trade for you, what with your talent takin' care of the little ones in the church nursery. When he found out your mama had lied to get you into that fancy boarding school instead of sending you to the teachers' college, well, he 'bout hit the roof."

So Papa wasn't behind sending her off to Miss Potter's school. That much she could believe. "Why didn't he come get me when he found out?"

She shrugged. "Well, he never said so to me, but I figure your mama convinced him it would all work out just fine. She's got a way of doin' that with your papa."

"Yes, she does." Lydia studied her hands for a moment, then lifted her gaze to meet May's stare. "Do you think Papa will come after me this time?"

May seemed to be considering the question. "I don't rightly know," she finally said. "But if I was you, I wouldn't count on him comin' right off. He gonna be in New York for two weeks—that's what your mama said. We been gone a week now, so that means he ain't even home yet. Far as he knows, you're still up in Georgia gettin' refined."

"But once he comes home, do you think he'll fetch me back then?"

May looked away. "I just don't know, Miss Lydia."

"Well, I do, May, and I'm just going to have to bide my time until he does."

She gave Lydia a look. "What have you done?"

Lydia shrugged. "I wrote my father a letter and mailed it back at the Menger. I'm sure as soon as he reads it he'll be on his way to fetch me back."

"Miss Lydia, when will you learn?" She shook her head. "Your papa, he don't disagree with this. He gave you a chance, and you didn't take it. If he comes at all, it'll be to see that you go through with it."

The words struck fear in her heart. Then on second consideration she dismissed them. "You can't be serious."

"I can't?" The older woman gave a tired sigh. "Think, chile. What does your papa want more than anything for your future?"

Trail dust swirled into the tiny coach. "That I be taken care of," she said before giving in to a fit of coughing.

May nodded. "And how has he tried to do that?"

Lydia blinked the dust from her eyes and swiped at them with the backs of her sleeves. "By raising me in a Christian home and seeing that I developed a relationship with the Lord."

"Uh-huh. And what else?"

She pondered a moment. "Well, by sending me to school

and, oh. . ." Her eyes filled with tears. "I've done this to myself, haven't I?"

May patted her hand again but said nothing.

Lydia lifted tear-filled eyes toward her former nursemaid. "What am I going to do now?"

"Only thing I know is if the Lord wants you home in New Orleans, He gonna stop all this foolishness, not you."

The coach rolled past a sign announcing their destination. Any moment the coach would stop, and her new life would begin.

"Yes, but what do I do in the meantime?"

"You do what the Lord tells you, Miss Lydia. That's always the right thing."

They lurched forward as the coach halted before a primitive wooden building with a hand-lettered sign above the first floor. In a series of movements that felt like walking through water, Lydia left the coach and stood on a dust-covered walkway made of rough boards and marked by the occasional hole or missing board. To the right was an old woman staring at her from the doorway, her demeanor less than friendly. To the left a trio of roughs eyed her curiously before the coachman shooed them into the saloon.

She glanced down at the instructions Mama had given May, then up at the hand-lettered sign. So this was to be her new home, at least for now. According to Mama, her rent was paid for exactly two weeks. After that she was on her own.

As the driver hefted the first of her trunks onto the boardwalk, a panic like she'd never known before gripped Lydia. After she prayed, she covered the rising fear the way she always had—by squaring her shoulders and walking straight into it. Or, in this case, walking straight into the path of a cowboy who wore a black hat and a crooked grin.

Chapter 3

'Scuse me, ma'am." Caleb took a step backward and helped the little lady back onto her feet, then removed his hat and gave her a nod. "I'm real sorry. My mind was elsewhere."

"As was mine. I do apologize."

She was a pretty thing, no bigger than a minute, but with a voice as smooth as silk and a pair of big brown eyes that could cause a man to forget his troubles.

Well, most men might. Not him, though. His troubles were impossible to forget.

Then again, something told him so was this gal.

"You comin', Cal?"

One more look at the big-eyed gal, and then he nodded and replaced his hat on his head. "Be right there, Ed. Pleased to make your acquaintance, ma'am."

He trotted across the street, then took another look at the lady. A force of nature, she'd already disappeared, leaving a stack of trunks and a dark-skinned maid in her wake.

"Probably best you didn't tangle with that one," he said

under his breath, although the sentiment didn't reach his heart.

Not that he'd want a gal who looked so fragile. No, he liked a woman with a little meat on her bones. And while dark hair was nice, he'd always fancied blonds.

"What are you thinking, Wilson? Remember that prayer you prayed? There isn't a woman alive who'd be interested in you, leastwise not until the Lord changes His mind."

Then there was the issue of his freedom.

Caleb shrugged off his miserable self-pity to step into the sheriff's office. The smell hit him first, then the dust. He reeled backward trying to sneeze and cough all at once and nearly tripped over a pile of lumber that looked to have once been part of the roof.

When he recovered, he saw Ed standing in the door. "You okay, Cal?"

Straightening, Caleb swiped at his mouth with the back of his hand. "Name's Caleb, Ed, and I'm fine. Just wasn't prepared, that's all."

"Yeah, looks like we got some cleaning and fixing to do in there." Ed shrugged. "To tell you the truth, ain't nobody been in there since Sheriff Merritt passed on last winter. The skunks must've moved in 'bout the time the sheriff moved out. The roof, well, you got me how that whole thing fell down like that. Must've happened when we had that big wind back in January. See, there's an old piece of roof. I reckon we must've had some rotten timbers that didn't cotton to being pounded."

Caleb let his gaze sweep the office and adjoining jail cell. No sheriff or prisoners since last winter?

That surely told a man what sort of town Dime Box was. Even if he weren't about to be the guest of the jailhouse, he might have considered staying around of his own accord. What were a few skunks when the townsfolk were a law-abiding sort? Compared to Tombstone, this place was paradise.

A thought occurred. "If the sheriff passed on last winter, who's been keeping the peace?"

Ed leaned against the door frame and crossed his arms over his chest. "Oh, we mostly been doing it ourselves, the menfolk, that is. Once in a while we get a tough customer who has to be taken over to Millville. Mostly, though, we see a few drunks and the occasional mischievous lad."

"I see." Caleb paused. "Well, then, I suppose we ought to be heading out. Millville's a half day's ride."

The Thompson fellow looked at Caleb as if he'd grown an extra ear. "What would we be wantin' to go to Millville for?"

"Well, I just figured, what with the jail not being usable you might want to put me over there."

To Caleb's surprise, Ed began to laugh. At first he chuckled; then he doubled over in full-fledged laughter. When he straightened, he had to wipe his eyes before he could speak.

"You're a real hoot, Cal." He gestured toward the place where they'd just come from. "I reckon you can head on over to the Widow Sykes's place and set yourself up in a room there. Last I heard she had two empty ones. Once we get the jailhouse back in shape, we can move you in here. That to your liking?"

To my liking? Caleb searched Ed Thompson's face for signs he was pulling a prank. What he saw looked to be concern.

"Anything wrong?" Ed asked.

"Wrong? Well, I guess I was wondering if you're serious or just pulling my leg."

There was that look again. "Why would I be pulling your leg? Don't you like the rooming house? I mean, I know things are fancier where you come from, but I figure a clean bed and a good meal's the same no matter where you get 'em."

"I reckon you're right." He reached out to shake Ed's hand. "I appreciate your trust in me, Ed, and you've got my word as a law-abiding man that I won't leave town."

"You're too much, Cal." His amused expression turned serious. "I wonder if we ought to keep this under our hats, though. I mean, once the townsfolk get wind of who you are, well, you and I won't have a moment's peace."

Caleb said a quick prayer of thanks for the reprieve, then beat a path to the rooming house before Ed changed his mind.

Caleb spent four nights at the Widow Sykes's place and five days at the jailhouse helping Ed repair the ceiling damage and remove all traces of the skunk family that had spent Christmas in the lone jail cell. When questioned as to his reasons for taking on such a task, Caleb had an easy answer: "If I'm going to be spending my time here, the least I can do is make it livable."

That response satisfied Ed, and just before sundown on the fifth day, they completed their work.

"I best go get cleaned up," Ed said. "The missus is particular about smelly menfolk at her supper table." He scratched his head, then glanced over at Caleb.

"Why don't you join us tonight, Cal? Evelyn sets a fine spread, and I know she'd welcome you. She's been after me to fetch you home, but I figured with you working yourself to the bone here the last thing you felt like was socializing of an evenin'."

Along the way he'd met quite a few of the townsfolk, most of them arriving carrying a baked good of some sort. They welcomed him like an honored guest rather than the inmate he was to become, and they all called him Cal, which struck him as odd. Still none of them had invited him to socialize.

He met Ed's gaze. "You sure about this, Ed? I mean, I'm a—"

"Pa, you still in there? Mama said to tell you she's buttering the corn bread."

Ed grinned. "Looks like I'm being called to supper. You comin' or what?"

Caleb pondered the invitation for a moment before shaking his head. He sure did like a good piece of buttered corn bread. In fact, he loved to eat.

"I really ought not to get used to such luxuries. You tell your wife I appreciate the invite, though."

Ed studied Caleb a moment, then shook his hand and headed out the door. A moment later he returned. "I know you're tired and all, but we need to talk about getting you moved in here. What say you fetch your things from the Widow Sykes's place after breakfast and meet me here? Say eight o'clock?"

"Eight it is." Caleb straightened his hat and walked out into the dying rays of the last sunset he would see as a free man—at least for quite a while.

"Lord," he said under his breath, "I sure would like another chance. If You'd see fit to let me get a clean start, I'd be much beholden."

Bypassing the dining room, Caleb made his way upstairs and kicked off his boots. It would be a shame to spend his last free night alone, yet he felt no need to go any farther than the table where'd he left his Bible.

A sound drifted up and pulled Caleb toward the window. There below, in the sliver of dirt and rocks the Widow Sykes called her garden, the dark form of a person huddled against the far wall. Upon closer inspection he could see skirts.

The sound found him again, and this time he knew it was the sound of a woman crying. While he watched, she doubled over, then sank to her knees.

His first instinct was to leave her be. A woman's tears were a more dangerous weapon than a gun or a knife, and he generally steered clear of a female packing a damp hankie.

But what if she's hurt? What if she's hiding from someone looking to do her harm? Despite what Ed said about Dime Box's low crime rate, plenty of bad guys were lurking out there, and they could just as likely be hiding here as anywhere.

Caleb ought to know. He used to be the worst of the worst, and his favorite hiding places were where the decent folk went. That's how he'd learned to pass himself off as a gentleman.

Some days he felt like he was still playing that game: an outlaw pretending to be a man of character. Then the good Lord would give him some reminder He had settled the score and wiped away the past.

Caleb waited a moment longer, then made his decision.

"Nothing like spending the night before I go to jail doing a good deed."

Shoving his feet into his boots, Caleb headed outside. He might not be able to do much with his immediate future, but the least he could do was help a woman who was obviously in some kind of distress.

Chapter 4

Lydia's breath came in gasps, and her eyes stung from the tears she'd held back all day. So much for making the best of the situation. The moment May fell asleep, the strong facade Lydia had kept all week crumbled.

Try as she might, she hadn't managed to believe the Lord intended her to be here.

In this place.

Doing what her mother insisted she must do.

A sob tore from her throat, and Lydia silenced it by taking a deep breath. The spot she'd chosen was private enough, with only one darkened room having a view; still she worried someone might happen upon her.

Funny how she had no trouble making a spectacle of herself to get sent home from all the finishing schools she'd attended over the years, yet she couldn't shed a single tear in front of a witness.

She dabbed at her eyes with her handkerchief. Always she had found a way out of her predicament, a way to get back home. This time, however, her situation seemed a bit more. . .dare she even think it?

Permanent.

Tears sprang afresh, and this time she gave them free rein to flow down her cheeks and soak her frock. To think Papa knew of this and still—

"Anything wrong, ma'am?"

Lydia scrambled to her feet, then reeled backward and thudded against the wall. Her head banged against the rough stones, and she cried out. A pair of strong arms lifted her off her feet.

"What are you doing? Put. Me. Down."

As if he hadn't heard her, the stranger whirled around with her in his arms and headed for the boardinghouse.

"Put. Me. Down!"

The man froze. A slice of moonlight cut across chiseled features she might have thought handsome had the oaf not just hauled her around like a sack of potatoes.

"What do you think you're doing?" she demanded.

He cocked his hat back, revealing more of the face she knew must have caused more than a few women to take notice. "I thought I was helping a lady in distress."

"The only distress I'm feeling is because I'm being tossed about by a complete stranger. Put me down before I call for the sheriff."

This time he complied, setting her feet on the rocky ground, then taking a step backward. "Go ahead."

Lydia gave him a look. "I mean it. I will."

The cowboy leaned against the side of the rooming house and crossed his arms over his chest. "Like I said. Go ahead. There's just one problem."

"What's that?"

He shrugged. "Far as I know, there's not a sheriff in Dime Box. Leastwise there wasn't one this afternoon."

No sheriff? This was interesting. Dare she hope?

"Since when is there not a sheriff?"

Another voice spoke up. "Ed says the sheriff is going to be sworn in tomorrow morning." The Widow Sykes turned the corner. "You ought to know that, Cal." She turned to Lydia. "Everything all right out here, Miss Bertrand? I was takin' a pie out of the oven and thought I heard some commotion."

She gave the stranger a look, then turned her attention to the innkeeper. "Yes, I'm fine. Will you excuse me? I'd like to return to my room."

"Let me go with you." The landlady gave the man named Cal a nod, then reached for Lydia's arm. "What say I walk with you just to be sure you're all right?"

"That's not necessary, really." A light breeze blew past, bringing the scent of something delicious in its wake. "What sort of pie is that? It smells wonderful."

"It's my mama's recipe. She called it a Jeff Davis pie. She was from Savannah, you know."

"Might I have the recipe?"

The older woman stopped short. "You like to cook, do you?"

"Very much," Lydia said, "although I haven't had the chance to do so in far too long."

"Now isn't that interesting? I was just asking the Lord for some kitchen help this mornin'. I can pay in wages or free rent. You interested?"

—∞—

The dark-haired gal reminded Caleb of his mama's banty rooster, and he would've told her so except he intended to leave there in one piece. He watched the Widow Sykes usher her out of sight, then lifted his gaze to the heavens. The stars shone bright.

Somewhere beyond them was his real home. Knowing this made what he faced tomorrow seem a little less awful.

It occurred to him that in all their time together Ed hadn't mentioned anything about the charges against him. Of course he hadn't asked, either, but then neither he nor Ed cared much for idle chatter. They'd worked most days in silence.

By the time Caleb climbed under the threadbare blanket and laid his head on the pillow, he'd come up with a sizable list of possible crimes he'd committed. Some he'd already confessed to, and a few others he might have forgotten.

Still others might have been blamed on the Wilson boys but committed by others. That happened occasionally.

A spark of hope rose. *What if I can prove I'm innocent? What if Ed's mistaken?*

He winced when he thought of the man he was. The Good Book said the Lord could wash a man clean and turn his scarlet sins to pure white.

If the Lord said it, Caleb believed it. Understanding it—now that was another matter.

But then, come tomorrow he'd have plenty of time to study on the idea.

That night he slept in short doses and met the Lord in His Word well before sunrise. Dressed and ready before six, Caleb wandered downstairs with the intention of taking one last walk around Dime Box before meeting Ed.

Passing the dining room, he turned down good coffee, then thought better of it and sat down to let the widow pour him a cup. One cup turned into two, and before he knew it, he had a plate of eggs and bacon sitting before him.

He stabbed a fork into his eggs and took a hefty bite, then washed it down with black coffee. Before his mug could hit the table, Widow Sykes wandered in from the kitchen and set a pan of biscuits on the table, then disappeared with a promise to bring more butter and some honey.

He grabbed three biscuits, then set one back on the plate. No sense being greedy, even though he sat alone in the dining room. Two more bites of eggs and he was ready for that butter and honey.

Once the bacon was gone, Caleb began to wonder if she'd forgotten. The biscuits smelled too good to ignore, so he decided to taste one plain. It was so good he had another.

Caleb winked. "They'd be even better with butter and some honey."

He thought to call his landlady's name just to see if she was heading this way, then decided he'd amble into the kitchen and help her find that butter and honey. One push on the door and he found it stuck. On the second try, it almost felt as if the door pushed back.

He gave it a good shove, and the door cooperated, swinging open to reveal the Widow Sykes standing at the black cookstove.

The door slammed against the wall, and a woman screamed.

Caleb took a step forward, then tripped.

About the time he landed on his posterior, he found the source of the roadblock—and presumably the caterwauling. There in all her honey- and butter-covered glory was the dark-haired gal from last night.

Chapter 5

Caleb tried to right himself under the glare of the sputtering woman but found nothing but slick floor boards beneath him. He tried rolling onto his stomach to push up from the floor but landed on his face.

A few more maneuvers, and he managed a sitting position. The pretty gal looked as if she wanted to wring his neck, and he fully expected the first words out of her mouth to be directed at him.

Instead, she surprised Caleb by looking past him. "Might I trouble you for a length of toweling, Mrs. Sykes?"

A length of toweling? She certainly wasn't from these parts.

She met his gaze, and her eyes narrowed. At that moment Caleb felt about as welcome as a wet dog at a church picnic.

"What are *you* doing here?"

It was more of a demand than a question, really, and with her glaring like that, Caleb had to think hard to remember how to respond. "I came to fetch the butter and honey," he finally managed.

She seemed less than impressed with his answer. Of course,

with honey smeared across the front of her dress and a streak of butter running from the corner of her mouth to her nose, she probably wasn't paying much attention.

"I thought I was helping," he decided to add. "Best batch of biscuits that ever come out of the cookstove, ma'am," he said to the widow.

Widow Sykes looked like she was about to double over laughing. "I appreciate that, Cal, but I'm not the one who mixed up that batch." She gestured to the dark-haired gal. "You've got Miss Bertrand to thank for that."

Caleb dared a sideways glance at Miss Bertrand. "Them's prize-winning biscuits, ma'am."

She lifted the corner of her apron to swipe at her cheek, smearing the butter in the process. "Glad you liked them," she said without much enthusiasm.

"Miss Bertrand's gonna be cooking for us. Least until she says her 'I-dos,' that is."

"Is that right?" When she didn't respond, he tried again. "So when's the hitchin'?"

"Hitchin'?"

"Your wedding. When's the wedding?" He reached for his hanky, clean as of this morning, and handed it to Miss Bertrand.

She dabbed at the butter, then handed it back. For a moment her expression softened. "I'm not exactly sure." Soon as the words were said, the temper returned. "I'm thankful it's not today. This was my only clean dress."

"Bein' as I'm not your intended, I'd rather not imagine you without a clean dress, ma'am."

His joke fell flat. Rather than smiling as he hoped, she deepened her frown. "Just what are you suggesting, sir?"

"I'm not suggesting anything, Miss Bertrand. It's just that you've unintentionally given me an image of you that a gentleman doesn't need to have."

Caleb dabbed his finger in the honey and tasted it for effect. Yes, it would be mighty fine on those biscuits waiting for him back in the dining room. From the look of his clothes, however, he probably ought to eat on the run.

Dare he hope the widow might see fit to send a meal or two his way while he was a guest of the jailhouse? He'd have to ask once he knew exactly how long a term he faced.

With that thought weighing on his mind, Caleb struggled to his feet and reached to offer help to Miss Bertrand. When she declined, he made his way back upstairs to step into the last set of clean clothes he owned: his Sunday suit.

He knew he looked ridiculous wearing it to jail on a Tuesday morning, but it was better than parading over to the jail in his long johns.

—w—

"Be still, Miss Lydia, or I'm never gonna get that honey outta your hair."

Lydia leaned farther over the basin while May poured yet another pitcher of water over her sticky hair. She gritted her teeth and entertained a few unsavory thoughts as the icy water splashed onto her neck then began to trickle down her back.

"That Wilson fellow is the most irritating man I've ever met. I mean, the nerve of him. Last night he hauled me around like a sack of potatoes. A sack of *potatoes*, May. Do you hear me?"

"Um-hum." May began to work lavender soap through Lydia's tangles. "Potatoes. I hear you."

"And today. If you'd been there, you would have seen what a cad the man is. Can you feature that he would actually be amused by causing me to spill butter and honey all over myself?"

May stopped scrubbing and reached for the pitcher.

"And of all the nerve. Do you know what he said to me? He said he was a gentleman, and he didn't want to imagine me in my—." Lydia yelped as icy water cascaded over her head. "Warn me next time, May."

"Cold water ain't what you need to be warned about, chile." She set the pitcher down. "You all done. Now let's get you dry."

Lydia stewed until May finished the process of drying and braiding her hair. When the last pin went in, she could stand it no more.

"What exactly do I need to be warned about, May?"

May pressed the wrinkles out of the skirt of the yellow frock Lydia had worn the day before, then held it out toward her. "I don't believe you really want an answer to that question, Miss Lydia."

She stepped into her dress and frowned. "And why not?"

"Why, indeed." Whirling Lydia around, May began fastening the row of buttons that ran down the back of the dress. "It most certainly wouldn't be to your likin'."

Lydia stepped away and turned to face May. "Try me."

The older woman shook her head. "Chile, you are as stubborn as your mama sometimes. When are you gonna learn that the Father knows what's best, and it ain't no use to run from Him or put off what He's a-wantin' you to do?"

"What do you mean?"

"I mean there's no use frettin' and fussin' when the good Lord brought you here for a purpose. You know why you're here—now you need to go present yourself."

Lydia swallowed hard. "You mean, just walk up to him and say, 'Hello, I'm Lydia, the bride you ordered'?"

May rested her hands on her hips. "That's exactly what I mean. Now you scoot outta here and do just that, or I'm gonna start worryin' you're gettin' sweet on that fella who 'bout ran you down in the kitchen."

"That man?" Lydia grimaced. "Trust me, May. He'd be the *last* man I'd ever be sweet on. I can promise you that."

"Oh, I don't know 'bout that." May made a soft clucking sound as she turned her back to empty the basin out the window. "I got me a feelin' 'bout you and that fella."

She pointed to the letter her mother had sent along with the one she'd written. The man who paid her way to Dime Box had penned this. The man who bought her lock, stock, and petticoat.

Lydia took one last look in the mirror. "Your feelings aren't worth anything when compared to that letter over there. Fetch it and let's go get this over with."

"How 'bout we take him a pie, Miss Lydia?"

She stopped short. "A pie? Whatever for?"

May shrugged. "Ain't nothin' a man likes better'n a good fresh-baked pie, and you done made an extra this mornin'. I doubt Miz Sykes'll mind."

"Oh, all right. But if this fellow's awful, I'm heading for the hills. You understand?"

May chuckled. "Oh, I been speakin' to the Lord, and I believe He's got a nice surprise for you."

Lydia squared her shoulders and refused to comment.

Chapter 6

Caleb had already reached the porch when he thought to go back inside and make his apologies to the landlady. He found her clearing the last of the honey from the floor with a mop. The room smelled of cleaning fluid and pie crust.

"I'd be obliged if you'd let me help," he said.

"It's nothing but a little spill." She shook her head and leaned up to give him an appraising look. "Now don't you look sportin'?"

"I suppose." He glanced down at his suit, then back at the Widow Sykes. "Let me pay for the dry goods I ruined."

"Oh, no, I wouldn't think of it." The widow climbed to her feet and gestured toward the stairs with her cleaning rag. "What with the answer to my prayers staying right under my roof, nothing bothers me today."

"The answer to your prayers?" Caleb chuckled. "That feisty gal?"

"Let me tell you something about feisty gals." She slung the rag over her shoulder, then crossed her arms over her chest.

"I'm of the opinion that behind most feisty gals is a little girl crying for attention. I figure once she settles down, so will her temper."

Caleb laughed out loud. "For the sake of her poor husband, I certainly hope so."

He chuckled all the way to the sheriff's office, then sobered his expression when he walked through the door. The room had been cleared of the tools they'd left last night, and someone had put a pie on the corner of the desk. Upon closer inspection, he decided it was a Jeff Davis pie.

"Just like Mama used to make," he said as he inhaled one more time.

Situated between close buildings, the office was darker than it seemed it ought to be. An old Regulator clock chimed, and he took note of the time. Fifteen minutes early. At least no one could accuse him of procrastination.

He gave the jail cell a wide berth, searching instead for some way to light the kerosene lamps in the dark corner of the office. A search produced a match, and soon enough he had sufficient light to see the wanted posters stuck up on the wall.

Right off he recognized three fellows he and his brothers had ridden with. Two were back home in Missouri, having retired to become gentleman farmers, and the third owned a dry goods store in Kansas City. Last he heard, Reuben made the place his favorite hideout when the law got too close.

Reuben.

The reminder of his brothers sliced like a knife to his gut, so he squared his shoulders and stepped away from the posters. Last thing he wanted was to see one of them up there.

Not that it would have surprised him.

"You're early." Ed stood just behind him, proof positive that Caleb's outlaw instincts were rusty.

"No sense putting off what I can't change." He walked over to the desk and removed his pistol, then set it and his holster on the desk. Without a word, he walked over to the cell and placed his hands on the bars.

"I'd be much obliged if you'd let the Widow Sykes know I appreciate her hospitality. I know I won't be takin' my meals at her place for a spell, but I left her some money in my room just the same." He turned to look Ed square in the eye. "I wonder if I might have her good home cooking carted over here every once in a while. I'd pay, of course."

"Well, I don't see as how that would be a problem. Although you could just as easily go fetch it."

Caleb shook his head. "But, Ed, I'll be—"

"There's the man of the hour." A burly redhead lumbered in and parked himself behind the desk. "What say we get this started?"

"Are you the judge?" Caleb asked.

"Judge?" The man slapped the surface of the desk with his open palm, then laughed. "I like that idea, Ed. Since you're the mayor, why don't you make me the judge?"

"Wouldn't that be like putting the wolf in charge of the henhouse, Elmer?"

The men shared another laugh while Caleb stood and watched. It was all well and fine that the fellows enjoyed one another, but did they have to do it while he waited to hear his crime and receive his sentence? He was about to ask them when Ed held up his hands and stopped his chuckling.

"Elmer, I don't believe you and Cal have been formally introduced. Cal Wilson, meet Elmer Wiggins. He's the barber and the undertaker. Guess you could say Elmer gets you comin' and goin'."

"Pleased to meet you, Mr. Wiggins." Caleb rubbed his chin. "I got a fine shave and haircut over to your place. Wasn't you who did the job, though."

Elmer shook his head. "No, that was my brother-in-law Pete. He generally only works on the corpses, but I let him try out his skills on live folks every once in a while."

Ed clapped his hands, then rubbed them together as if he actually looked forward to what was about to happen. Elmer looked more interested in the pie than anything else.

Neither of them seemed to give a second thought to the prospective inmate.

Caleb felt his temper rise, then reminded himself he was no longer that sort of man. "Let's get on with it then."

Elmer rose and pushed away from the desk, giving the pie one last look. "That from your wife?" he asked Ed.

"The Widow Sykes, actually." Ed gestured to the door. "I got a surprise for you, Cal."

A surprise? Outside?

That's when he heard it. The sound of people. Caleb leaned toward the window and lifted the red-checked curtain. Sure enough, half the town was waiting for him in the middle of Main Street.

If the good folks of Dime Box, Arizona, wanted to lynch him, they'd have to find him first. His gaze darted around the room in search of a back exit.

Finding none, he contemplated a different means of escape. In the old days, he would have shot his way out, risking any number of innocent lives in the process.

A hand clamped down on his shoulder, and Caleb looked around to find Ed had joined him at the window. "Cal, as mayor, I want to be the one to—"

The door burst open, allowing the sound of cheering to drift in from outside. Miss Bertrand practically fell into the room, followed by the same dark-skinned maid he'd noticed with her earlier.

Oblivious to Caleb's presence, Miss Bertrand addressed Elmer. "I need to speak to the sheriff."

Her voice sounded as if she'd run all the way from the boardinghouse. Under her arm she carried a tin of what he hoped were more of her biscuits. While the feisty gal irritated him to no end, she sure could cook.

"Hold on there, girlie," Elmer said. "The menfolk are carrying on important business here. Is this here an emergency?"

"Emergency? You could call it that." She set the tin on the desk beside the pie, then caught sight of Caleb. "What are *you* doing here?"

Ed released his grasp on Caleb's shoulder to slap him on the back. "Haven't you heard? Cal here's the new—"

The Widow Sykes came bustling in. "Ed Thompson, what's taking so long? You got everyone in town out there waiting. If you're not gonna make the announcement, then leastwise go and tell them so." She shifted her attention from Ed to Caleb. "Hello there, Mr. Wilson. What're you doing here?"

"That's what I asked." Miss Bertrand inched forward and swiped at the spot on her cheek where butter and honey had been only an hour ago. "Did the law finally catch up with you?"

A few responses came to mind, none of which was particularly nice. He settled for ignoring the question.

"In a manner of speaking," Elmer said with a chuckle. "You might say he's gonna make the jailhouse his home now."

"Hush, Elmer, you old fool." Ed pressed past the ladies to reach for the door knob. "Come on, Cal. Let's get this over with."

Irritation turned to white-hot anger. Now both of them were grinning. Meeting his Maker was one thing, but enduring ridicule was another.

"Now hold on a minute, Ed," Caleb said. "I got some rights here, and before I go out there, I'd like to know exactly what you're charging me with."

"What we're chargin' you with?" Elmer guffawed. "We're chargin' you with being the new sheriff."

"Sheriff? Hold on." Caleb shook his head. "You got the wrong man, Ed. I'm Caleb Wilson."

Ed slapped Caleb on the back and pushed him toward the open door. "That's right. You're Sheriff Caleb Wilson."

"I'm who?" He shook his head. "Is this a joke?"

While Elmer guffawed, Caleb took a step backward to try to make some sense of the situation. Somehow he'd obviously been mistaken for a man whose name was similar to his. In nothing flat, he'd gone from inmate to jailer.

Caleb took a deep breath. He ought to set them straight, ought to say right out that he was Caleb Wilson, not Cal

Wilson, and that six months ago he'd been cooling his heels at the Huntsville prison. Then he had another thought. Had God heard his prayer and given him a chance at a new life?

"*He's* the sheriff?" Miss Bertrand looked as if she might fall down right where she stood. "*You're* the man I'm supposed to marry?"

"Sheriff Wilson, I knowed it, I did." The dark-skinned maid waved a paper in Caleb's direction. "It's all right here in your letter. You the one who sent for Miss Lydia."

"Say somethin', Cal." Elmer pointed to Miss Bertrand. "Tell these women who you are."

Caleb took the paper and unfolded it. There on the top were written the words that nearly sent him to the floor.

"Contract to marry?" He looked up at the maid who nodded; then he shoved the paper back at her. "You've got the wrong man."

She gave him a look that would chase off a polecat. "You the sheriff, ain't you?"

Under her scrutiny he almost cracked. Almost told the whole town they were about to pin a badge on the wrong man. Then he looked over at Miss Bertrand and couldn't say a thing.

Elmer answered for him. "Sure he's the sheriff. Tell her, Cal. We been waitin' for Cal Wilson nigh on six months. We was beginnin' t'think he'd run off with our travelin' money, so Ed went lookin' for him, and here he is." He returned the maid's scathing stare. "Who'd you think he was, one of the prisoners?"

Chapter 7

The next thing Lydia remembered was waking up in a jail cell. May dabbed a damp cloth against her forehead, and a man with red hair paced nearby.

Someone called, "She's awake."

Another said, "Fetch the bride out to meet the folks."

The bride.

It all came tumbling back. The contract to marry, the conversation with May, and her first look at her groom-to-be. Then the realization hit that she was to wed the man who plowed her down in Mrs. Sykes's kitchen.

At this reminder she groaned.

"You hit your noggin, hon?" This from May who ran her hand across the back of Lydia's head.

Mrs. Sykes stood in the door of the cell shaking her head. "To think I had both of you under my roof and I didn't know a thing."

Lydia climbed to her feet and shook off May's attentions. "Well, I didn't know, either."

Without bothering to explain, she straightened her shoulders and rose. Putting one foot in front of the other, she headed for the door and her intended—or maybe she'd just keep walking until she'd shaken off the dust of Dime Box, Arizona.

Whichever choice she made, she first had to make good her escape. With the only exit being the front door, she took a deep breath and stepped through. The claps and cheers should have stopped her, but they didn't. Rather, she walked all the way to the end of the sidewalk before she turned to see Cal Wilson staring at her.

By pausing, she was well and truly caught, for several ladies reached her and began to talk about dress fabric and wedding dates. She might have been there indefinitely had Mrs. Sykes not made her apologies to the ladies, taken her by the arm, and led her back down the sidewalk.

"There she is, folks." The red-haired man pointed to Lydia. "She's a little shy. Let's make the sheriff's intended feel welcome. Folks, welcome Lydia Bertrand, soon to be the new Mrs. Wilson."

Lydia's stomach did a flip-flop, and tears sprang to her eyes. The crowd parted to reveal the new sheriff standing by his side. Odd, but the lawman looked as miserable as Lydia felt.

Could it be that the goods he purchased had not met his expectations? Had he decided she wasn't all he hoped her to be?

Well, of all the nerve. What was wrong with her? Why, half the boys in New Orleans of marrying age had been trotted through their parlor, and not a one of them had made *that* face at her.

Why him? Why now? Eyes narrowed, Lydia strode over to the man to ask him.

Before she could take two steps, May intercepted her. "Now don't you go making a spectacle of yourself, Lydia Bertrand. You done been raised better than that."

Lydia pasted on a smile and aimed it at the lawman. "Well, of course I have, May. That's why I'm going to go over there and show my intended just how glad I am he's chosen me."

May whirled her around and stared at her hard. "And how do you intend to do that?"

"I'm just going to go over there and be polite." She shrugged. "If he's going to marry me, he needs to meet me proper, don't you think?"

May gave her a sideways look. "I didn't think you wanted to marry him."

"I don't." She upped the smile and aimed it in Sheriff Wilson's direction. "I just want *him* to *want* to marry *me*."

"That don't make no sense," May muttered. "That just don't make no sense."

She left her maid shaking her head on the sidewalk and headed for the spot where the mayor of Dime Box was introducing Cal Wilson as their new sheriff. Something gleamed in the sun as she approached. The badge, she realized.

"Would you like to do the honors, Miss Bertrand?" the mayor asked.

"I'd be delighted, Mr. Mayor."

—∞—

The crowd cheered as the Bertrand woman flounced over to

give the mayor her biggest smile. As she drew near, badge in hand, Caleb instinctively put his hand over his heart. From the look in her eye, she'd either stab it or steal it.

She lifted up on tiptoe, then met his gaze. For a moment she almost smiled. Then the woman looked down and went to work fastening the tin star on his shirt. Her fingers trembled, he noticed, and he couldn't help but wonder if his old charm had returned.

Then she looked into his eyes. She looked more determined than smitten. But determined to do what?

"So when's the date, Sheriff?"

He looked over at Elmer, who seemed to take great pleasure in Caleb's discomfort. Ed, however, looked as if he might come to the rescue any minute.

"Honestly, we haven't discussed a date." Miss Bertrand's smile could have lit a room.

"That's right," Caleb added as he plotted how to get himself out of this fix.

All he had to do was admit he and Cal Wilson were two different folks. That would get him out of the marriage contract. It would also set the townsfolk straight. The only trouble with the truth was that it didn't seem to fit with the answer to prayer he so clearly felt he'd received.

He'd asked the Lord to give him a second chance, and here He'd gone and let a reformed outlaw become sheriff. By speaking up now, he could very well ruin the plans the Lord had made for him.

Something in that logic chewed at his conscience, but Caleb ignored it. Instead, he smiled and shook hands and made small talk with the people he'd been entrusted to protect. He noticed the Bertrand woman was doing the same thing. She might be as pretty as a newborn calf, but he'd have to find some way of getting out of this contract.

The last thing Caleb Wilson needed right now was a wife.

Finally, the mayor stepped up and put his hand on Caleb's shoulder. "Folks, let's leave these two alone for a spell. I'm sure they've got some catchin' up to do."

A few hoots and hollers later, the people of Dime Box went back to their business, leaving Caleb to attend to his. He shook Ed's hand and stepped inside to take his place behind the big wooden desk.

Caleb and Ed had cleared the mess off the top of it, but he'd never looked to see what was inside. He did that now, starting with the top right drawer. Inside he found a layer of dust and a stack of papers. He lifted them out and set them on the desk. Topmost on the pile was a letter written on the stationery of the Wentworth Hotel in Wichita, Kansas, promising that one Cal Wilson's arrival would fall somewhere between the end of January and the middle of February.

No wonder Ed and the boys were getting impatient. He set the letter aside and, two posters down in the stack, found a familiar face staring up at him from a wanted poster: his brother Colt.

Caleb tore it in half and wadded up the pieces. He knew for a fact that Colt had done his time on this charge. He'd just missed seeing him in Huntsville.

The temptation to dwell on family pressed hard on him, and Caleb had to force himself to ignore it. He had more than enough to worry about, what with a feisty gal with marriage on her mind and a new job on the other side of the law.

He leaned back in the chair and set his boot heels on the desk. Given time, he'd find a way out of that predicament.

"A moment of your time, Sheriff." The object of his thoughts barged through the door, her maid following in hot pursuit.

"A moment?" He looked her up one side and down the other. She had her feathers ruffled for sure. "Looks like you aim to take more than that." He pushed two chairs up to the desk. "Set yourself down and speak your piece."

Both women spoke at once, leaving Caleb to shake his head and call for quiet. The maid clamped her mouth shut and handed over the paper she'd showed him earlier. Right there on the bottom line was the signature of a man named Calvin Wilson. Proof positive it couldn't be him.

He was about to say so when the Bertrand woman cleared her throat and aimed her attention in his direction. She wore yellow, an idiotic thing to notice considering the situation, but it did make her look pretty as a picture.

"Mr. Wilson," she said in her prim and proper way, "you and I have a contract. We also have a situation."

Caleb nodded. "Yes, indeed, I'd say we do."

"You got a *situation*, all right," the maid said. "The situation is you brought this gal all the way out to this place, and you are goin' to marry up with her right and proper—or I'll know the reason why."

Miss Bertrand placed her gloved hand on the maid's arm. "Let me handle this, May."

She addressed Caleb. "As May said, I've traveled from New

Orleans to fulfill my end of the contract, Mr. Wilson. I am interested as to whether you intend to fulfill yours."

"Well, now, just a minute here." Caleb's mind raced through the possible excuses for holding off on a wedding, coming to a stop at the most likely one. "You and I, we barely know one another, Miss Bertrand. I suspect you don't relish the thought of being married to a total stranger. Besides, we haven't exactly had a good start, have we?"

Her look gave him the impression she didn't relish the idea of being married to him at all. If he hadn't been so set on getting out of the deal himself, he'd be offended.

"This is true." She shifted positions and cast a quick glance at the maid. "But the townsfolk are calling for a wedding date, sir."

"I'm aware of that." Caleb set his boots on the desk again and tried to look as if he hadn't a care in the world. "What do you think of a summer wedding, Miss Bertrand? Say June?"

"June? Why, that's several months away." Her tone signaled displeasure, but the twinkle in her eye told him she felt otherwise.

"It is indeed," he said slowly. "But don't you think we need the Lord's blessing on this? You *are* a God-fearing woman, aren't you?"

"I am," she said. "And I think your idea is an excellent one. There's just one problem. I was not prepared for such a lengthy engagement."

He crossed his legs at the ankle. "Meaning?"

"Meaning we will be in need of a place to stay. I'm sure Mrs. Sykes won't be pleased when we have no more funds to pay for our room."

"Well, now, that is a problem. Let me ponder on it a spell." She rose, and Caleb set his feet on the ground and did the same. "I suppose I ought to come calling now that we're going to get hitched, Miss Bertrand."

She looked less than pleased at the idea. To her credit she recovered quickly. "That would be lovely, Sheriff. Please, call me Lydia."

"Lydia." He looked past her to see the maid frowning at him. "I'm Caleb."

The maid's frown deepened, but she said nothing.

"The mayor and his wife are having me to supper tonight. What say I fetch you round about six and we walk over together?"

Lydia aimed a smile in his direction. "Are you asking me to supper, Caleb?"

He hitched up a grin. "I reckon I am."

"Then you'll have to do better than that. I'm used to spending time with gentlemen."

With that she swept out of the office like the queen of England. Rather than follow, the maid leaned toward him.

"I'm on t'you, Sheriff," she said softly. "But I'm gonna speak t'the Lord afore I say another word t'anybody."

"While you're talking to Him, would you mind mentioning that I'd take any help He might want to send my way?"

She lifted a dark brow. "If'n you're gonna have anything t'do with that 'un, you're gonna need all the help He can send."

Caleb watched the swirl of yellow skirts disappear from sight and sighed. "Ma'am, I believe you're right."

Chapter 8

For some reason unknown to him, Caleb showed up at the boardinghouse at a quarter to six. Hat in hand, he had Widow Sykes announce his presence in the parlor. Courting came about as natural to him as breathing before he met the Lord. Now he seemed to be sadly lacking in the fine art of wooing a lady.

Not that he intended to woo Lydia Bertrand. Rather, he sought to pass the time until the Lord got him out of the mess he'd gotten himself into. In the meantime, it didn't seem proper to ignore the woman the whole town thought he was to marry.

He practiced his speech a couple of times while he waited. He'd tell her he was sorry they'd gotten off on the wrong foot, sorrier still he'd brought her all the way to Dime Box just to find out the wedding wasn't going to happen.

Sure, he'd said June, but after giving the matter some thought, he'd figured she would see the logic in holding off on getting hitched. Then she stepped into the room, and every word he planned scattered like dust on a stiff breeze.

This time she wore green, and it occurred to Caleb that he'd never once noticed the color of a woman's dress before today. Proof positive he had to steer clear of Lydia Bertrand.

"Mrs. Sykes said you wanted to speak to me."

"I did, actually," he said, hat in hand. "I felt like I had some apologizing to do, and now seemed as good a time as any." He shook his head. "What I mean to say is, I know you and I didn't get along right off, but I was wondering if you might consider putting that aside and accompanying me to the mayor's house for supper. I didn't ask right the first time, and for that I do apologize."

She seemed to consider his offer. "I'm not sure I have the time, Caleb. It's rather bad form for you to come waltzing in on short notice and expect me to jump at your command."

The woman certainly didn't intend to make his apology an easy one. "Yes," he said, "I do appreciate the problem here, but I believe if you'll think on it, you'll see that I did mention it earlier in the day. I just didn't use the right words."

Caleb straightened his shoulders and took a deep breath. He'd learned much about being humble over the past year, but he did have his limits.

"I can see I've made a mistake in coming here." He set his hat on his head and pressed past Lydia to head for the front door. "I'm sorry I wasted your time. Do have a good evening, Lydia."

He hadn't even reached the street before the Bertrand woman caught up with him. "My, but you walk fast, Caleb."

"I thought. . ." He looked down and saw all the fire had gone from her expression. "My mistake, Lydia. I assumed you'd be dining with the Widow Sykes tonight."

"It was an option," she said as she gathered her shawl about her shoulders. They walked in silence for a bit; then she spoke up again. "Apology accepted," she said softly. "Would you accept mine, as well?"

Caleb nodded and kept walking. The less they talked, the more he liked it.

With the mayor's house in view, Caleb stopped short and reached for Lydia's hand. "What say we start over, you and me? I mean, long as folks think we're a pair, we might as well be civil."

"About that." Lydia studied the ground for a minute, then swung her attention up to meet his stare. "I should have said something sooner, but if I had my way, I'd be back home in New Orleans. I really don't want to marry you, Sheriff."

"You don't?" Caleb's shock rendered further words impossible for a full minute, maybe longer. When he recovered, he shook his head. "If you're telling me the truth, you're the first woman I've ever met who wasn't looking to snag a husband."

Her giggle surprised him. "I suppose that makes me one of a kind then, doesn't it?"

The mayor's wife called Lydia's name, and he watched her wave and pick up her pace in response. Caleb caught up with Lydia and grasped her wrist, halting her progress.

"Wait a minute," he said. "You really *don't* want to marry me?"

Lydia's smile lit her face. "Not in the least."

—∞—

Dinner seemed to last forever. Making small talk with Amanda Thompson didn't hold a candle to besting Caleb in a discussion about weddings. While Amanda ladled gravy over the roast, Lydia recalled the entire conversation in the street. Every time she thought about telling the sheriff she had no interest in marrying him, she smiled.

"Penny for your thoughts, Miss Bertrand," the mayor said.

"I'm sure she's planning our wedding." Caleb leaned over to squeeze Lydia's hand. "Her face just lights up when she's thinking about getting hitched."

Lydia kicked Caleb under the table, then she watched with satisfaction as he winced then propped his smile back into place. "Oh, yes," she said to the mayor as she extricated her fingers from Caleb's grasp. "I do so love to think of my Caleb. He's such a fine catch, don't you think, Amanda?"

The poor woman seemed at a loss for words. The mayor, however, offered a quick blessing over the food, then asked for the corn bread to be passed in his direction.

"So when is that wedding, Caleb?" the mayor asked.

Caleb stabbed his fork into a slab of beef and unloaded it onto his plate. "Lydia and I were just talking about that today. Why don't you tell them, dear?"

She gave Caleb a smile, then turned to face Mr. Thompson. "Caleb's a gentleman, you know, and so protective of me." She patted Caleb's hand. "He suggested a June wedding to give me time to adjust to living here in your lovely community."

"June?" The mayor shook his head. "That's thinkin' positive. We usually don't get a parson in here till late summer."

Lydia nearly dropped her fork. "You mean you don't have a preacher in town who can marry us? What about the fellow who's been doing Sunday services?"

"Elmer Winslow?" The mayor cut a swipe through the

air with his hand. "He's nothin' but a farmer from north of here. He offered to fill in until we got a full-time preacher. He's right good at carrying on a Sunday service or speaking at funerals, but he don't have no marryin' abilities."

Relief shot through Lydia. Perhaps there was a way out of this mess after all. "And you say you expect a preacher in July?"

"Or August," Amanda said. "That's when the circuit riders come through. 'Course, it could be sooner."

Caleb looked in her direction and smiled. "Well, dear, looks like you'll have to wait longer than you wanted to get hitched."

"Oh, I don't know," she said in her sweetest voice. "For you I'd wait forever." She leaned close to Caleb. "Actually, forever sounds like just the right amount of time to wait."

The evening stretched on until Lydia thought she'd never see the end of it. After supper the men headed out onto the porch to talk politics while Lydia followed Amanda into the kitchen to help with the cleanup.

"You didn't wash many dishes back in New Orleans, did you, Lydia?" Amanda asked.

"Truthfully I didn't." She dabbed at the plate in her hand with the towel. "How could you tell?"

Amanda took the plate from her and finished the task, setting it on the drain board. She turned to Lydia and removed her apron. "If I'm being nosey, you just go ahead and tell me."

Lydia folded her apron and set it atop Amanda's. "Of course."

She leaned against the edge of the cabinet and dried her

hands, then looked up sharply. "I was a mail-order bride, too." She held up her hand. "Ed and I haven't shared that fact with anyone in Dime Box, so I'd appreciate it if you'd keep this to yourself."

"Of course."

Amanda led her to a chair by the fire, then settled in the rocker beside her. "My first husband passed on and left me with my son to raise. Ed here is a fine man, and he never held it against me when his mail-order bride showed up with a mail-order baby." She chuckled at the joke, then grew serious. "I'm telling you this because I want you to understand that God engineered the circumstances. Remember He does that. Often He does it in spite of us."

"Yes, I'm reminded of that frequently," Lydia said.

Amanda nodded. "Please know that I understand you're afraid, and you have every right to feel that way. You're far from home without a mama or papa to advise you, and now you're about to gain a husband."

Tears clouded Lydia's eyes, but she refused to allow them to fall. Rather, she took a deep breath and let it out slowly.

"Cal Wilson's a fine man," Amanda said. "My Ed says he comes highly recommended, and after working beside him nigh onto a week getting that jailhouse back in shape, he claims Cal's a hard worker, too."

Lydia shifted positions, suddenly uncomfortable. "I wouldn't know."

"I've seen him in worship, Lydia. That man loves the Lord. It's plain on his face when he's singing the hymns."

"You make him sound like a saint, Amanda."

"Oh, honey, none of us are saints." Amanda set the towel across the clean dishes. "Remember that when you go judging the man the Lord gives you."

"But I'm not judging," she protested. "It's just that I don't want to be married to a man who. . ." Lydia found she had no words to complete the sentence. She hung her head. "Yes, I suppose I am judging him. It's just that every time we're together something happens to irritate me." She sighed. "I can't explain it."

Amanda patted Lydia's shoulder and smiled. "There's a fine line between irritating and interesting."

"Are we being spoken of, wife?" Ed Thompson rounded the corner and embraced his wife, who merely grinned. "I was tellin' your intended that we're lookin' at buildin' a new Sunday go-to-meetin' place. One of our parishioners donated her property before she left to go back East. Now all we have to do is figure out how to turn it into a proper place of worship."

"Anything would be better than the little place we use now. Why, it's so small we barely have room to squeeze everyone in. But you know all about that, don't you, Cal?"

"I do indeed, ma'am." From where she stood, Lydia could feel the sheriff staring. She braved a glance and saw Caleb leaning against the doorpost, hands crossed over his chest. His grin took her by surprise.

"I'm going to send a bowl of cobbler to your landlady, Lydia. I promised I'd send some next time I made it."

While Amanda spooned dessert into a bowl, Lydia noticed Ed studying Caleb. She watched the mayor for a moment before turning her attention to the sheriff. To her surprise, he walked over and placed his hand atop hers. Lydia swiftly removed her fingers from his grasp and reached for the cobbler.

"It's been a real pleasure," Caleb said to their hosts before taking Lydia's elbow. "Once Lydia and I set up housekeeping, you're going to have to teach her how to make that delicious roast, Mrs. Thompson."

Chapter 9

"I want a recipe for roast?" Lydia walked two steps ahead of the sheriff, stalking off her irritation. "Do you think I can't make a roast?"

Caleb shrugged, a grin forming. "Can you?"

She made her way around a puddle, then turned to head for the boardinghouse. "That's beside the point."

He came up beside Lydia, then stepped in front of her. "What *is* the point, Lydia?"

Lydia stopped short then tried to walk around him. The persistent sheriff caught her elbow and whirled her around. This time when she looked into his eyes, she saw no hint of teasing.

"That contract—is it real?" He blinked hard. "What I mean is, did you actually come all this way to marry me?"

Her heart thumped against her chest. "You're not funny, Caleb. Not at all."

The moonlight cut a slice across his face. "I wasn't trying to be."

"You're the one who sent for me," she managed. "I never asked to be here."

Caleb's expression softened. "Care to explain?"

"No." She turned to go, then thought better of it. What did it matter if she told him?

"What's your story, Lydia? I'm not going to ask again."

"Miss Lydia, that you, chile?"

She glanced over her shoulder to see May sitting on the porch. "Yes, it's me. I'll be right in."

"See that you do. You ain't hitched t'this man yet, and your mama would have my hide if'n something were to happen."

"I was just leaving." Caleb turned his attention to Lydia. "You let me know when you're ready to finish this conversation."

—m—

As it turned out, the next day Caleb was too busy to finish any conversations. His first full day as sheriff was spent helping Ed Thompson and Elmer Wiggins fetch a wagonload of supplies from Millsville. The lengthy trip gave them plenty of time for conversation, much of which Caleb only listened to.

Occasionally Ed would ask a question of him or make a comment that required an answer, but most times Caleb drove the wagon and let the older men do their jawin'. Round about an hour from Dime Box on the return trip, Elmer fell silent. Caleb glanced over his shoulder to see the red-haired man sound asleep leaning against the pile of supplies.

"Mind if I join you, son?" Ed asked as he climbed up on the seat beside Caleb. "I'm of a mind to give some advice. You of a mind t'listen?"

"I suppose," Caleb said.

Ed stretched his legs out in front of him and leaned back

against the seat. "I'm wonderin' something, Sheriff Wilson."

A dry wind blew dust across Caleb's face, and he lifted his bandanna to cover his mouth and nose. "What's that?"

"I'm wonderin' what your intentions are toward Miss Bertrand."

Caleb gave Ed a sideways look. "What set you to wondering about that?"

The older man shrugged. "You didn't fool me," he said slowly. "I know you and that girl are complete strangers." He clapped a hand on Caleb's shoulder. "Oh, don't worry. Amanda and me are the only ones who've figured it out."

"Figured what out?"

"Figured out you mail-ordered your bride from back East." He shook his head. "Now there's nothin' to be ashamed of. Why, that's how I got my Amanda."

"It is?"

He nodded. "They's some fine women who start married life as a stranger to their husbands." Ed paused. "And they's some husbands who don't cotton to gettin' hitched to the gal they paid for. I reckon they figure they can do better elsewhere, but I say you stay with what God brings ya."

"What are you trying to tell me, Ed?"

"If I ain't makin' myself clear, then I don't figure I ought t'keep talkin'." He crossed his arms over his chest and got comfortable. "Wake me up when we reach town, would ya?"

"Yes, sir, I will." He chuckled. "And, Ed?"

He lowered his hat, then lifted one eyelid to regard Caleb with a sleepy gaze. "Yep?"

"You're making yourself crystal clear." He tightened his grip on the reins. "And thanks for saying what I needed to hear."

"Question is, what're you gonna do about it?"

"I don't rightly know."

He crossed his legs at the ankles. "Well, maybe I ain't done with my advice. Maybe you got some wooin' t'do with your bride-to-be."

Caleb shook his head. "Ed, I don't even know if I want her to be my bride. She's the most exasperating woman I've ever had the displeasure to know."

"Well, that settles it then." Ed straightened up and set his hat back on his head. "Marry her. That's love if I ever heard it."

"I don't think you were listening, Ed. That woman drives me to distraction."

Ed tipped his hat back down over his eyes. "I don't think you were listening to me, Caleb. If a woman drives you to distraction, it's a sure sign the Lord must've put her in your life. I don't know why that is, but that's how I've seen it work out."

—∞—

Caleb pondered on Ed's words for four days straight. Rather than face Lydia directly, he took his meals at the office or out on the work site. Each time he saw her, he pretended he hadn't. He felt pretty sure she did the same.

Every time one of Dime Box's citizens addressed him as Sheriff Wilson, he felt a little more uneasy. He jumped whenever someone called his name, because he figured someone had found him out.

Each night he pestered the Lord about his predicament. What he got back scared him.

God wanted him to have a new start, but Caleb had taken the timing into his own hands. Clean hands didn't come from a life built on lies.

Caleb chewed on Ed Thompson's advice almost as hard as his situation with the sheriff's office. Much as he hated to admit it, Ed's words mostly rang true.

The only thing he couldn't figure was whether Lydia had been sent by the Lord or had become his punishment for not telling the truth. In either case, he had a woman on his mind and a serious danger to his heart. If he kept the truth to himself, he'd get to keep her without a doubt. If he told the truth, she might get away.

Trouble was, Caleb didn't know which way he preferred things to go. He decided to do as Ed said and take to wooing his bride-to-be. That way, if the Lord released him from his obligations, at least he could part ways with Lydia knowing he'd done his best.

The next evening, Caleb arrived at the boardinghouse with a handful of penny candy he'd picked up in Millville. He'd thought to keep the sweets in his desk and savor one or two when he felt the urge. Instead, he'd gone against good sense and made a present of them.

"I hope you like them," he'd planned to say when he saw her. "I brought them from Millville," he might add.

But when she swept into the parlor smelling like flowers and wearing a dress that made her look fresher than springtime, he lost all ability to be clever. He thrust the handkerchief he'd carried them in toward her, then took a step backward.

"For me?"

He nodded.

"Thank you."

Again he nodded.

Lydia popped a sour into her mouth, then made a face. A puckering face. At that moment Caleb was horrified to realize he wanted to kiss her square on her puckered lips.

Chapter 10

Lydia offered Caleb a piece of candy, but he couldn't look at anything except those pretty puckered lips.

"No, thank you," he finally managed. "In fact, I can't stay. I just thought you might like a sweet."

"Thank you."

She took his hand to shake it, but he brought her fingers to his lips instead. An awkward moment passed between them until Caleb released his grasp.

She walked to the window and lifted the lace curtains. "A lovely evening for a stroll, don't you think?"

Caleb rocked back on his heels. "Stroll?"

"Do I need to spell it out? I'm going for a walk, and I'd like you to accompany me." She paused to let the curtain fall back into place, then turned to face Caleb. "That is, if you'd like to. I'm quite capable of going out alone." Without waiting for his answer, Lydia reached for her shawl and wrapped it around her shoulders.

"Hold on there, darlin'." Caleb grabbed his hat and set it back on his head. "You don't have to be in such a hurry."

"I do if I don't want to lose my nerve."

"Your nerve?" The screen door slammed behind him, and Caleb hurried to catch up. "What're you talking about?"

She pointed to the garden, the same place where he'd seen her crying what seemed ages ago. "I'll be honest. I lured you out here to tell you my story without fear of being overheard."

Caleb nodded. "I appreciate that you trust me enough to share it."

Lydia stopped short and looked up into his eyes. "It's not you I trust. It's God." She swallowed hard. "I need to tell you about me, Caleb. About why I'm here in Dime Box."

He gave her a sideways look. "All right. Why's that?"

She took a deep breath and prayed the right words would come. "I'm an only child and quite a disappointment to my parents. You see, I—"

"Who's out there?"

Lydia saw Mrs. Sykes standing at the garden wall in her dressing gown. "It's me—Lydia. I'm with the sheriff."

Mrs. Sykes waved and disappeared inside the rooming house. Lydia stepped away from the wall, and Caleb followed. Somewhere between the garden and the street Caleb slipped his hand around hers.

She walked beside him in silence, allowing Caleb to lead the way. Before long they were strolling down the sidewalk toward the sheriff's office.

"We can keep walking or talk in here," he said.

Lydia peered inside the office, then nodded. "Here's fine."

Caleb bustled around lighting lamps and putting on a pot of coffee while Lydia watched. Before she knew it, he sat across the desk from her with a pair of mugs in hand. He set one in front of her, then leaned back in his chair.

The time had come. Lydia watched the steam rise from the black coffee, then began. "As I said, I'm an only child." She lifted her gaze to meet Caleb's stare. "I'm sure my father expected more from his daughter. My mama, well, I know she did."

To his credit, Caleb remained silent.

"Mama was from a distinguished family. Old money, I guess you could say. Papa, well, he is a preacher. He loves the Lord and my mama." She paused to take a sip of the best coffee she'd tasted since leaving New Orleans. "He loves me, too, but I'm afraid I disappoint him regularly."

Caleb looked concerned. "How so?"

"Silly things to you, I suppose, but to Mama my antics have been an embarrassment."

"Antics?"

Lydia felt the heat rise in her cheeks. "Yes, you see I've been in boarding schools since I was ten. Mama felt it would be good for me to broaden my experiences, but all I wanted was to go home." She sighed. "I soon learned that fine line between misbehaving and things that could get me sent home."

Caleb leaned forward. "Like?"

She shrugged. "Like dipping my slippers in the punch bowl or dancing a jig in the town fountain." Before he could speak, she held up her hand to silence him. "I was modest about it, I promise."

His grin disappeared. "So how did you end up in Dime Box?"

"Well, actually, this was Mama's doing. With Papa's approval."

She blinked back tears. "She—or rather, they—felt it in my best interest to send me away to find a husband."

"I see." He steepled his hands and stared hard into her eyes. "And how do you feel about this?"

Lydia let out the breath she'd been holding. "I feel like God must've sent me to marry Cal Wilson, so that's what I am supposed to do."

Caleb rose abruptly and set his mug on the desk. He walked around to her and reached for her hand. Rising, Lydia found herself dangerously near to the sheriff.

"Is that what you want to do, Lydia?"

She looked up into eyes that glittered with emotion. They were gray, she noticed, the color of the New Orleans sky just before a storm.

Before she could answer, before she could manage to put together a thought as to how she felt, Caleb Wilson kissed her. Lydia stepped back, touching her lips.

No man had ever been so bold with her. No kiss had ever been so welcome. With all her heart, Lydia knew God had led her to this place, to this man. Fear slipped away, and peace took its place.

"This changes everything." Had she spoken or merely thought this?

"Yes, it does." Caleb stepped back and leaned against the desk. "I'm not who you think I am, Lydia. I believe it's time you heard my story. You see, I'm not Sheriff Cal Wilson. I'm Caleb Wilson, outlaw. Well, reformed outlaw, that is."

"This sounds like quite a story. Do you mind if I sit down?"

Lydia settled back on the chair while Caleb paced the room and told her of his life as part of the Wilson gang. When he finished, he had his back to her and his attention focused on the wall of wanted posters.

"I know personally more than half the men on this wall." He turned to face her. "But I know one man who makes all this not matter anymore. See, I found Jesus behind the prison walls. I was locked up, but He set me free. I wanted to do something good for Him, but I haven't gone about it the right way. I need to go talk to Ed and make this right."

"Would you like me to come with you?"

Caleb shook his head. "I need to do this alone."

Chapter 11

Caleb stole another kiss before he left Lydia at the boardinghouse. Any other time he would have whistled his way home, but tonight he felt like he was walking in lead boots. He knocked on Ed's door and prayed he would be able to handle whatever punishment he got after he spilled his story.

Amanda Thompson let him in, then called for her husband. She left them in the kitchen with a plate of cobbler and two glasses of milk.

Ed shoveled a healthy amount of dessert onto his plate, then regarded Caleb with a frown. "You look like you're heading for the gallows, Cal. What's the problem?"

"In a way I might be." Caleb refused Ed's offer of cobbler. "I'm not who you think I am, Ed."

"I wouldn't be so sure about that, but go on and tell me about it."

Caleb started at the beginning. When he finished his tale, exhausted after repeating it for the second time in one night, he sat back and waited for Ed to react.

To Caleb's surprise, the man continued to eat his cobbler.

"Did you hear me, Ed? I'm Caleb Wilson. I'm an outlaw, or rather I was until Jesus got hold of me."

Ed set his spoon down and reached for the milk. After taking a healthy swig, he set the glass on the table. "I reckon we all got a story, Caleb. Yours, well, I'll grant you it's not like most." He leaned forward and rested his elbows on the table. "I 'preciate you comin' clean with me. Now, I wonder if you're gonna be at the church house tomorrow, because it looks as if we're gonna need a few extra hands. We're shorin' up the ceiling, and we're gonna have our hands full with keeping it from fallin' in around our heads before we build the new one."

Caleb shook his head. "I don't believe you heard me. I'm a criminal. An outlaw. It just happens my name is similar to the man you were expecting. Doesn't that mean anything to you?"

" 'Course it does." Ed met Caleb's gaze. "It means the Lord works in mysterious ways. But then we both knew that."

He pushed back from the table and stood. "I need to come clean with this, Ed. I've got to admit to the folks of Dime Box that I'm not the man you all were expecting."

Ed rose and straightened his lapels. "You know Elmer Wiggins?"

"I do."

"You respect him, do you?"

Caleb scratched his head. "Yes, I heard him preach last Sunday, and he did a good job. I'd say he's a fine man."

"No, he's a reformed horse thief. Ben Mulligan over t'the general store? He used t'rob stages until he got a good shot of the Holy Ghost." Ed shrugged. "I could tell you stories that would curl your hair. The Widow Sykes, well, suffice it t'say she can pick a fine lock if she still had a mind to. There's a reason she don't live in Savannah anymore. And Ma, the gal who owns the restaurant?"

He nodded. "Now she's a rough-looking character."

Ed chuckled. "And yet she gives just about every penny she makes to the orphanage back in Dallas where she grew up. Nobody in town but me knows this, so I'd appreciate you keepin' it quiet. She brings me the money every month and has me send it 'cause she don't want the man at the bank t'know she's the one makin' the donations."

Caleb hung his head. Of all the things he'd thought about Ma, picturing her like this was not one of them. "I guess you never know about people."

Ed clamped his hand tight on Caleb's shoulder. "No, you don't. Folks don't come to Dime Box, Arizona, for the good weather and fine food. They come, most of 'em anyway, t'forget who they were and concentrate on bein' who they ought to be. Ever wonder why there ain't hardly no crime?"

"I guess I hadn't."

"Well, I have a theory on that. I figure the Lord's got His hand on this place. I don't know for sure, but I'd like t'think maybe He created Dime Box as a place where sinners are forgiven."

Ed's son burst into the room nearly out of breath. "Pa, there's a coach a-comin'."

"A coach?" He looked up at the clock. "It's a quarter of nine. You sure it's a coach?'

"Sure as can be," he said.

Ed nodded. "Looks like I've got work t'do down at the livery. Son, you head on down there and light the lamps." He waited until his son had gone, then thrust his hand in Caleb's direction. "I 'preciate you comin' clean, son, but I have to confess I figured out who you were right off."

Caleb shook his head. "You knew who I was from the beginning?"

"Sure," Ed said. "You told me."

"I did?"

Ed made his way to the door as the sound of a team of horses drew near. "I called you Cal Wilson, and you corrected me right off. Did that a couple of times. So you never did deceive me, boy. Whilst I was jawin' with you that day, I felt the Lord tell me you were the one we'd been waitin' for. Now I've got work to do. I believe you need to go home and study on what I told you."

Caleb walked out with Ed and watched as a stage halted outside the livery. The driver jumped down to open the door. Two men spilled out into the semidarkness.

"Welcome to Dime Box," Ed said. "They's rooms at the boardinghouse across the street and a good meal to be had there, too. Where you all comin' from?"

As Ed continued his mostly one-sided discussion with the weary travelers, Caleb walked away with his heart light and his conscience clean. Before he did anything else, he went straight to the garden beside the boardinghouse and picked up a small rock. He lobbed it against the darkened window of Lydia's room, then waited for her.

"Who done been throwin' rocks?" The maid appeared at

the window. "It's you. What you want?"

"I'd like to speak to Lydia."

"What you want with Miss Lydia?'

"That's enough, May." Lydia appeared at the window. Her hair hung loose, and she appeared to have been sleeping. "I'm here."

"I need to talk to you. Can you come downstairs?"

She leaned forward as she began braiding her hair. "To the garden? Now?"

"No, to the parlor. I'll wait on the porch." Without allowing her to say no, he made his escape from the garden.

He watched the activity at the livery until Lydia opened the door. "This is highly irregular," he heard the Widow Sykes call from somewhere upstairs. "So speak your piece and go on home so decent folk can get their sleep."

Decent folk. Caleb swallowed hard. Indeed, tonight he felt as if he could be counted among the decent folk. "Yes'm," he called back. "I thank you for allowing the interruption."

"Anything for a man in love."

A man in love? Yes, that just might fit him.

He followed Lydia into the parlor. While she chose to sit, he knew he couldn't. "I'll stand, thank you."

"So how did Mr. Thompson take the news?"

Caleb began pacing. "He said he knew all along who I was. Said it was the Lord's will I showed up when I did. He told me I was meant to be here." He stopped to look down at Lydia. "What do you think about that? Or, I guess the better question is, what do you think about me? Will you still have anything to do with me now that you know about me?"

Lydia rose to fall into Caleb's embrace. "Don't be silly. Of course I will."

Caleb held her tight. She was a pretty thing, no bigger than a minute, but with a voice as smooth as silk and a pair of big brown eyes that could cause a man to forget his troubles.

And she was all his.

Or she could be soon as he asked right and proper.

Caleb let her go and dropped to his knee, taking her hand in his. "Lydia Bertrand, I'd be right proud to wake up to your biscuits every morning for the rest of my life. Will you do me the honor of—?"

"Lydia? Oh, sweetheart, is that really you?"

His intended let go of his hand and sprinted past him as if he hadn't said a word. Caleb scrambled to his feet and watched as Lydia fell into another man's embrace.

"Hold on here," Caleb said. "Who is this man?"

The fellow stared back at him with a surprised look. "I might say the same thing. Who are you?"

"The name's Wilson," Caleb said. "I'm the new sheriff 'round these parts."

"You're a liar, sir. I just rode into town with Sheriff Wilson. He's at the livery at this very moment."

Chapter 12

Lydia slipped from the man's embrace to reach for Caleb's hand. "Caleb, I'd like you to meet my papa, Reverend Augustus Bertrand." She turned to the older man. "Papa, this is Caleb Wilson, and I don't care who you rode in with—*he's* the sheriff of Dime Box. He's also going to be my husband."

If he weren't in such a sudden fix with her papa at that moment, Caleb would have kissed her for sure. Instead, he tried to think of a way to get out of this mess. He had no doubt the older man had ridden in with Cal Wilson. It would be about right to have the real sheriff finally show up when he'd made his peace with keeping the job.

Caleb felt her squeeze his hand, and he squeezed back before offering his palm to Reverend Bertrand. "Pleased to make your acquaintance, sir. I assure you I am Caleb Wilson."

"He is who he says he is, and I'm here to vouch for him." Ed Thompson walked into the parlor and shook hands with the pastor. "He's a fine, God-fearin' man who's been helpin' with the church when he isn't busy keepin' the peace." He turned his attention to Caleb. "I'd like you to meet someone, Caleb. This here's Cal Wilson."

A portly fellow tipped his hat at Caleb. "I hear tell you took my job."

"I suppose I did."

The fellow reached over to shake Caleb's hand. "I'd just like to thank you."

He shook his head. "You want to what?"

"You see, I was headed this way to take the job when I come across the loveliest gal a man ever set eyes on. Suffice it to say, I made the gal my wife in short order, which left me with two problems: the job and the woman I'd sent for from New Orleans."

The pastor gestured toward Lydia. "That would be my daughter, Lydia."

Lydia smiled in his direction. "Pleased to make your acquaintance."

"Likewise, I'm sure." He turned to Caleb. "I'm not here to take your job, but I do need to set some things to rights." He looked at Ed. "First off, I need to repay you for the money you wired, Mr. Thompson. The whole hundred dollars is in there. You count it and be sure." He handed the mayor a thick envelope. "And then there's the matter of my betrothed."

He took a step toward Lydia. "My dear, you are lovely. I deeply regret any trouble I've caused by sending for you and then failing to be a gentleman and fulfill my end of the contract."

"Actually, I'm grateful for how things turned out." Lydia looked past him to where Caleb stood. When she smiled, his heart nearly turned over. "At least I think I am. Caleb was in the middle of an important question earlier, and he never did finish asking it."

"Reverend Bertrand, I'd like to do this right and proper. Would you do me the honor of allowing me to marry up with your daughter? I'll see she never wants for a thing as long as I draw a breath."

"Is this what you want, daughter?"

When Lydia nodded, Caleb dropped to his knee again. "Will you marry me, Lydia Bertrand, and not in June but as soon as your papa's willing to perform the ceremony?"

—∞—

Lydia looked down at the man who'd stolen her heart and smiled. Tears began to fall, and she didn't care who saw them.

"I'd be honored to become your wife."

Caleb rose to embrace her, then kissed her quickly before shaking hands with her father. Only one thing kept the moment from being perfect.

"Papa, where's Mama?"

Her father smiled. "She's out in the coach. She was afraid to come in until I checked things out. For some reason she thought you might be a bit miffed at her. It was her idea we make this trip."

"It was?" A thought occurred to her. "Papa, were you offered the position in New York?"

He nodded. "I was, but I turned it down."

"You did?"

Papa smiled. "I had a better offer, but I'll let your mother tell you about it."

He stepped out and returned with Mama, who cried and professed love and apologies all in the same breath. "There's nothing to forgive, Mama," Lydia said. "Meet Caleb Wilson, the man I intend to marry."

Her handsome husband-to-be charmed Mama in no time flat. She knew Mama approved when she looked over toward Lydia and nodded.

Mrs. Sykes called from the kitchen that coffee and a hot meal awaited the travelers. The portly former sheriff headed off, but Mama and Papa lingered behind.

"So what's this about a new assignment?" Lydia asked.

Mama smiled. "Yes, your father has taken a prestigious assignment with an up-and-coming church. I'm so very proud. He will be the first pastor to preach in their new building."

Lydia turned to her father. "Where is it?"

"Right here in Dime Box, dear. Mr. Thompson was very kind to allow me to break the news. You see, Lydia, I've been plotting this ever since I returned from New York. Rather, your mother has been. Isn't that right, dear?"

Mama kissed Papa, then nodded.

Caleb shook Papa's hand. "Welcome to Dime Box, sir." He gathered Lydia into an embrace, then kissed the top of her head. "I know from experience that when you're where the Lord wants you to be, there's not a better feeling."

KATHLEEN MILLER Y'BARBO

Kathleen is a multipublished award-winning author of Christian fiction who also writes under the name Kathleen Y'Barbo. A tenth-generation Texan, she holds a marketing degree from Texas A&M University and a certificate in paralegal studies. She is the former treasurer of American Christian Fiction Writers, as well as a member of Words for the Journey Christian Writers' Guild, Inspirational Writers Alive, Fellowship of Christian Writers, Writers' Information Network, Houston Paralegal Association, and the Writers' Guild. The proud mother of a daughter and three sons, she makes her home in Texas (where else?).

Kathleen's historicals often include settings in the Old West, which is her favorite topic for research. From Texas Rangers to Arizona outlaws, she loves learning about the Old West and the men and women who settled there.

A Gamble on Love

by Tamela Hancock Murray

Dedication

A father to the fatherless, a defender of widows,
is God in his holy dwelling.

Psalm 68:5 NIV

Chapter 1

Denmark, Texas—Summer 1882

"Another round for the boys, Pearl." Balancing his chair on its back legs, a sober Benjamin Wilson kept his facial expression unreadable and studied the playing cards he held.

"I already knew what you were thinking, darlin'." With an oval-shaped fingernail, Pearl tapped the half-empty bottle. She batted her eyelashes and swayed her hips in Benjamin's direction, motions that always left him wishing he could be alone with her instead of sitting at a card table surrounded by cowpokes, whiskey, and tobacco smoke.

Benjamin winked at her. Though Pearl said she loved him, she spurned his advances beyond an occasional kiss. But at the moment, Pearl winked back at him as she tipped the bottle toward the dry glass of a young self-proclaimed cattle rustler, a man they knew only by the name of Owen.

"No more for me." Owen looked up at Pearl and placed his flat hand over the top of his glass. "Or cards, either. I'll hold 'em." He pulled on his mustache.

"Are you sure you don't want another round, Owen?" Pearl tilted the bottle, hovering it over the empty glass. "There's plenty."

Benjamin didn't take his gaze off the cards. "Plenty" was a code word. His hand was better than Owen's. With seventeen dollars on the table, Benjamin didn't want to lose this round. Pearl lived up to her name, all right. She was a jewel.

Another habitual card player, Cyrus, threw his cards on the table. "I'm out."

Benjamin held back a smile. *If I can just hold on, I'll get a good take.*

He caught Sadie studying him from her perch on a settee near the front door. No doubt her silent observations went something along the lines of how foolish his companions were to fall for his tricks—again. Blue-eyed and baby-faced, with dark blond stubble that matched longish blond hair, Benjamin knew his innocent-looking demeanor misled many players into thinking they could beat him at the card games he had long since mastered.

Pearl's coded talk interrupted his musings. "There's plenty more here for you, too, W.C."

With a nod, W.C., a man whose wealth derived itself from suspicious origins, accepted the drink. "I'll raise you." He tossed some coins in the pot.

Since W.C.'s hand also lacked the cards to win, Benjamin kept the game going. "I'll see you and raise you."

A look from Pearl told him he'd done the right thing—according to the rules of a cheating gambler. But in the world beyond Sadie's, Benjamin was doing wrong, according to what they said at church. That's why he seldom attended worship.

If the preacher had his way, he'd take away whiskey, cards, and tobacco and even shut down Sadie's business. While whiskey and tobacco didn't impress Benjamin, he realized those threats didn't touch his penchant for cheating. But he let the boys win once in a while so they had their fun. Just often enough so the local gamblers and out-of-towners passing through wouldn't catch on to Benjamin's guile. He knew he should feel guilty, but he couldn't. He'd been cheated in life when his brothers dumped him off at Sadie's at the age of six. Why shouldn't he be rewarded now?

Benjamin had begged to go along with his older outlaw brothers, but they would have none of it. The last remembrance he harbored was watching them ride out of town. Only Reuben looked back at him. Having been thrust unceremoniously into manhood, he never whimpered or complained after that, but the hole his brothers left in his heart had never healed. He tried to fix the hurt by gambling, but no amount of money soothed his wounds.

At least on this night he'd get a temporary lift from winning. According to Pearl's signals, Benjamin had the best hand at the table. He held out until the call, showed his hand, and watched as his gaming companions threw down their cards in defeat, snorting and frowning.

"I'm gonna be in a right nice fix with my wife tonight. That was her egg money." Luke, a young farmer with a wild streak, rose from his seat.

Benjamin resisted the urge to sympathize. No one had

forced Luke to join the game. Every man who played knew the chances of losing were greater than those of winning. As for Luke, well, he'd spent over three quarters of his wife's egg money on whiskey before he even sat down at the table.

"You know," W.C. said with a menacing tone that gave Benjamin pause, "you seem to have a powerful lot of good luck at cards."

"His luck will run out soon. I'll be here next week to win my money back." Wagging his finger, Owen seemed more cheerful, his mood no doubt brought on by one shot too many of libations.

"Sure, we'll play next week. I'm not that hard to find." Benjamin looked around, but he didn't see Pearl. Wisely, she had disappeared from view. He smiled to himself. Pearl wasn't that hard to find, either.

—∞—

Pearl drew two silk frocks from the narrow oak wardrobe occupying the small room she had called home for the past year. Colorful dresses, fashioned to flatter, were part of the allure that first brought her to Denmark, Texas. But fancy clothes couldn't compensate for disappointment. Life at Sadie's hadn't been glamorous or exciting, as she imagined when she first left Pa's ranch in a misguided attempt to earn easy money. Why she had listened to grand promises from the loose girls back home, she never knew. Their advice had proven dismally wrong.

Pearl should have known earning money was never easy, but back then she wanted to try. Pa had died and, with him, Ma's dreams of making the ranch go. Most of the livestock were sold off, and only the garden crop, one cow, two pigs, and some chickens remained. Pearl's fantasies were grander. She wanted to make the ranch a going concern. Not only that, but she dreamed of sending money to her favorite sister, a young widow with five small children, living in Abilene. Both efforts required money.

She thought back to her entrance at Sadie's only a few short months before. When Pearl eyed Benjamin, she thought herself fortunate. But not all the men were like gentle and handsome Benjamin, and on that first evening there, she hadn't been talking to one of the cowpokes ten minutes when she realized what she had done. She ran upstairs to the shelter of her room, crying. Sadie demanded that Pearl pack her bags and leave. But when Benjamin offered her a chance to help him win at cards, she took it. She knew cheating was wrong, but the alternatives—including returning home in defeat—seemed worse.

Returning to the present moment, she remembered the letter she had tucked away in a little box where she kept correspondence from home. In the box was a missive from her sister Rachel letting her know that Ma needed Pearl, and so she had to go back to the ranch. Pearl was ready to return. If only she didn't have to leave Benjamin.

A tear dropped down her cheek. She let it flow.

Benjamin found Pearl in her room. Little red veins appeared in the whites of her brown eyes, and the lids were red, too. Her skin, though still creamy, looked splotchy. He'd caught her crying before and surmised she was thinking about her home. At least, that's what she always told him when sadness overcame her.

She looked up from folding a dress and gasped. "Benjamin! What are you doing, sneaking up on a body like that?" When she looked away from him and resumed folding, he understood she wanted him to ignore her saddened state.

Leaning against the door frame, he dressed his face in its best smile. "Gettin' ready to go to a party later?"

She shook her head but didn't look at him.

After ascertaining no one would overhear them, he approached Pearl. "You must be plannin' on something important. You haven't even asked me how much the take was." He kept his voice low in volume.

That got her attention. She regarded him. "How much?"

"Here's your share for the week." He handed her twenty dollars.

"Not bad." She inspected the bills and then hid them in her bodice. "Now you wouldn't cheat me, would you, Benjamin?"

"Never. Not you." He smiled as if he meant it, and he did. He and Pearl always joked about how they would cheat gamblers, but never each other. Stroking her cheek, he noticed her gardenia perfume. "And even if I did, you could forgive me, couldn't you?"

"Maybe." She smiled. "But you better not try."

He laughed and stepped back. "You'd better not try any fast maneuvers on me, either. Even though I could forgive you anything."

"Could you really?" She cocked her head.

"Yes. I do believe I could."

"Maybe you better watch what you say," she advised.

"Oh? How come?"

"Because you won't like what I'm about to tell you." Her coy manner evaporated as she took in a breath and let it out. "Today was my last with Sadie, and with you. I'm leaving tonight."

"What? What do you mean, leaving?" Anger overtook shock. "You can't do that to me."

Pearl flinched and covered her face.

"Now you know I would never haul off and hit you, Pearl. But I tell you, you can't do that. Don't you see what you're losing? We have the perfect business. Why would you want to leave?"

"It's my ma. She's sick. Real sick." Pearl cried anew.

His heart softened, and he took her into his arms. As soon as he did, her sobbing increased, tears wetting his shirt. "I'm sorry. I didn't realize. But you know what? I'll wait for you to come back. Why, I'll even take a vacation, a little break. Maybe I can visit Reuben's family in Wyoming. How does that sound?"

"I—I don't want you to wait for me. You don't need to worry. Plenty of other women would be glad to take my place." He could tell by her anxious expression the suggestion pained her.

"But I don't want anyone else to work with me. We're a team, Pearl."

"I know it." Her sobs increased. "But Ma needs me. I gotta go. You—you can make do without me."

"No, I can't."

"Sure you can. You're skilled—and lucky—at gambling. Why, I think you'd win most every time even without me."

"It's not just the gambling, Pearl. You know that. Don't you? Without you I'd have no heart left at all."

She drew back and sniffled.

He reached in his pocket and handed her his red bandanna.

She accepted the kerchief and wiped her eyes. "Neither will I, Benjamin. Neither will I."

"Then don't go. I know you love your ma, but can't one of your brothers or sisters go to her?"

Pearl shrugged. "You know I'm the youngest of ten. They've all long moved on to their own broods. I'm the only one who's not tied down to hearth and home. So I'm the one who takes the responsibility now."

Seeing Pearl's pretty face lined with care saddened him. He knew what he was going to do. And no one would be able to stop him.

Chapter 2

The next day, hoping no one would see him, Benjamin strode toward the front door of Sadie's. She was the only person who knew he planned to leave. He wanted to keep it that way.

He had only a few more paces to the exit when a familiar female voice stopped him. "Say, Bennie, whatcha doin'?"

Letting out a sigh, he turned to face Eliza. "Why are you up at ten in the morning? Aren't you usually in bed at this hour, still getting your beauty rest? Not that you need it." He sent her the sardonic grin he knew she loved.

She drew closer. "Flattery will get you everywhere, except out of answerin' my question. Are you thinkin' of leavin' us?"

Benjamin looked down at the trunk that housed every possession he owned. Their number was not great. He hadn't ever needed much. His life hadn't been one of fond memories tracked by souvenirs, so two changes of clothes and some toiletries were all he ever needed.

"You won't answer. You must be leavin'."

He twisted the heel of his boot into the floor. "Matter of fact, I am."

She placed her hand on her hip. "Where?"

"Out of town."

"For how long?"

"Don't rightly know. Not sure if I'll ever come back."

Eliza's painted face fell. "Not sure if you'll ever come back? Whatcha mean by that kind of crazy talk?"

"It's no crazy talk." Benjamin didn't want to admit he planned to follow Pearl because he couldn't stand to be without her—and because he saw a new opportunity in relocating. "I need to leave town, to—to—help out a friend."

"Pearl." Eliza grimaced and crossed her arms.

He didn't answer but looked at the pine floor.

"Don't try to fool me. I know she left yesterday. Something about her ma dyin'. But she didn't say nothin' about you goin', too."

He looked into Eliza's face. "That's because she doesn't know."

Eliza shook her head. "This gets crazier by the minute. If Pearl didn't invite you, why are you goin'? There's plenty of us around here who'd love to take her place."

When Eliza swayed her hips, the motions had no effect on his heart or emotions. The realization only made him long for Pearl.

Eliza persisted. "I'll bet Sadie doesn't like that you're leavin'."

"No. She doesn't like it at all," Benjamin admitted. "And Pearl might not like it, either. But I'm a man who's hard to stop once I set my mind to something."

"That I know. But don't stay too long."

Benjamin didn't make such a promise but tipped his hat as Sadie had taught him and left.

As he made his way to the corner where he was supposed to meet the coach, he tried not to look back. Leaving the familiar house presented new opportunities, but he hadn't remembered feeling so anxious since his brothers dropped him off there years ago. He wondered what awaited him at Pearl's family ranch.

Minutes later, to his surprise, among the crowd Benjamin saw Pearl approach the corner of Main and First. Like him she had only one trunk. But instead of her familiar red rouge, darkened lips, and black lines around her eyes, she had left her face bare. He studied her countenance, hoping his admiration wasn't obvious. Her cheeks contained natural color, a soft pink rather than the red circles to which he was accustomed. Even without paint accentuating her eyes, their chestnut color stood out, dotting skin the color of cream. Red color no longer covered her lips, but her full mouth still looked appealing. Pearl had always possessed beautiful black hair. The sun caught reddish highlights he had never before noticed. He hadn't thought it possible, but she looked more ravishing on that day than she ever had at Sadie's.

Feeling curious and amused stares upon him, he remembered they stood amid three others awaiting rides out of town. Apparently he had been observing Pearl too long, and his fellow sojourners had taken notice.

At that moment, Pearl's glance caught his. Her mouth slackened, and he watched surprise turn to vexation. "What are you doing here?" she asked, keeping her voice just above a whisper.

"Waiting for a coach. What are you doing here? I thought you left these parts yesterday."

"I was planning to, but the coach I was supposed to be on broke down. So they said I could ride out on the next one."

"But I didn't see you at Sadie's last night."

Pearl shook her head. "I'd said my good-byes. I couldn't return. I stayed at Mrs. Hoffman's."

"Mrs. Hoffman's?" He started to say more, then thought better of it.

"I know what you're thinking. She wouldn't want a woman like me in her place. But without my face paint, I'm not sure she realized who I was." She averted her eyes. "But that doesn't explain why you're here. You aren't leaving because of me, are you?"

He took her aside, out of earshot of the others. "I decided on my own to leave town. To start a new life. Time to move on before the gamblers around town catch on to my tricks." Remembering W.C.'s veiled threat, he held back a shudder.

"I wouldn't worry about that. They have their fun. Where would they be without you to offer them a challenge?"

"I suppose. Sort of like trying to outgun a sharpshooter. Haven't been caught yet. Well, except for that one time when that traveler caught on and landed me a pretty good punch in the jaw." Benjamin rubbed the now-healed spot. His account attracted the attention of one of the ladies. She clutched her bag closer to her, apparently afraid that Benjamin might be interested in her cash, too.

"Yes, you do present a challenge," Pearl conceded and smiled.

He liked her familiar smile, even though it wasn't painted on.

Soon the coach arrived, jangling to a stop. Minding his manners, he acted the gentleman, letting the ladies board before him and taking the least desirable seat by the window. Dust always came through there the most, especially landing on those who faced forward. Pearl's posture relaxed, and he felt comfortable.

After five hours of riding down bumpy trails, away to another world Benjamin didn't know anything about, the coach finally stopped for dinner at a town even smaller than Denmark. The inn in question wasn't much better than a bunkhouse. The meal offered was a watery soup of beans and carrots.

He stuck near Pearl, glad to have her as a dinner companion until he sat beside her at a corner table.

"What is the meaning of all this?" she hissed.

"All this?" Peering around her, he noticed no one else was nearby. No wonder Pearl didn't mind speaking freely. He didn't like the ire he saw in her flashing brown eyes. Clearly she had saved her wrath just for his ears. "Why the change in attitude? You seemed fine before."

"I only seemed fine. I don't like making a public spectacle of myself. Now that we're alone, I want to know what you mean by following me like this. You have no right. I'm finished with that life—for good. I don't ask or expect you to change for me. Why don't you go back to the life you know? The life where you have plenty of money and more than enough eager women." She rose from her seat. A fresh tear dripped down her cheek. "You can start by eating dinner by yourself."

Her angry words notwithstanding, Benjamin knew he had made the right decision to join her. The tear told him all he needed to know. Desperate to stop her, he blurted, "I'm changing my ways, too."

She stopped in midmotion, nearly spilling her soup before returning to her seat. "You are?"

He crossed his fingers behind his back. "Yes."

She looked at him cockeyed. "I hope you really mean that, because I have news for you. If you go home with me, you're going straight whether you like it or not."

"Oh?" He looked at her without flinching or blinking, a skill garnered from years of gambling.

"Ma won't allow any illegal or immoral activities on her ranch. In fact, she might not even let you stay since she knows you're a link to a part of my life she doesn't approve of."

He stirred his soup as he clenched his back teeth under closed lips. His plans to convince Pearl to help him win a few dollars from bored ranch hands looked as doomed as a man holding a hand of twenty-two in blackjack. But he wasn't giving up that easily. Not with his way of living at stake. "If she doesn't approve of your past, why are you running back to her now?"

"Because she's my ma, that's why. Not that I can expect you to understand that."

He hadn't seen that coming. This time Benjamin winced.

"I'm sorry," Pearl blurted. "The way you were brought up isn't your fault." She reached across the table and placed a comforting hand on his arm. She swallowed. "Truth be told, out of all my sisters, I'm not Ma's first choice. She's only letting me come back home because she's desperate for help." Her crying had slowed as she spoke, but now fresh tears poured down her cheeks unabated.

Benjamin reached into his pocket and pulled out his red bandanna. "Here you go."

She accepted the gesture, and they heard the driver calling out the room assignments for the night's lodging.

Benjamin took the opportunity to embrace Pearl, not caring about the stares and odd glances they received. "I know your ma has been judgmental and condemning of you in the past. Don't worry. You can always come to me for a shoulder to cry on. I'll protect you," he murmured into her ear.

She pulled away. "I don't need protection. Not from you, not from anybody."

When pride tugged at Pearl, arguing was useless. Benjamin tried another tactic. "If you'll let me tag along, I'll consider it a personal favor. You can do a good deed for an old friend, can't you?"

"I—I don't know."

He searched a satchel he carried and found the bottle of perfume he'd been saving for just the right time. The tuberose scent was Pearl's favorite and one the shopkeeper didn't always have in stock. Benjamin had been lucky to get the last bottle.

She gasped when she saw the pink glass vessel.

"This sweetens the deal, wouldn't you say?"

She uncorked it and inhaled. A dreamy look entered her eyes, and she indulged by dipping the bottle upside down so the cork would absorb some of the scent and then using it to apply a drop behind each ear. Before she closed the bottle, she took another whiff.

"I'm glad you're enjoying your gift already."

"I'd better while I can. Ma won't abide the scent of perfume around her. Says virtuous women don't need any aroma other than soap."

Benjamin wondered how good business would be at Sadie's place if the women didn't keep themselves painted and smelling pretty, but he decided not to make reference to the life Pearl was leaving. "You'll just have to wear it when she's not around."

"Maybe." She slipped the bottle into her dress pocket. He had a feeling she'd hold on to it the whole trip.

"So you'll consent to me following you?"

"Against my better judgment," she agreed.

Benjamin grinned. "Whether your judgment is good or bad remains to be seen."

Chapter 3

Pearl didn't say much during the second day of the trip. Worried, she fiddled with her skirt, a simple brown cotton affair she had worn on the day she first went to Sadie's and hadn't donned again until that morning. Ma would be glad to see her in a drab house dress, even though the hem had muddied from the trip. If she tried to approach her mother while wearing silk, despite Ma's desperate illness, she'd throw Pearl out faster than a gunslinger could draw his pistol.

Why she hadn't given the silk frocks in her trunk to her friend Eliza, Pearl didn't know. Why were the dresses—a literal outward show of the past she wanted to shake—so hard to shed?

Musing, she realized the dresses symbolized another link. To Benjamin. She was thankful he'd followed her, even though she pretended to be mad at him about it. She could only hope he wouldn't buckle under the pressure of Ma's discipline and insistence that everyone in her house walk the straight and narrow. Though Ma was ill, she'd find a way to control them. She didn't know how she could stop it.

Lord, I know I haven't talked to You much, but I pray You'll keep me strong now. I'm teetering on the edge of the new life and the old. Don't let me fall off the fence and land in the muck.

—∞—

They reached Rope A Steer, Texas, that afternoon. Pearl hired a buckboard to carry them to her mother's place.

"The ranch sure is beautiful," Benjamin remarked as they approached an unpainted gate. The sign said "M&H," which stood for Milk and Honey. Pearl had told him the name represented the Bible's promise and her father's hope. The horse pulled them past a stand of brush, over a shallow creek, and down a fenced field. The simple frame home looked to be missing a few roof shingles. The house wasn't much, but he hadn't expected to be so taken with the acres upon acres of flat land stretching as far as he could see. Nearby a cow grazed on more land than she needed, rich green grass offering a veritable feast.

"I've always thought it was beautiful out here." A wistful look covered Pearl's face. "You should see the fields in spring when the bluebonnets are at their peak."

"I can only imagine how pretty that must look." Benjamin noted that Pearl couldn't seem to take her gaze away from the land. From the moment she had stepped into Sadie's, Benjamin knew Pearl wasn't meant for that kind of life. Now she was back home, and the radiance in her face showed she had landed right where she needed to be. "You really missed the ranch, didn't you?"

"I suppose I did." Pearl cleared her throat as she put her hand on the front door latch and looked him in the eye, much like Sadie used to do when she was about to lecture him on how to be a gentleman. "Now Ma isn't expecting you, so you need to be real quiet and let me handle her, you hear?"

"I hear."

Pearl straightened her shoulders and crossed the threshold. Her surefootedness surprised him, considering Pearl had said Ma was quite a character. Perhaps since Pearl no longer bore the marks of one of Sadie's girls, her ma could overlook her brief mistake, and they could start anew. At least that's what he hoped for Pearl. He set down both of the trunks he carried—his and Pearl's—on the kitchen floor.

"I'll go ahead and put on some coffee. You can help yourself to a cup while you wait for me to greet Ma," Pearl instructed. "I'll let you know when you can meet her."

Benjamin nodded and took a seat at the rickety oak table. Seemed a mite small if they were expecting to serve a number of ranch hands their meals. He shrugged. Maybe the hands ate in separate quarters. Smiling to himself, he fantasized about easy pickings from bored gamblers. He'd seen that the nearest town, Rope A Steer, offered an inn, a blacksmith shop, and a tiny dry goods store. Not much in the way of entertainment. Surely the men here would be more than happy to go a round or two of cards. He'd make sure to hit them for a game on payday.

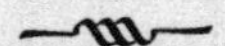

Pearl said a quick, silent prayer for courage before she entered the sickroom. No matter what Ma said, she was determined to be as cheerful as any paid nurse or companion. Even more so. She remembered how Ma's favorite daughter, Rachel, conducted herself. Rachel's sweet demeanor and radiant peace brought life to her plain features and made Pearl wish she could be more like her. Pearl decided she'd do her best to emulate her older sister.

Opening the door, Pearl found Ma lying in the finely carved four-poster bed Pa had built out of pine years ago for his new bride. Though her eyes were shut and she lay in repose, Ma's face looked haggard and pale. Had she really aged ten years when Pearl had been away only a few months? Her mother's mortality, and her own, struck her.

Before Pearl could ponder her new role as a nursemaid in silence, Ma opened one eye then the other. "Well, look what the cat dragged in."

Pearl had been prepared for a cool greeting, so her heart didn't twinge, nor did she draw near to her mother for a kiss. She summoned her best impression of Rachel. "I'm happy to see you, Ma."

"Sure you are."

"I'm pleased to hear your voice sounding strong even though you look a mite peaked."

"Of course my voice is strong. It had better be if I have any intention of convincing a sinner like you to stay out here in God's country. Sure would have been easier on me, not having to preach while I'm sick. If Minnie had come, I'd never have to say a word to her. And Emmie would open the Bible right along. I don't suppose you have a Bible with you, do you?"

She flinched. "No, ma'am."

"Never mind. Mine's right here on the table. You'll be reading at least a chapter a day to me, you know. Maybe you should start with the tale of the prodigal daughter."

"You mean son."

Ma's eyes narrowed. "You would know, wouldn't you? Guess I can't expect to bear ten children and not have one turn out to be a black sheep." Ma pulled herself up on her elbows.

"You sure you're up to sitting?"

"Sure I'm sure. Wouldn't try it if I wasn't."

Pearl rushed to her side, placing pillows so the older woman could situate herself in comfort.

Ma inspected Pearl with sharp brown eyes. "I see you're wearing the same dress you wore when you left."

Pearl winced. "You won't be seeing any colorful silks around here, Ma."

"That's good. You know red's not a good color to wear around a bull. Maybe it works real good around a two-legged bull, but not one with four legs. Did I tell you our bull died?"

"No. I'm sorry." Pearl pursed her lips. The bull's death had no doubt been yet another setback for her mother and the struggling ranch. She was sure the event had only added to Ma's agitation, which was greater than Pearl expected. She didn't want to break the news about Benjamin's arrival to her mother. "I'll be fixing supper shortly. Maybe I can fry up one of those cheese omelets you like so well."

"That's one thing you can do, is make a cheese omelet. And I've got some cheese and a few eggs in the house—what I was able to gather before I got so sick I had to send for you." Ma let out a labored sigh. "I'm mighty tired of livin' off the atrocious food Mrs. Wilkins brings by. Not that I'm not grateful for whatever that good Christian soul is willin' to do for me. She's mighty obedient, livin' the Lord's commandment to love your neighbor as yourself. But her cookin' is somethin' awful."

Pearl laughed out loud in spite of herself. "Now, Ma, you're mighty picky for someone so sick."

"A sick person needs edible food." Ma crossed her arms, but Pearl detected the slightest upward curve to her lips.

Since her expression was the closest to congenial she'd seen in the few minutes she'd been there, Pearl decided to broach the subject of Benjamin. "I—I didn't come here alone."

All pleasantness evaporated. "What are you sayin', child?"

"Someone followed me here. Benjamin."

"Benjamin? Who is that?"

"I didn't ask him to follow me, but he did." Pearl decided she might as well tell the whole truth. "He's the man I love. And he loves me, too."

"Is that so?" Ma eyed Pearl's left hand. "Then why don't I see a weddin' band on your finger?"

Without meaning to, Pearl inspected her ringless hand. "Maybe you will one day."

"That's what he wants you to think."

"I don't ask you to approve of Benjamin, but I do ask you to meet him," Pearl said.

"Fine. Stuck in bed as I am, I have no other choice." Ma looked down at her night shift. Though the garment was fashioned from opaque cotton and the collar covered her neck, she grabbed her bed jacket from the foot of the bed and donned it, fastening the buttons with quick expertise that reminded Pearl of how Ma used to dress her.

After a nod from Ma, Pearl went to the door and motioned at Benjamin. Without hesitation he set down his coffee and made his way into the room.

Ma tilted her head and peered at him through narrowed eyes. "Well, well, lookee here. Cat's been busy today."

Benjamin was obviously taken aback by Ma's odd greeting. "Come again, ma'am?"

"Ma's just being Ma," Pearl said, rushing to intervene before she made the introductions.

Ma looked Benjamin up and down. "You must think a mighty lot of my daughter to follow her all this way. Though only the good Lord can understand why."

Benjamin shot Pearl a distressed look before he answered. "I think your daughter is a fine woman, Mrs. Hubert."

"You do, do you? Turn around and let me see you."

Benjamin hesitated.

"Go on, boy. What's the matter with you—got some sort of defect you don't want me to see?"

"Ma!" Pearl objected. With his fine features and strong physique, Benjamin had nothing to be ashamed of in his appearance.

"Now, you shush. I want to see what kind of man would follow you all this way."

Benjamin, looking stunned, complied.

"I think you'll do." Ma nodded. "You'll do just fine working here on the ranch."

"What?" Benjamin and Pearl said in unison.

"You came all this way. What else were you plannin' to do?" Ma's tone feigned innocence.

"He didn't come out here to be a ranch hand." Pearl looked at Benjamin. "Did you?"

"No, I've never worked the land a day in my life."

Ma sniffed. "I won't bother to ask how you do make a living."

Pearl decided not to enlighten her. "I'm sure Benjamin wouldn't mind doing a little work around here in exchange for room and board."

"Room and board? No, that won't do. I can't have a man livin' here with you the way you are and me too sick to stop whatever it is he plans to do. No, he'll live in Rope A Steer and report to work every day just like he was a paid employee."

"You can't expect him to work for free," Pearl said.

"I suppose you're right about that," Ma conceded with a sigh. "We'll pay what we can."

Pearl turned to Benjamin. "You don't have to work here."

Benjamin set his gaze on the open window that offered a view of the land, land that appealed to him. Though the idea of winning money from the ranch hands crossed his mind, Pearl was more important. He wanted to stay near her. How could he refuse her ma's invitation?

"No, I don't have to work here," he answered Pearl. "But I will." He looked toward the older woman. "I accept your offer, Mrs. Hubert."

Chapter 4

Later that evening, after Pearl had served her mother the omelet she promised, she sat with Benjamin at the table. She took delight in how he savored every mouthful of omelet and the satisfied grin that accompanied each bite. Though it was much too soon to entertain such thoughts, she couldn't help but dream about dining with Benjamin every evening. His presence lifted her spirits and soothed her mind in the face of Ma's criticisms.

Pearl didn't want to consider the possibility that he regretted promising Ma he'd work at the ranch. Yet she felt she had to offer him a way out, just in case. Courage to broach the topic arrived over after-supper coffee.

She cleared her throat. "I know Ma must have taken you aback today with her offer of a job. Truth be told, it surprised me, too. I have to ask, are you sure you want to work here?"

He didn't hesitate. "I'm sure. The idea's kind of grown on me." He swirled his half-full cup in circles with more enthusiasm than was required to melt the two lumps of sugar he took. "Uh, I realize I won't get treatment this good every night.

Reckon I'll be eating with the ranch hands from here on out. Living with them, too." He looked up. "You don't mind showing me the quarters after supper, do you?"

"The—the quarters?" She set down her cup and patted her lips with her napkin.

"Uh-oh. Are you telling me you don't have an extra bed?" He shrugged. "Well, I can sleep on the floor if you can spare a blanket." He downed his coffee. "How many hands do you all employ, anyway?"

She stiffened. "Employ?"

A chuckle escaped his lips. "Yeah. You know. Like a man works for you, and then you pay him. We have this here paper in the U.S. of A. that we call money. The same paper we used to win at our games." He winked.

Instead of consoling her, his wink made her uneasy. Because she knew Benjamin's schemes, her mind didn't take long to form an unhappy conclusion. "Games, huh? I hope you weren't thinking you'd win the ranch hands' paychecks. Now you wouldn't be thinking that way, would you?"

His lips twisted into a little grin. "You know me too well. All right. I admit it. I confess I followed you out here because I couldn't stand the thought of being without you." He placed his elbow on the table and set his chin in his palm.

Pearl knew him well enough to realize the blue-eyed puppy dog look he gave her was contrived to melt her heart. Though it was working, she decided to remain steely. "But?"

"But." The puppy look disappeared, replaced by a mischievous light as he retreated by leaning back in his chair. "In the back of my mind, I thought maybe I could rustle up a few extra dollars from the ranch hands."

"Benjamin! You'd take advantage of our ranch hands?"

"I wouldn't call it taking advantage. Gambling's a form of entertainment, the way I see it. Everybody knows there's a risk. But for your sake, I wouldn't have taken too much of their money." Sincerity coursed through his voice.

"I believe you," she answered.

"I must say, things have changed a little since your ma hired me. So I'll go you one better. Now that you've got me working, eating, and living with them, I won't be taking any of their money by cheating. I'll win every game fair and square." He lifted his forefinger to emphasize his point.

"Are you sure?"

"Of course. Why would I lie to you?"

"I don't think you're lying. I just think you don't possess the conviction to keep your promise." She sighed. "Maybe you'd see the real need to be an honest man if you knew God. I wish you weren't so mad at Him."

"I'm not mad at God. I know He's there. He must be, for all those people to pour into church every Sunday morning. He just hasn't showed up a whole lot for me, that's all." Benjamin's voice betrayed sadness and defeat.

"I reckon He's not too easy to find in a place like Sadie's. I know I didn't see much of Him there. Not that I looked too hard." She let out a breath. "Lately I've been thinking a lot about my life."

Benjamin surveyed the room. "Being out here does that to you, doesn't it?"

"Yes. Not too much music and talk to distract you." Pearl

let out a little laugh.

"You know, I thought I'd miss all the noise, but I don't. Isn't that strange?"

"Strange in a good way. Maybe the good Lord's telling you how you don't need all those distractions after all."

"Maybe. But I interrupted you. What have you been thinking?"

"Oh." Pearl got her thoughts back on track. "When I left home, I was hoping for a lot of things. I wanted to help Ma by sending money to her and my widowed sister, too. I thought living in a bigger town would be exciting and talking to men would be an easy way to get money. After all, Ma kept reminding me how I attracted too many men for my own good. And I have admitted to the Lord that a part of me wanted to get away from Ma's strict rules. But I didn't know until I got to Sadie's how high the cost of escaping Ma's domineering ways would be. These past months away from home were the worst I've ever had. I wouldn't have survived if not for you. I'll always be grateful to you for being there during my darkest hour. But now it's time for me to see the light and to try to walk with God once more."

Benjamin didn't answer right away. Pearl gave him time to absorb all she had shared. "Where does that leave me?" His voice was quiet.

She placed her hand on his knee and gazed into his eyes. "Walking beside me, I hope."

"But I am right with you, by working here. Right?"

"There's more to it than that." When she hesitated, the silent air seemed to oppress the room. "I–I'd like you to start going to church with me."

His eyes widened. "Church?"

"Is that so bad?"

He chuckled and nodded at once. "I don't reckon so. You know you can make me do almost anything when you look at me like that."

Pearl laughed. "I hope so. But I'm leaving the heavy work up to the Lord."

"You're going to need Him to convince me to repent. Churchgoing and all is nice for a lot of folks, but you know it's not something I'm used to. Maybe things would have been different if Pa hadn't died. But my outlaw brothers had plans for me that didn't include God."

"They did the best they could."

"I know it. And I understand they've changed—although I haven't seen them in years to find out one way or another." He leaned closer and, with his blue eyes, searched her face. "You don't think I'm like them, do you?"

"I—I never thought much about it."

"Well, I'm not. I might cheat a little at cards, but I never stole outright from anybody. I never robbed a bank and sure never shot anybody over money or anything else. And how many other men would live at Sadie's and still resist the ladies?"

"You—you have?" Though she'd never seen him act untoward to any of the women there, she didn't realize he had maintained his virtue. In her eyes he was becoming more and more heroic.

His face reddened, and he pulled away from her. "Don't tell anybody what I told you. Some of the men would never let me live it down."

"I wouldn't tell anybody if my life depended on it," Pearl promised. And she meant it. They were silent for a moment before she spoke once more. "I won't even tell anyone if you decide to go to church." She smiled.

"Do I have a choice? I'll bet your ma makes all the ranch hands go to church every Sunday, doesn't she?"

Sorry he had returned their conversation to a raw topic, she took her hand off his knee and didn't look him in the eye. "I have to tell you. We—we don't have any ranch hands out here. This is a small enterprise. My parents ran it themselves. Ma owns a few acres, but she and Pa just subsisted."

His expression took on a confused light. "What? You mean you don't own all this land I see?"

"Not all of it by any means. No, most of it belongs to Oliver O'Connell, proprietor of the Double O Ranch next door. Now that's a man who owns some acreage."

"Then why do you insist on calling this place a ranch?"

"That's what they planned for it to be one day. Pa hoped to buy more land in the future. But he became ill soon after he settled our little parcel, so he was never able to bring the ranch up to its potential. Now Ma doesn't even farm except for keeping a little livestock and growing a few vegetables to eat. When she's well enough, which isn't often, Ma takes in sewing and laundry and sells eggs to make enough money to buy the dry goods she can get by on. Of course, I've always sent her a good part of the money I made at Sadie's. Now don't you mention it to her, because she'd never admit it. She thinks my money is dirty." Pearl slumped in her seat, and her voice grew quiet. "Maybe it is."

"You need money to live, though, don't you?"

"Yes, but maybe we'd all be better off with a little less money and a little more ingenuity. Although I was glad for what I earned with you. I sent a good part of it to my widowed sister. With four boys and a girl, she needs all the help she can get."

He could do nothing but shake his head in amazement and admiration. "I had no idea. I thought all your money went to pretty dresses and perfume."

"Had you fooled, didn't I? I'm pretty good with a thread and needle, so I managed to keep myself in fancy costumes." She looked down at the plain gray housedress she wore at that moment. "Truth be told, I'm happier wearing this."

Benjamin studied her. He remembered how she once looked in low-cut, beaded gowns fashioned from silks in colorful hues. The way she looked now, with a simple kitchen as her backdrop, made him comfortable. Pearl presented the vision of a strong woman, capable of hard work. "Truth be told, you look even better dressed like that than the way you looked at Sadie's."

"Now you're just funning me."

"No, I'm not."

Pearl looked beyond him through the open window. "The sun's getting low. You'd better be going. Why don't you use one of our horses for a ride into town? Get yourself a room at the inn."

—ꟺ—

A half hour after he left Pearl's, Benjamin rode a gentle horse into Rope A Steer. His second look at the dust-ridden town revealed that his first impression had been right. The place felt dead. He spotted only one sign of promise—HOOT N HOLLER INN. Not that the wooden structure, in dire need of paint, looked like anything to hoot or holler about.

The inside didn't offer much more promise. An old man sat behind a tall counter boasting a sign that read NO PAY, NO STAY in bold letters. The rack housing three rifles on the wall behind him indicated he planned to enforce his policy.

"Got a room I can stay in for a couple of months? Maybe more?" Benjamin asked.

"I got something for a dollar a week if you're not too picky."

"I'm not."

The innkeeper held out his palm. "That'll be two weeks in advance."

Benjamin peeled two dollar bills off his roll of cash and relinquished them.

"You can call me Mr. Dimsbury." He handed Benjamin a key. "Third floor. You won't have trouble finding it since it's the only one up there."

The idea of an attic room hadn't occurred to Benjamin, but considering he hadn't seen any other inns, he figured he'd best take it without complaint. Once he navigated the narrow stairs, his fears of a tiny room with a pointed ceiling proved true. The bed looked no larger than a coffin, and there wasn't even a desk. He figured it was a good thing he wasn't much of a writer or scholar.

Unpacking, he was almost grateful he couldn't stay at Pearl's. Had he remained on the ranch after work hours, she might have sensed his mood and realized how distressed and shocked he felt. He'd come all this way only to find a pathetic little enterprise with no ranch hands to cheat? The idea of leaving suddenly seemed fine. But if he did, what would life be like without his Pearl? Making money by cheating a few ignorant and bored ranch hands appealed to him, but Pearl appealed to him more. He couldn't leave her. He was going to stay, even though that meant rooming in a hole in the wall in a tiny speck on the road that considered itself a town, where no one knew him.

As soon as he set himself up in his new quarters, Benjamin looked for a saloon. He didn't see much prospect of being paid to work at the ranch no matter how noble the Huberts' intentions. Sure, Pearl had decided to walk the straight and narrow, but even without her he could make money. Why, maybe even better money than before. With that thought he allowed himself a triumphant smile.

He hadn't been in the Drunken Steer Tavern a moment before he attracted the attention of a woman wearing a revealing dress. "Hey, handsome, you new around these parts?"

"Sure am. Thought I might set up a little card game." He cocked his head toward an empty table.

She shrugged. "I don't mind, but Bart might want a cut of your winnings. He's the owner."

Benjamin hadn't thought of such a possibility. Then again, Sadie had always been his friend and knew Benjamin's card games attracted customers. At least this woman hadn't asked to be his partner. If she had, he'd have turned her down. No one could take Pearl's place.

That fact became more evident as he played that night.

He won, but not as handily as usual. Without Pearl's help, Benjamin wasn't gambling in the fine form to which he had become accustomed. He had to convince Pearl to change back to her old ways. And fast.

Chapter 5

The following morning Pearl opened the door to her mother's sickroom, expecting her to be asleep. Instead, Ma sat in bed, looking outside through the open window. Her Bible rested in her lap.

"You got my bed jacket?" she asked Pearl.

"Yes, ma'am. All nice and clean, fresh off the clothes line." Pearl walked toward the bed and handed the garment to her mother.

"Took you long enough." Ma brought the article of clothing to her nose and inhaled. Pearl expected to be complimented on how fresh it smelled, but Ma had other ideas. "This is still damp."

"It is?" Pearl reached for the bed jacket and squeezed the cotton until she felt a tinge of dampness on one edge. "I suppose I could have let it stay out there a little longer, but I thought you wanted it back."

"I know you're tryin' real hard, and I appreciate it, but you burned my bread and forgot to put the sugar in my coffee this morning," Ma pointed out. "You haven't been yourself ever since you got back. It's that man, isn't it?"

"You mean Benjamin?"

"Of course that's who I mean. Who else? He's all you can think about, isn't he?" Ma didn't wait for an answer. "He's a handsome one, all right. But he ain't no good for you. Not until he gets right with the Lord."

"I know. I'm worried about him finding trouble in town. Even though Rope A Steer is hardly as sophisticated as I imagine a big city back East is."

"True. I know what you're thinkin', young lady." Ma wagged her forefinger at Pearl. "The answer is no. He ain't staying here with us overnight. There's too much temptation for that. I can see in the little time you've been here that you're tryin' to do better. And, sick or not, I'm your ma, and it's up to me to help you get back where you should be with the Lord. That means avoiding temptation."

"But, Ma—"

"Now don't you sass me." She held up her palm. "I can look into your eyes and his and see that. I might be old and sick, but I remember what it's like to be young. Just barely do I remember, mind you, but I remember. You know what your grandpa would say if he was still kickin'? He'd say we ought to work Benjamin so hard he'd be too tired to think about anything else at night but sleepin'. And speakin' of work, where is he, anyhow?"

Benjamin was indeed late, but Pearl didn't want to dwell on that subject. At that moment, they heard a horse's hoofbeats. Pearl looked through the window to see Benjamin approach, looking like a fine gentleman on his borrowed horse rather than the gambler he was. Her heart beat harder upon eyeing Benjamin. Ma was right. He offered her nothing but temptation. Temptation she didn't need.

"Is that your man?" Ma asked. "It's about time that he showed up."

"It's Benjamin." Pearl noticed the trotting horse stirred up red dust. "I'd better get the rest of the clothes off the line before they're ruined."

She hurried out the front door to greet Benjamin. She noticed the wind blew in the opposite direction of her clean clothes, so the dust would have little effect. Watching him hitch the horse, she summoned all her willpower to keep herself from running. Only a day had passed since he had last been to the ranch. Why did it seem more like a month? Or a year?

"Did you miss me?" he teased.

She felt her cheeks warm up. "What's the matter? Do I look like a forlorn coyote or something?"

"Nope. You look better than that. Much better."

She laughed. "You're full of flattery today. You aren't seeking shelter, running from the sheriff, are you?" She realized her question, made in jest, held a hint of fear and seriousness.

He didn't seem to be offended. "Naw, I stayed out of trouble so far."

"You found a room at the inn?"

He shrugged. "More like a broom closet. But it will do."

"What were you expecting in such a small town? A fancy hotel?" She motioned for him to follow her into the house. "I promised you breakfast every morning. I'll scramble you some eggs. Unless you've already eaten."

"Not yet." He rubbed his stomach. "Breakfast sounds good."

Soon they entered the kitchen. "Go on and wash up now."

"Yes, ma'am," Benjamin said with good humor.

"I've already milked Pansy this morning, so she won't need attention until this afternoon. So probably the best place for you to start your day after you eat is to see if all the fences are in good repair. Our land runs up through the creek on the south side."

"You've gotten mighty bossy." His tone sounded teasing.

"Have to be. I'm the boss." She squared her shoulders and broke an egg into the frying pan. "I've got some cured bacon, too. You'd better eat a slice or two. You'll need to keep up your energy if you want to put in an honest day's work on a ranch, even if it isn't much of a ranch."

"You seem to be enjoying being bossy." He dried his hands on the plain white towel that hung from the side of the basin.

She peered out the kitchen window and thought about how much a coach ride had transformed her. From a life where she was subject to the whims of others, to telling Benjamin what to do. The change felt good.

"So you don't want to answer me. I reckon that dashes my hopes."

"I'm sorry. I was caught up in my own thoughts. What hopes are you talking about?" Pearl scooped up the eggs onto a plate.

"I was hoping maybe you'd like some excitement. How about coming to town and being my partner again?"

"Benjamin, you know I can't." She set his plate before him. "Give me a moment and I'll slice you some bread."

"You mean you're happy serving me breakfast and tending to your ma? What kind of life is that?"

"The kind of life I'm leading now." She slackened her posture. "You wouldn't be asking me to abandon my own ma, now would you?"

"No. I just was hoping you might be a little tired of your ma's preaching by now. I know I was after I was with her only ten minutes. Not that I mean any disrespect."

"I know. Ma takes some getting used to." Pearl sat at the table. "But now that I'm home, she's softening up a little. Why, just this morning she told me how much I'm trying." Pearl decided to omit the criticism of her cooking that accompanied such faint praise.

"Well, that's fine, but you still do a lot of work. Wouldn't you like to get out of the house one or two nights a week? You could put on a fancy dress like you used to. Paint your lips pretty. Don't women like to do those things?"

The persuasion in his voice made the prospect sound almost too good to pass up. Without meaning to, Pearl studied her hands. In a short time they had grown pink. Not too much, but enough that she could tell she'd been scrubbing pans, washing clothes, and tending to livestock. She could only guess what they, once soft and pretty, would look like in no time at all.

On second thought, she didn't have to guess. They'd look like Ma's. Coarse, with blue veins evident. And in years to come irregular brown spots would appear on the backs of her hands and grow larger and larger. Soon the skin was destined to deteriorate to the point where wearing a ring or bracelet would only call attention to her age and the facts of what was turning into a hardscrabble life.

Pearl shuddered.

"You didn't answer me." Benjamin picked up a slice of bacon.

She turned her gaze from her hands to his face. "Sure, I like pretty clothes. But this dress I have on is a lot more comfortable."

He snorted. "That doesn't sound like the Pearl I know."

"The Pearl you know isn't around anymore."

"Is that so?" He leaned toward her, close enough that she could take in his clean yet manly scent. His nearness made her want more. But Benjamin represented a life she had left behind. A life to which she could not return.

She rose from her seat and made much ado about pouring herself a cup of coffee and him one, as well. "I know that. But I can't live with my ma and act one way in the daytime, just to go out with you and cheat men at cards every night."

"I'm not asking for every night. Just one or two nights a week." His mischievous eyes were impossible for her to resist. Nearly. But she had to resist.

"No. I can't."

"So you're going to bargain, are you? Can't say that I blame you. Fact is, I admire you for getting smarter so fast." She was only half surprised when he withdrew a box from his satchel. "Here you are. I got this for you before I left Denmark."

Returning to her seat, she remembered the bottle of perfume he gave her at the station. "Just how many gifts did you get, Benjamin? Looks to me like you might have bought out every store in Denmark."

"I'd do that if I thought it would make you happy. I just wanted to be prepared, Pearl. And I'm glad I had that foresight. The general store in town has mighty slim pickin's."

"Our needs out here are simple."

"Judging from the goods that Simpson fellow carries, I'd agree."

"I know adjusting to life here must be hard for you, Benjamin. Out here, our way of looking at life is different. Our lives revolve around church, not saloons. At least, my life does." She swallowed and looked at her napkin on the table.

"So you don't miss Sadie's at all?"

Pearl shook her head. "But I would have missed you if you hadn't followed me out here. I sure am glad you did."

He looked toward her ma's room. "I don't think everyone shares that opinion."

"Ma wants me to find a churchgoing man." She looked at him plaintively. "What do you say, Benjamin? Would you give church a chance? Maybe you and I could go together next Sunday."

"I don't know, Pearl. I've done a little Bible reading, even been to socials at church a couple of times."

"Really? You went to church?"

"Once or twice. When I was younger."

"I always thought the people in church were nice. Don't you think so?"

"Yep. Even nicer than most, I reckon," he admitted.

"So what made you stop going?"

"Gambling. Whenever I stepped near any church, the

preacher man would try to make me give up gambling."

"And that made you mad."

"No. Not really. I knew the preacher had to say such stuff and nonsense. He had to make a living just like everybody else."

Pearl laughed even though she wasn't sure she agreed with his logic.

"Laugh all you like, but I don't know any other way to make a living."

"Now you're the one talking stuff and nonsense. You sure do know how to make a living."

"How's that?"

"Why, you can make a living right here, earning more than the pittance we can pay you now. You don't realize it, Benjamin Wilson, but I have big plans for this place."

Chapter 6

Benjamin looked into Pearl's shining brown eyes. For the first time since he'd met her, they sparkled with joy. He propped his elbow on the kitchen table and stroked his clean-shaven chin. "What are your plans? And, uh, do they include me?"

"They can if you want them to." Pearl averted her gaze, then looked back up at him. "If you really do want to get away from life at Sadie's. I mean, I think you do. You followed me out here. And so far you haven't hightailed it back to Denmark in spite of Ma's preaching."

He leaned back in his chair. "Her preaching must not bother you much. You're still here."

Pearl shook her head. "And I want to stay here. Listen—I know Ma must seem peculiar to you. She's not at all like the women who raised you. I know she takes some getting used to; but she's my ma, and I love her."

"You're a fine daughter."

Pearl's grin looked wry. "I'm trying to improve."

Her words stung. In the solitude of the country, he could

see where he needed to improve, too. Maybe it would be nice to take a break from his life of gambling. Sleeping in late every day, up all night—what kind of life was that? Besides, maybe taking a new turn would elevate him in Pearl's eyes. Funny, he had come out here to talk her into changing her life back to the way it was, and instead, she had convinced him to try a new way of living.

"So do you think you can help me realize my dream of making this a real ranch?" Pearl asked.

"I'd like to, but what use do you think I'd be around here? I don't know anything about ranching, and anyhow, it seems to me there isn't much of a ranch to handle. You told me your ma only grows enough vegetables to keep herself fed."

"Yes."

"I've seen your stable. You don't have horses to break, and even if you did, there's not much room for them to run. You do a pretty good job on your own of taking care of the chickens, and how much work is it to take care of two pigs, a few chickens, and one cow? Even your ma could do that much on her own before she got sick."

"True. But I have plans, and you can be a part of them. If you joined us here on the ranch, we could buy more livestock and eventually hire more people and make this ranch a real going concern, not just a little farm where one or two people can barely eke out a living."

"Sounds ambitious. You really do have dreams for this place, don't you?"

"I suppose so. I didn't realize it myself until I came back." She leaned toward him. "What do you say? Will you help me?"

Those eyes held too much interest for him to refuse. "All right. I will."

That afternoon Benjamin reentered the house, and Pearl joined him in the kitchen.

"How's she doing?" he asked.

Pearl shushed him, though not in an unkind way. "She's asleep."

He nodded and lowered his voice to just above a whisper. "Everything looks to be in good repair, except I saw a few places where the chicken coop could use some work. I should be able to get to that this week."

She nodded. "Thank you."

The absence of food on the table told him he'd finished his chores well before supper, much to his regret. According to his rumbling stomach, he could use a bite to eat. He could only hope the inn would have something good on their menu. "I'd best be getting along. See you tomorrow."

Raised eyebrows indicated Pearl's surprise. "You milked Pansy already?"

Pansy! He'd forgotten. And he wished Pearl had forgotten, too. Afraid of failure since he'd never milked a cow, he was desperate to escape the chore. He looked out a window to the sky, hoping the sun hadn't settled too far. "It's a little early for milking, isn't it?"

"No. In fact, your timing couldn't be better. You'll find the bucket and milk stool in the barn."

Instead of expressing gratitude for her guidance, Benjamin

shuffled his foot from one side to the other and stared at the tip of his brown leather boot. "Oh."

"What's the matter? Has the sun gotten to you? Are you feeling too poorly to milk Pansy?" She peered into his face, her expression much like that of a concerned nurse. "My, but sweat is just pouring down the sides of your face. I reckon the sun can get pretty hot out there when you're used to being inside all day." Pearl glided to the kitchen counter and picked up a transparent pitcher. "Here. Let me get you a glass of water. That might cool you off."

Benjamin wanted to lie and tell Pearl that indeed he felt sickly and wanted to go back to his room at the inn right away. But he realized that excuse would only buy him that afternoon. The next day he'd have to tell her the truth. Besides, if he was going to be more like the man Pearl wanted him to be, he couldn't start out by lying to her now.

He cleared his throat. "A glass of water would be nice, but I'm right as rain physically."

Pearl handed him the water. "That's good to hear. But you seem hesitant. Why?"

Stalling for time, he took a gulp of water. Never could he remember feeling so stupid. "I—I don't think I can milk Pansy."

"Why ever not?"

He paused. "Truth be told, I don't know how."

She opened her mouth as if to say something, then burst into laughter.

This time it was Benjamin's turn to shush her. "Do you want to wake your ma? Besides, I don't see what's so funny."

"I'm sorry. It's just that it never occurred to me you wouldn't know what to do. But why would you? You've never had to tend livestock before in your life." Pearl looked toward her mother's open door and back. "I think Ma should be fine. Come on. I'll give you a lesson."

Embarrassed that Pearl had to discover his ineptitude but grateful she was willing to help him learn, Benjamin watched her lure Pansy to the barn with the ease of a woman familiar with the task. Soon they were situated. A honey brown creature with big brown eyes, Pansy chewed her feed while regarding him with what seemed to be nonchalant disdain.

"I'll be gentle, Pansy," he assured her.

"She doesn't look too worried." Pearl placed a bucket underneath the animal's udders. She set the stool beside the cow and sat down.

Benjamin noticed the cow's bag looked plenty big, and he wondered how long the process of extracting the milk would take.

"Here's how it's done." Pearl reached for a teat, gripped it, and squeezed a stream of milk into the pail as though the motion were the most natural thing in the world. The cow remained unperturbed, chewing and swishing her tail. Pearl drew two more streams of milk into the bucket, the liquid hitting the bottom of the metal bucket with force.

"You make that look easy enough."

"It is easy. You'll learn in no time." She rose from the stool. "Now you try."

"I was hoping you were having so much fun you'd keep at it yourself," he only half jested.

Pearl smiled and pointed to the stool.

Benjamin took the seat. He chose the nearest udder and gripped it gently. For some reason, the animal's warmth, conveyed through thick pink skin covered with sparse but coarse white hairs, took him aback. He let go.

"Everything all right?"

He nodded. "Yep." Taking a breath, he tried again, forcing himself to become accustomed to the cow. This time he pulled. No milk resulted.

"You have to pull a little harder," Pearl advised. "Try an udder on the other side. Don't be scared. Pansy can sense your fear."

His manly pride took a blow at such a term, but he knew Pearl meant well. He nodded and yanked. This time a stream of milk came at him, and good. The milk missed the bucket and landed on his thigh.

"Don't get discouraged. Happens to all of us." Pearl grinned, looking as though she'd held back a big guffaw.

The idea that Pearl was amused by his clumsiness left him in ire. Determined to succeed, he grabbed a back udder and aimed it at the bucket. He yanked.

He heard Pansy's angry moo, then felt a kick. With a sharp hoof the animal struck him in the leg with such force that Benjamin fell off the stool and yelped.

"Benjamin!" Pearl knelt beside him, all traces of mirth absent from her expression. "Are you all right?"

He righted himself though pain reminded him of the encounter with Pansy. "I reckon so." He grimaced.

"Don't try to stand up. Not yet. Just stay there for a moment."

Benjamin didn't argue. Intense pain left him with little choice.

"You don't think your leg is broken, do you?" Fear penetrated her voice.

Benjamin shook his head. "I'm just bruised, that's all."

"You'll have a right good bruise, I'm sure," Pearl speculated. "Do you feel like getting up yet?"

He nodded and, with some difficulty, rose in stages.

Pearl nodded toward a bale of hay. "You sit on down."

He hobbled to the hay, wishing he'd been gentler with Pansy. He'd let his foolish pride irk him and was suffering the consequences.

Meanwhile, Pearl consoled Pansy, patting the cow and rubbing her. Soon the beast breathed more slowly and resumed feeding.

Benjamin imagined Pansy was calmer than he was. "I'm sorry I made Pansy mad."

"You didn't mean to." Pearl gave the animal one final pat then nodded toward the house. "Come on. Let's go back. I'll tend to you and then come back here and finish up later."

If Benjamin were prone to blushing, he would have at that moment. He had proven a colossal failure. How could he ever expect to be of any use to Pearl?

"Don't worry," she consoled him. "You can try again tomorrow."

Benjamin didn't answer. He wasn't sure he ever wanted to see another cow.

Chapter 7

Weeks later, Benjamin rose early on Sunday morning to escort Pearl to church. After long days of physical labor, he looked forward to an hour or so of sitting on a pew, listening to Preacher Giles, and praying and singing.

Since he was running late, he hurried with shaving and dressing and soon retrieved the Huberts' buggy, which he had borrowed since he'd be taking Pearl to church. Trotting toward the ranch, he thought back on his time there, being part of Pearl's new life. The first few days after he agreed to help bring the ranch up to its potential, he didn't think he would survive. Pansy's kick had been a setback, and his injured leg had impeded his progress as he tried to learn the ins and outs of ranching. But once he and Pansy became friends, he learned to milk her with as much ease as Pearl. He found that such a chore, along with the other labor, brought its own sense of pride in accomplishment. Even in the past, when he had outwitted other gamblers and taken home their money, he never felt proud of his day's labor. On the ranch he did.

Pearl had said the ranch was small, and he reckoned it was by Texas standards, but the amount of work it entailed made it seem gigantic to him. First he had invested some time in making sure the fences, barn, and chicken coops were in good repair. As he approached Milk and Honey Ranch, he admired his handiwork.

He admired Pearl even more when he saw her waiting for him. Nearly unable to control himself, he took in a breath. Her Sunday dress, though simple, made her appear even more radiant than usual. He had barely called the horse to a stop before Pearl ran toward him and jumped into the buggy.

Benjamin marveled at how she managed to maintain a grip on her Bible while leaping into position. "Good morning!" He twisted his mouth into a wry grin.

"I hope it's good. We're late." She looked straight ahead.

"I know. I'm sorry. I overslept a mite."

"I hope that means we'll only be a mite late."

He pulled the buggy out of the drive with more force than he intended. Pearl jostled and grabbed her hat.

"Sorry."

"Never mind. I can take a little bump if it means not being late for church."

"How's your ma this morning?"

"Not so good. She didn't eat breakfast. Just turned back over and went to sleep. I almost decided to skip worship service, but I figured that would upset Ma more than me leaving."

"I'm sorry she's still feeling poorly. But you can't do anything to help her when she's sleeping," Benjamin consoled. "That's probably the best thing. Did Dr. Spencer have anything much to say when he saw her yesterday?"

Pearl shook her head. "There's nothing he can do. I think he just wants me to make her comfortable."

Benjamin didn't respond. The idea of watching Pearl's ma wither away wasn't a happy one. Pearl remained silent for a moment. He wondered if her thoughts were similar to his own.

She changed the subject. "I do have some good news. News I think has cheered up Ma, too. It's about the ranch."

"Oh?"

"Remember the Angus bull and two cows I was thinking about buying? Well, I took the leap. They're all mine." Excitement colored her tone.

He let out a low whistle. "You must have saved more money than I thought."

"Ma had a few dollars hidden away, and I drove a hard bargain with our neighbor." She smiled and nodded once, a sure sign of triumph. "Now your job is simple. Make sure they stay healthy so we can expect to deliver some calves soon."

Benjamin wasn't sure he was up to the job, but he wanted to do right by Pearl. "I'll do my best."

"And I have a few other chores to keep you busy. I'd like to procure a few more chickens, so do you think we can build another coop?"

"I reckon." He tried to sound enthusiastic but failed.

Pearl didn't seem to notice. "Good!"

"I'm glad we're in sight of the church. If it was too much farther away, you might find other things for me to do."

"Oh," Pearl jested in turn, "we haven't ridden home yet."

Later, as they entered the sanctuary, Benjamin didn't feel

apprehensive. Weeks ago, the first time he darkened the door of the little frame building that also served as the schoolhouse, he'd felt like a speckled sheep among a lily white flock. Jittery since he wasn't sure how to act in such a holy place, he tried not to notice curious glances thrown his way. But the glances had melted, and he greeted people he had come to know.

That day he didn't squirm in boredom as Pastor Giles preached about the Ten Commandments. Benjamin couldn't recite but two by heart—the ones on lying and covetousness—but he decided to memorize all ten that week.

"Now I ask you, my friends," Pastor Giles shouted, "do you want to be thrown into the pit? Into hell's fire?"

Several answers in the negative resounded.

"Then you must obey these commandments!" With each word the pastor touched the Bible he held with his forefinger. The pastor was so fired up that Benjamin thought he could almost see the flames of hell.

Choruses of "Amen!" filled the sanctuary.

Benjamin knew he hadn't been obedient, especially about bearing false witness. And he reckoned that coveting other people's goods had led him to cheating. Not so long ago, the thought wouldn't have worried him. But now that he had seen a better way to live, sorrow visited him. He realized that each time he attended church he'd become more certain he had to change. For good.

Pastor Giles preached. "Now I ask you today, do you know where you are going when you die?"

The pastor looked right at Benjamin. He tried not to wince. But Pastor Giles was right. Benjamin didn't know where he'd be headed when he died.

"Some of you young folks might think you have all the time in the world to repent," the pastor said. "But you may not. For tonight your very life might be required of you."

Benjamin shook his head in surprise and regret. Such a thought had never occurred to him.

"You don't believe me?" Preacher Giles's stare focused on Benjamin, who responded by looking at the back of the pew in front of him. The pastor continued. "Turn in your Bibles to Luke chapter 12, verse 16, and read along with me the words of our Lord Jesus Christ."

They read:

> *And he spake a parable unto them, saying, The ground of a certain rich man brought forth plentifully: And he thought within himself, saying, What shall I do, because I have no room where to bestow my fruits? And he said, This will I do: I will pull down my barns, and build greater; and there will I bestow all my fruits and my goods. And I will say to my soul, Soul, thou hast much goods laid up for many years; take thine ease, eat, drink, and be merry. But God said unto him, Thou fool, this night thy soul shall be required of thee: then whose shall those things be, which thou hast provided? So is he that layeth up treasure for himself, and is not rich toward God.*

The words shook Benjamin. He had no reason to think God would take him anytime soon, but what if He did? Farm work offered plenty of chances for accidents. He remembered Pansy's kick. What if the blow had landed on his head? He shuddered.

Pearl laid a gloved hand on his arm and whispered, "Are you all right, Benjamin?"

He wasn't sure.

"Are you like this man? If you are, I ask you today to come to the altar and make a proclamation to God. Ask Jesus to forgive your sins and make you clean."

Benjamin felt so drawn to the altar that he had no other choice. He had to go. Rising from his seat, he walked to the front of the sanctuary and knelt at the altar. Pastor Giles kept preaching, and he heard shouts of joy from the congregation; otherwise, all was a blank to Benjamin. He just prayed. Tears rolled down his cheeks unabated.

He had come home.

Throughout the ride back to the ranch and even as she prepared Sunday dinner, Pearl didn't hold back her expressions of joy. "Oh, Benjamin! I'm still stunned about the day's events. I never expected you to take the altar call. I've never been happier!"

"Me, neither." Though he spoke the truth, he didn't want to admit he felt scared. The new life he promised God sounded hard to live. But he could try.

"I wish I had planned something more special for dinner than my same old fried chicken."

"Your fried chicken is special any day," Benjamin assured her. "Besides, now that I've come to Jesus, I'll bet every day will be special regardless of what I eat." He flinched. "Oh, I reckon I shouldn't use the word *bet* anymore."

Pearl laughed. "I know what you mean." She picked up a silver tray that held a small meal and an abbreviated glass of milk. "As soon as I take this in to Ma, I'll set ours on the table."

"Sure you don't want me to help?"

"Thanks, but you do enough around here. But you can come on in and talk to Ma. She'd like to hear your news."

Benjamin nodded. For the first time, he didn't feel fearful about seeing Pearl's mother.

Pearl poked her head through the sickroom door. "Ma? You decent?"

"Yes," a weak voice responded.

Benjamin followed Pearl.

"I've got lunch," Pearl announced. "I'm hoping you'll eat something."

"I'm not hungry right now. Leave it on the nightstand, will you?"

"Would you rather have an omelet?"

Pearl's mother barely shook her head.

Pearl set down the tray and drew closer to her mother. "Ma, I've got news. It's about Benjamin. He accepted the altar call at church today."

Ma opened both eyes. "He did?"

"I sure did, Mrs. Hubert," Benjamin assured her.

"Well, praise God." Her voice sounded stronger although she didn't sit upright. "So when is the baptism?"

"Baptism?"

"You mean, you've already been baptized?" Pearl's mother asked.

Benjamin hesitated. "If I have, I don't remember."

"Well, we'll have to take care of that," Pearl said. "Don't you worry about a thing, Benjamin. I'll take care of everything."

Later that week, Benjamin arrived in Pearl's kitchen for his usual breakfast. When he entered, bacon and eggs awaited.

"Sure smells good, Pearl."

"Me or the food?" she asked.

Her playful mood offered a pleasant surprise, and Benjamin decided to play along. "Both."

"I have a feeling this time of morning the bacon and eggs take precedence over the smell of my soap."

"I notice you don't wear the perfume I gave you much." He pulled up a chair and sat at the table. "Kinda hurts my feelings a mite," he teased.

"I'm saving that perfume for special occasions. Besides, didn't I tell you Ma doesn't allow perfume around here? Thinks it makes a woman smell—well. . ." Pearl looked into the frying pan and seemed to concentrate a little too much on dishing four thick slices of bacon and two eggs sunny-side up onto his plate. She buttered a slice of bread to go along with the food. He noticed a splotch of red on each cheek.

"The scent makes your ma think of your past, doesn't it?" he asked as he took his seat.

She nodded and set his plate before him. "And me, too. I don't want to go back."

"Neither do I."

"Oh, that reminds me. Pastor Giles says he'll baptize you in Trinity River whenever you're ready. But he doesn't want to wait too long."

"I know. But there's something that would mean a lot to me, if we can get it to happen." Benjamin's voice became quiet. "I'd like my brothers to be there to see it."

"Are you sure?"

"Part of getting my life where it should be is forgiving them. Isn't it?"

"Sure." Pearl fetched the coffeepot.

"You're afraid of them, aren't you? Afraid because they're outlaws?"

Pearl nodded. "I wish I could say different."

"I understand. But they won't do any harm around here. They might still be outlaws, but they always made sure I was protected. So will you help me find them?"

"If it means that much to you, sure, I'll help," Pearl said as she poured coffee. "I wonder if they'll recognize you."

"They might not—it's been so many years."

"I hardly recognize you myself. Your skin isn't as sallow as it used to be, and you walk with more vigor than you ever did at Sadie's."

He chuckled. "Vigor? I wonder how, considering how tired I am every day."

Pearl laughed as she served the coffee. "Physical work is a challenge, isn't it? I find it rewarding. Don't you?"

"Yes, I reckon I do."

She took her seat. "We need to say a blessing."

Chastened, Benjamin set down his fork. He'd already taken a bite of egg. "If it's not too late."

"As long as we're living and breathing, it's never too late to be thankful."

She bowed her head, and Benjamin knew she expected him to offer the prayer, a practice to which he still hadn't become accustomed or comfortable. Nevertheless, he managed to utter a few words, and they proceeded with breakfast.

"So you haven't been tempted to gamble?" she asked.

He shook his head. "Not so far. Nobody in town knows me as a card player, so that helps, I think."

"I would venture you sleep easier at night knowing you haven't cheated anybody."

"I'd have to agree with that." He chuckled, then turned serious. "I'm glad I put the past behind me."

"You mean that?"

An idea occurred to him. "Yes, I do. Do you want to see how much?"

"Sure, but I don't know how you'd show me."

"Go get that bottle of perfume. And you'll see."

"Now I am wondering what you've got up that sleeve of yours," she said, then disappeared into her own room.

Benjamin was just finishing the last of his eggs when she returned.

"Here you go." She set the perfume on the table.

Benjamin picked up the bottle. He imagined the squat shape, with a little bulb on top to spray out the fragrance, would seem pretty to a woman. He'd spent a lot of money on that bottle of tuberose scent for her. Money he'd risked a lot to earn.

"So why did you want to see the bottle of perfume?" Pearl persisted.

"I'll be right back. I have to go get something." He picked up the bottle. "Meet me outside."

Benjamin hurried to the shed to retrieve the hammer he'd been using to make repairs. For a moment he indulged in the luxury of examining the tool, thinking about what he planned to do. The smooth metal felt slightly chilled, warming quickly under his touch. He never thought he'd think in such a way, but the worn wooden handle fit his fingers as if it had been fashioned for him. He marveled at how the hammer, instrumental in creating buildings and fences and maintaining their usefulness, would now be used for destruction. He slipped the tool into his back pocket and made his way back to the stoop where Pearl waited.

"What are you doing?" she prodded.

"Would you set the bottle down for me?" He pointed to a step.

Pearl shook her head ever so slightly but didn't argue.

"Stand back." As she stepped backward, he retrieved the hammer and showed it to her. "Take one last good look at that bottle of perfume. In a few seconds it will be history."

She gasped. "But you paid a lot of money for that perfume. Are you sure you want to do that?"

"I'm not going to think about the money now. I'd ask you to give the perfume to a friend, but I doubt any respectable woman around these parts would wear it. Am I right?"

After the briefest interlude she responded. "You're right." She looked at the bottle and gulped.

"Sure you don't mind?" Benjamin asked.

Pearl took in a breath that broke the morning stillness. She nodded. "Oh, I mind, but I think you should do it."

Benjamin nodded. Before Pearl could have a chance to reconsider, Benjamin took the hammer and gave the bottle a good, hard strike. The bottle split into several pieces, spilling tuberose perfume. The pungent, sickly sweet odor, so lovely in small doses, sent both of them to coughing with the power of its unabated volume.

"I sure hope Ma doesn't smell that, for a lot of reasons." Pearl furrowed her brow with a concern Benjamin hadn't seen in some time. "The scent will remind her of my venture to Denmark, but even worse, it might make her physically sick."

"Really? Tuberose can be a bit strong, but—"

"No, it's not that." Pearl shook her head. "It's just that Ma's been feeling even more poorly lately. Odors, even nice ones, seem to bother her an awful lot. And when she's not flushed, she looks more pale and sickly. She's not eating much. I'm really worried."

Benjamin didn't know what he could say. When Pearl left Denmark, she knew her ma was near death's door. "I suppose you're never ready for the death of a loved one, even when you've been expecting it."

"I'm not ready," Pearl admitted. "I wish I had been a better daughter."

"I think you've been a wonderful daughter. Probably better than she deserves."

"I doubt that, but thank you." Pearl's voice was just above a whisper, and she kept her gaze on the shattered bottle.

They remained quiet for a time. Benjamin contemplated the broken bottle and everything it had meant to them both. Judging from the faraway look in Pearl's brown eyes, she shared his thoughts.

Finally, he broke the silence. "Are you going to be all right, Pearl?"

She nodded. "Benjamin, I never thought I'd say such a thing about a broken bottle of perfume, but you've made me glad. I feel like you've unlocked shackles from around my feet."

He understood all too well what she meant.

Chapter 8

The next week, Benjamin arrived as usual at the inn, tired even though his body and spirit had grown accustomed to the physical work the ranch required. He had planned to go straight to his room, wash up, and go to bed since Pearl had seen to it he enjoyed a good supper before he left her place. They had lingered over coffee. He treasured those times with her.

When he entered the small area that passed for the inn's lobby, he halted. Leaning on the counter toward the proprietor was a tall, lean man Benjamin recognized as Owen. Back in Denmark, he'd cheated Owen at cards many a time. He wondered if he was in town trying to get Benjamin to pay back some of the money. If so, was he willing to draw pistols over it? Or maybe Owen's errand was something else altogether. A terrible thought that Sadie might be ill entered his mind.

Worried, Benjamin debated whether to duck from Owen's view or to approach him with a warm greeting. Maybe Owen was traveling through town and merely looking for a place to stay for the night. He hoped he was on his way to somewhere else and that somewhere else was California. A long, long way from Benjamin and Pearl.

Summoning his courage, he strode toward Owen. Suddenly he became aware of how loud his heels sounded clacking against the worn wooden floor.

Owen turned toward him, and recognition flickered upon his features. "Benjamin!"

He tipped his hat. "Evening, Owen."

Owen excused himself long enough to get a key from Dimsbury.

"You two know each other?" the innkeeper asked.

"Sure do. We were friends back in Denmark," Benjamin said.

"Well, just make sure the two of you stay friendly," he warned. "I don't want no trouble around here."

"You won't have any trouble," Benjamin assured him.

Owen nodded, which seemed to satisfy Dimsbury. He'd put up a sign saying he'd be away a spell, then disappeared as he always did at that time of day. Benjamin always assumed he took dinner next door since it was the right time and he was always punctual about leaving for an hour.

Owen turned to Benjamin. The two men walked a few steps away from the counter before resuming their greetings.

"What are you doin' here?" Owen asked. "I knew you were somewhere in these parts, but I didn't think I'd find you like this, in a speck of a place out in the middle of nowhere."

"If this is such a speck in the road," Benjamin quipped, "then what are you doing here?"

"I'm passing through on my way to California. My aunt

died, and she left me a house in San Francisco."

Benjamin chuckled. "You want to live way out there in a city?"

Owen shrugged. "I figure I can at least go and see the house. At the worst, I can sell it and make some money. Maybe replace some I lost to you." He folded his arms. "Speaking of that, I don't have anything to do tonight. I noticed there's a saloon next door. How about we get up a game of cards?"

Benjamin hesitated. What could he say to Owen that his former gambling buddy would believe?

Owen drew closer. "I'll bet you already know most of the saloon girls by now and probably have a set of regular card players, don't you? Just like back home."

He squirmed for a response. "This isn't the same place."

"Of course not. But women are the same everywhere. They all swoon when they see a handsome fella. If I looked anything like you, I'd be married with ten kids by now."

"You'd be married if Ellie had her way." Benjamin grinned.

"I know it. Maybe if I like this house out in San Francisco and I don't see no other woman that looks better, I might send for Ellie. She's not the best-looking woman in the world, but she'd make a good enough wife."

Benjamin didn't want to agree that Ellie was one of the homeliest women in Denmark. Considering the likelihood Owen would find another woman in San Francisco, Benjamin visualized Ellie's slim chances with Owen evaporating.

A sly grin covered Owen's features. "Seeing as how we don't got any women to worry us, what about that card game?"

Benjamin shook his head. "I'd better not."

"Aw, come on now. You must know a few men who'd like to play a hand or two."

"Nope. I haven't visited the saloon but once since I first got here."

Owen's mouth dropped. "Come again?"

"You heard right."

"I don't believe it."

Benjamin shrugged. "I can't help whether you believe it or not. It's true. I've been working on a ranch."

Owen whistled. "You've been getting your hands dirty? That's a switch for you."

Benjamin knew he deserved Owen's disdain. "It's about time I started to make an honest living, don't you think?"

"Men who make an honest living during the day often don't mind a little bit of what they call 'recreation' at night. Time's a-wasting. Let's go get up a game."

As much as he hated to admit it, even to himself, Owen's offer tempted Benjamin. He hesitated. "I've changed since I've been working on Pearl's ranch."

"I can't imagine you lifting a finger outdoors." Owen eyed him. "But I have to say, you do look a mite tanned. But that don't mean you can't play cards."

Benjamin shook his head.

"What's the matter?" Owen scoffed. "Scared Pearl might find out? Pshaw, she's no better than we are."

Such words sent Benjamin's blood raging. Without thinking, he laid his fist into Owen's jaw. Owen reeled but recovered.

Benjamin heard chair legs on the front porch shuffle, wood

meeting wood, making a scratching sound. Two men rushed into the front room.

"What's wrong, Benjamin?" inquired a boarder Benjamin knew only as Harry. "This here stranger bothering you?"

"We don't take much of a hankering to that kind of thing here in these parts," Harry's friend added.

"He's not bothering me," Benjamin rushed to explain.

"More like he's bothering me," Owen said. "Laid a mean punch on me over a misunderstanding."

The two would-be rescuers regarded Benjamin, then glared at Owen, then returned their gazes to Benjamin. "You sure about that? 'Cause we can beat him up pretty good if you need us to."

"I'm sure," Benjamin confirmed. "But all is well here."

Owen looked whipped, but Benjamin wanted to be sure a sour word about Pearl never again crossed Owen's lips. He spoke to the man in a lowered voice. "Pearl has more goodness in her little finger than you and I have in our whole bodies and souls put together."

Owen rubbed his jaw and stared at Benjamin. "Whatever you and your friends say."

Benjamin wanted to point out that the two men were always looking for a fight and weren't really his friends and he could have taken care of himself. But he decided to omit all three statements. The fact that he had resisted Owen's suggestion to go back to his old ways—an easy way to make money, to be sure—was victory enough.

Benjamin smiled at his friend from Denmark. "Look—I'm sorry I flew off the handle like that. Punching someone never solves anything. And I know you wouldn't even be standing here still if we hadn't known each other a long time."

"You got that one right," Owen said.

"How about I get you a cup of coffee?" Benjamin offered.

"No, I'm not in the mood for coffee. I think I'll go to the saloon and try my luck there to find a night's entertainment." Owen studied Benjamin. "You really have changed. Never thought I'd see the day."

"Like Preacher Giles said in church last Sunday, with God all things are possible."

Owen put his hands on his hips and looked at Benjamin cockeyed. "Is that from the Bible?"

"I think so. I'm not entirely sure. But if Pastor Giles said it, it's pretty close."

"So you're a pew-sitter now? Either you've gone crazy, or I have."

Benjamin laughed. "Maybe you ought to try it sometime. Maybe you'll find yourself a pretty girl."

A week later Pearl and Benjamin had just entered the house when Ma called.

"Pearl?" Ma's weak voice sounded from her room.

Pearl sighed and sent Benjamin a look and set down the tomatoes she had picked. Just as quickly she regretted her show of impatience. Her mother couldn't help being sick. But some days she was more demanding than others. On this particular day, she had called Pearl five times in the span of an hour.

Pearl softened her expression and set her voice to a happy pitch. "Yeah, Ma?"

"Can you come here? And bring that man of yours with you."

So Ma wanted Benjamin? Pearl wondered what could be the matter. She motioned to Benjamin, who was just finishing breakfast. "Come on."

Without delay he complied.

"We're here, Ma. What's the matter?" Pearl noticed that Ma had consumed all the water in the pitcher in her night table. "Do you need more water?"

"I will, but not now."

Pearl sat on the side of her mother's bed. Strands of the older woman's hair clung to the sides of her face, saturated with sweat. Wet droplets marked her forehead. Her cheeks looked flushed, and she was thrashing. Pearl hadn't seen such a sight since one of Sadie's girls died of consumption, spreading fear throughout the house. Pearl remembered that was the one time she had asked the Lord to spare her, though she didn't deserve His mercy after traveling away from His protection for so long. Yet He had seen fit to answer her prayer. In a flash, she wondered if the Holy Spirit had brought that remembrance to her mind. Was it time to pay Him back?

Pearl noticed her mother's sheets had twisted and turned. "Here. Let me smooth these for you." She set about her task.

"You would have made a good nurse if you hadn't of. . ." Ma regarded Benjamin. "I'm glad you're here, too. I'm in desperate need of prayer, and I'll take petitions from anyone with a voice."

Pearl dried her mother's forehead with a clean cloth. "Your head is as hot as a branding iron." Pearl's throat tightened.

"I know it. And I feel mighty puny."

It wasn't like Ma to admit she didn't feel well. The confession worried Pearl.

"I don't want to die. Not yet."

Die! "You're not gonna die, Ma." Pearl hoped her words would prove true.

Ma took Pearl's hands. "Please. Please pray for me."

"I will, Ma. But first there's something we need to do." Pearl turned to Benjamin. "Fetch the preacher. If he's not at church, try the parsonage next door."

Benjamin nodded. "Right away."

Ma's voice rang out in the room. "No!"

"Ma! Don't you want the preacher?"

"There's not enough time. I know there isn't. You'll have to do."

Ignoring her mother's veiled insult, Pearl dropped to her knees and set her elbows on the side of the sickbed. "Lord, I pray You'll see fit not to take my ma. I know the mansion You built for her in heaven is much better than anything she can have here, but she's not ready to leave us yet. She feels so bad, Lord. Can't You see her tossing and turning, doing her best to sweat out the fever? I know she has a lot of life left in her, and she wants to live it. Please grant her a few more years with us. Please." Pearl felt tears drop down her cheeks.

She kept praying, not keeping track of time. During that spell, she noticed Benjamin's presence beside her. He had joined her by the bed and was on his knees, too. Though he didn't speak, his nearness consoled her. The fact that he had joined her in prayer made her sob.

She felt Benjamin's arm around her. "Shh. You'll wake her

up with all that boo-hooing."

"Wake her up?" Pearl studied her mother. Indeed, she had fallen sound asleep.

Ma's aged features had softened far beyond anything Pearl could have imagined only a few moments ago. Deep wrinkles, brought on by years of toiling in the sun, weren't as apparent as usual.

Unwilling to rise from her knees, Pearl scooted along the floor until her hand could reach her mother's forehead and cheeks. When she touched her mother's face, Pearl was relieved to find that her skin didn't feel nearly as heated as it had before they prayed. The redness had left her cheeks, leaving in its stead the soft pink color she was accustomed to seeing in her mother. The woman's breathing had become even. An occasional rattle that could once be heard in Ma's chest had left. It was as if the years had floated away and a youthful Ma was taking a nap while her little children played.

Benjamin took her hand and lifted her to her feet. "Let's go," he whispered. "There's nothing more we can do."

Chapter 9

A few minutes later Benjamin and Pearl returned to the kitchen.

"I can't believe Ma is resting so well." Pearl kept her voice low.

"After the way she was acting so sick before, I can't believe it, either. Let's just hope she stays that way. Restful and feeling better." Benjamin took his usual seat at the table and then looked at the entrance to the sickroom. "God sure acted fast, didn't He?"

Pearl joined him at the table. "He sure did. Not that He always works that quickly. But I'm glad He did this time. Ma was suffering."

Benjamin looked back at Pearl. "So you think our prayers had something to do with your ma's fever breaking?"

"What else could it be? She begged us to pray for relief. As soon as we did, the fever broke."

"We've been here awhile now. Wonder why she picked that moment in time to ask us?"

"I think she was too sick and desperate not to."

Benjamin was thoughtful. "Maybe God does help people, after all."

"Of course He does." Pearl remembered Benjamin's bitterness over how his brothers had deserted him at Sadie's. "Just because you had a tough childhood doesn't mean God wasn't there."

"But how could He expect me to find Him at Sadie's? I didn't go there on my own. But when I ended up there, I naturally fell into the gambling life. What else could I have done? If I'd had my druthers, I'd have done something else with my life if God hadn't abandoned me."

"Like what?" Pearl kept her voice gentle. She wanted to challenge him to think, not to alienate the only man she had ever loved.

Benjamin shrugged. "I don't know. I might have been a blacksmith's apprentice. Or worked at a shop in town. Or maybe even been a rancher."

"You're a rancher now. Of sorts."

"I suppose I am." Benjamin crossed his arms. "But it's taken me an awful long time to get here."

"Maybe God had a reason for you to take the long way around."

"You took the long way around, too," he pointed out.

"I'd like to think of my time in Denmark as a mistake. I learned a lot from straying off the path. I never will stray again."

"I'm glad," Benjamin said. "I don't mean any disrespect against your ma, but I can see by the way she talks to you that you haven't always had it easy. You never have had it easy, really."

"Maybe not. But I haven't had it as hard as some people. At least I do have a ma, and she does love me enough not to want me to suffer for an eternity out of the presence of God. I don't want you to suffer, either," Pearl said. "I want you to know God, but not because you've made some sort of bargain or deal with Him. You must seek His face because you want to know the Lord and because you want the Lord to be part of your life through all times, not just bad times."

"Things have gotten better since I stopped gambling and cheating people out of their money. I feel much better now in my heart. I can see now, by the way things have turned out in my life, that God never abandoned me while I was at Sadie's. But I sure can see a difference in my life now compared to then."

"I can see the difference in you. And I can feel the difference in me, too. That was no life for me. Or you," Pearl added.

"I do want a new life, Pearl. Pastor Giles said I can get baptized. I think I want to do that."

Pearl gasped and touched Benjamin's arm. "You do! Oh, Benjamin, I'm so glad to hear you say that. You've made me so happy!"

Ma called from the next room. "Pearl!" Her voice sounded strong.

"Ma!" Pearl jumped from her seat and rushed into her mother's room. "How are you—?" She stopped. "Ma!"

The older woman was sitting upright in her bed without her back touching the pillow. Sickness had melted from her being. A smile decorated her face.

Pearl gasped. "Ma! What happened?"

"I—I feel better than I have in weeks. Why, I do believe the Lord cured me! Hallelujah!" Ma lifted her arms in praise. "Thank You, God, and thank you both for your prayers." She threw back the covers and started to exit the bed.

Pearl hastened to stop her. "Don't leap out of bed just yet. You might not be as strong as you think."

"What do you mean? I should be able to get up and fix supper. Remember Peter's mother-in-law in Matthew, how Jesus healed her of a fever? 'And when Jesus was come into Peter's house, he saw his wife's mother laid, and sick of a fever. And he touched her hand, and the fever left her: and she arose, and ministered unto them.' " She shook her head at the young couple. "And if there's anybody who needs ministering to, it's the two of you."

Pearl let out an exasperated sigh and watched her mother try to bound out of bed. As soon as she did, she sat back down.

"I'm a bit dizzy. Must be the vertigo," Ma conceded.

Pearl helped Ma position herself back into a reclining position. "I'm not sure it's vertigo. What I am sure of is that you've been in bed a long time, and you're still weak. That's nothing to be ashamed of. You'll be as well as Peter's mother-in-law was soon enough. Then you can minister to us all you want. And cook supper, too."

"I'd like that."

"Let me bring you some hot soup in the meantime."

"I'd like that, too." Ma's voice sounded gentler than usual. She placed her hand on Pearl's. "Thank you, Pearl. And thank you, Benjamin."

Pearl nodded, unwilling to say anything that might discourage Ma's gentleness. Perhaps her healing marked the beginning of a new era. A new era for them all.

—ɷ—

"Now won't you have another helping of chicken, Benjamin?" Ma asked him two weeks later as she served supper.

Benjamin set a clean drumstick bone on his plate. "Don't mind if I do, Ma." She'd asked him to call her by that name, but it still sounded strange to his ears. "It's mighty good chicken."

"I know I'll never cook chicken as good as Ma can," Pearl conceded, though she declined a second piece.

"Sure you can fry up a bird as good as I can," Ma protested. "I'll show you how. Again."

Benjamin cut Pearl a look and tried to withhold a grin. Ma's acerbic tongue would outlive her, most likely. "Pearl cooks just fine, Ma. No husband of hers would ever starve to death."

"Is that so? Well, then, why don't you find out?"

"What do you mean?" Benjamin knew exactly what she meant, but he wanted to hear her put her feelings into words.

"I mean, what are you waitin' for, boy? Do you think a woman as pretty as my Pearl is goin' to sit around here forever and wait for you?"

"Now, Ma," Pearl protested, "you're embarrassing me!" Reddened cheeks confirmed her statement.

"I thought you were long past the point where anything could embarrass you, Pearl. Although I must say, you do seem more modest than you used to."

"I reckon I should thank you?"

"That's a compliment. But if you're lookin' for an insult, I can give you plenty of those, too."

"Ain't that the truth?" Pearl asked no one in particular.

"Now, if you keep on talkin' that way, I'll tell Benjamin here that he can forget about asking you to marry him. He can go on about his business, and I'll get Zeke Callihan to work for us in his place."

"Zeke?" Pearl scoffed. "Now, Ma, I know you mean well, but I don't want Benjamin to ask me to marry him just because you say he should. You wouldn't do that, would you, Benjamin?"

He grinned. "I think you know the answer to that."

With her fork, Pearl played with her mashed potatoes and didn't look up. Benjamin had delivered the quip without the least bit of hesitation. Maybe he wasn't planning to ask her hand in marriage after all. Not that she could blame him. She had asked an awful lot of him, that he come to a saving knowledge of the Lord and change his ways. From all appearances, he had done both.

Lord, You know what's best. If Benjamin isn't the one for me, let me know quick. I can't stand the idea of waiting and wondering. But if he's the one You have picked for me, please let him ask me real soon.

"What are you daydreamin' about, Pearl?" Ma asked. "Never mind. You'd best get goin' on your chores. You took on a powerful lot more work while I was sick, and now you've got to be sure it all gets done."

—∞—

Leaving the general store in Rope A Steer, Benjamin reached

into his pocket and fingered the little ring he'd bought for Pearl. He wouldn't rest until he got it safely on her beautiful finger.

Walking to the inn, he contemplated his life. Never would he have guessed that he'd marry Pearl, the woman who once helped him cheat at cards. But now he expected she'd help him in a better way—God's way. She would be the person who walked beside him, making a go of the ranch with him, bringing it up to its full potential. He imagined a full herd of dairy cattle in his future and plenty of money from the milk, cheese, and butter he could sell. He'd earn every penny. The hard work of farming already told him that. But each fiber of his muscles pulsated with energy and vigor. Sunshine hit the part of his face not sheltered by his brimmed hat, tickling his skin. After the harvest, Pearl would put up their food for the winter, and fall would begin in full force.

He could only hope the river wouldn't be too cold on the day of his baptism. After he broached the topic with Pearl the day Ma was healed, he hadn't mentioned baptism again. Thoughts of such a momentous event left him ecstatic and fearful. A new life of walking in the Lord's path presented a challenge for the reformed gambler, but the rewards of an honest living and a clear conscience seemed worth it all.

Not to mention the best prize. Pearl. She would be his forever. And not in the shadows, but in the full light of day, as his wife.

If she'll have me.

Crossing the inn's threshold, he fingered the ring again. He'd ask when the time was right. He knew when that would be. The day he proclaimed once and for all that his life belonged to the Lord.

On the day of the baptism, Pearl fanned herself more than she usually did during church. Nervousness, not just the heat, spurred her to take such action. She had a surprise for Benjamin. Today that surprise would come to fruition. She tried to restrain herself from looking out the window too much, but self-control wasn't easy. Every once in a while she cut her gaze to the sunshine outdoors without moving her head.

Ma knew about the surprise. And, though Pearl could feel nervous energy emanating from her, too, Ma watched Pearl and poked her in the ribs so she'd pay attention to the sermon on new beginnings. Meanwhile, Benjamin appeared to keep a close and anxious eye on Pearl, as well. No doubt in his own excitement he didn't realize they had something planned. A good thing, too, because any other time he would have caught on to their nervousness and wormed the information out of them.

Noon approached, and the last hymn was sung. Pearl didn't linger to talk with her friends. Instead, she hurried Benjamin outside. She couldn't wait any longer for what was to transpire.

In the churchyard, as planned, three men awaited. Pearl didn't have to ask who they were. She would have known them anywhere because she could see traces of her beloved Benjamin in them all.

"What? What are they doing here?" Benjamin stopped in his tracks and studied his brothers.

Pearl could hear murmurings from the other congregants

behind her, but she wasn't about to answer questions. She wanted to savor the reunion she had planned for Benjamin.

He let out a whoop and ran to each brother, embracing him in turn. Slaps on the back and happy greetings resulted.

"Do you know what's happening today?" Benjamin asked them.

Reuben nodded. "Pearl told us."

"Pearl?" Benjamin gasped and turned toward her. "I guess I'm not surprised." He strode over to her, then took her by the arm so he could guide her closer to his brothers.

Since they were outlaws, Pearl half expected lusty looks and whistles, but each man, while looking at her approvingly, took off his hat and greeted her with respect. The love they had for their youngest brother showed in their eyes, even though their demeanor was stiff since the reunion had been a long time in coming.

Preacher Giles joined them. "Are these the brothers you've talked about before, Benjamin?"

"Sure are, preacher." Benjamin introduced Colt, Caleb, and Reuben.

The pastor nodded and shook hands with each brother. He knew all about their past, but no judgment expressed itself on his face or in his demeanor. "I'm looking forward to knowing you all, but we have a baptism to get to now."

"That's a fact," Pearl agreed.

Preacher Giles grinned. "You ready, Benjamin?"

"I sure am. Now more than ever."

Benjamin squeezed Pearl's hand, and then they walked back to church together. Benjamin needed a few moments to change out of his Sunday suit and into attire more suitable for being drenched in water. After the baptism, a churchwide picnic was planned as a celebration.

Before he left her side, Benjamin embraced Pearl. "You kept your promise. I never doubted you would try, but I can't believe you found them all. And you never said a word."

"It wasn't easy, but I tracked them down with a little persistence and a whole lot of prayer."

"I didn't think this day could get any better, but it sure has." Benjamin's eyes misted. "Thank you, Pearl."

Later Pearl watched Benjamin rise from the water. Drenched in water and prayer, he'd never looked better.

People in church congratulated him. Many had developed a genuine fondness for Benjamin. He glowed amid their friendship and support. Time with Benjamin's brothers had been brief, but Pearl knew they would have a few days to get to know them before they returned home. After that, she planned to be instrumental in never letting Benjamin lose touch with them again. She made this resolution with no fear or trepidation.

Instead of the outlaws Benjamin had described to her, the three men had changed. Caleb was a sheriff out in Arizona and happily married with a baby on the way. Reuben stood with quiet confidence, unlike the outward bravado she had expected because of what Benjamin had told her about him. Pearl wished she could have met his wife, but she had stayed behind in Wyoming because she, too, was in a family way. Colt had a beautiful wife and two daughters who adored him, plus a little one. Pearl could see the baby was the spittin' image of his daddy. Surely the Lord had touched them all, even as He had touched her Benjamin.

Pearl waited for everyone, including Ma, to convey kind words to Benjamin before she took her turn. By the time she approached, the sun had almost dried him. "Oh, Benjamin, I'm so glad you got baptized."

"Me, too, Pearl. I never thought the day would come." He set his gaze on the ground and spoke softly. "Can I talk to you for a minute?"

"Why, sure, Benjamin." She could tell by the excitement in his eyes that something was urgent. But what?

He led her underneath a tree outside, where they had sought shade many a time. His expression conveyed tenseness, but he didn't seem unhappy.

Pearl couldn't stand the suspense. "What is it, Benjamin?"

He cleared his throat. "I have something to tell you. Or to ask you, that is."

Her heart beat faster. Was it finally time?

Benjamin reached into his trousers pocket and pulled out a little box. "I—I was hoping you might take this as a gift. You've been so good to me." He opened the box and showed her a brilliant garnet ring.

She gasped. "Oh, Benjamin! It's beautiful! But I—I can't accept something so expensive!"

"Sure you can."

"But where did you get so much money? Surely not from what I'm paying you."

"I had some left from my gambling days. In fact, I spent

all that money on this ring for you. I want you to think of it as a symbol of what God did for us—protecting us through our dark times and staying with us until we found Him again. So please accept it." He paused and looked into her eyes. "If you're planning to be my wife."

"Your wife!" The phrase sounded so good falling from her lips.

He smiled shyly. "If you'll have me."

"Have you? Why, I'd be a fool not to say yes!"

Benjamin chuckled and placed the ring on her finger. "I don't know about that, but I do know I've loved you ever since I first set eyes on you."

Pearl looked into his eyes, which shone brighter even than the stunning garnet. "And I've always loved you, too. Isn't it something how God used that awful detour I took to bring me to you, and you to Him?"

"He sure can do a lot of things, Pearl."

"Yes. Yes, He can."

Benjamin took her in his arms. "I'll always be grateful to Him till the day I die, for giving me you."

As his lips touched hers, affirming the true love they shared, the love that would last a lifetime, Pearl knew Benjamin meant every word.

TAMELA HANCOCK MURRAY

Tamela Hancock Murray lives in northern Virginia with her hero and two lovely daughters. She enjoys reading, church work, and time spent with family and friends. Tamela finds writing about the Old West fascinating because of its rich history. Often the wide-open land and free-spirited atmosphere attracted lawless adventurers, but God could be found by those who sought Him.

A Letter to Our Readers

Dear Readers:

In order that we might better contribute to your reading enjoyment, we would appreciate your taking a few minutes to respond to the following questions. When completed, please return to the following: Fiction Editor, Barbour Publishing, Inc., P.O. Box 719, Uhrichsville, OH 44683.

1. Did you enjoy reading *Brothers of the Outlaw Trail*?
   - ❑ Very much—I would like to see more books like this.
   - ❑ Moderately—I would have enjoyed it more if ______________

   ____

   ____

2. What influenced your decision to purchase this book? (Check those that apply.)
   - ❑ Cover ❑ Back cover copy ❑ Title ❑ Price
   - ❑ Friends ❑ Publicity ❑ Other

3. Which story was your favorite?
   - ❑ *Reuben's Atonement* ❑ *Outlaw Sheriff*
   - ❑ *The Peacemaker* ❑ *A Gamble on Love*

4. Please check your age range:
   - ❑ Under 18 ❑ 18–24 ❑ 25–34
   - ❑ 35–45 ❑ 46–55 ❑ Over 55

5. How many hours per week do you read? ______________

Name ____

Occupation ___________________________________

Address ______________________________________

City__________________ State___________ Zip___________

E-mail____